A
Compromising
Affair

A
Compromising
Affair

GWYNNE
FORSTER

ARABESQUE®

Recycling programs
for this product may
not exist in your area.

A COMPROMISING AFFAIR

ISBN-13: 978-0-373-53451-7

Copyright © 2011 by Gwendolyn Johnson Acsadi

All rights reserved. The reproduction, transmission or utilization of this work in whole or in part in any form by any electronic, mechanical or other means, now known or hereafter invented, including xerography, photocopying and recording, or in any information storage or retrieval system, is forbidden without written permission. For permission please contact Kimani Press, Editorial Office, 233 Broadway, New York, NY 10279 U.S.A.

This is a work of fiction. Names, characters, places and incidents are either the product of the author's imagination or are used fictitiously, and any resemblance to actual persons, living or dead, business establishments, events or locales is entirely coincidental.

® and TM are trademarks. Trademarks indicated with ® are registered in the United States Patent and Trademark Office, the Canadian Trade Marks Office and/or other countries.

www.kimanipress.com

Printed in U.S.A.

Dear Reader,

I hope you have enjoyed the first four books featuring the Harrington family. Over the years, many of you wrote urging me to write another story about this engaging family, and so the saga continues. The first story, *Once in a Lifetime*, introduced the three brothers and featured Telford, the eldest Harrington. Following Telford's romance, *After the Loving* profiled the story of fiery and stubborn Russ Harrington, the middle brother, whose sizzling but often rocky relationship ended in wedded bliss. The third story, *Love Me or Leave Me*, featured strikingly handsome yet enigmatic Drake, the youngest of the three brothers, who was serious-minded and devoted to his family *and* the woman he loved.

In *Love Me Tonight*, Judson Phillips, a man searching for his biological parents, discovers that he is related to the Harrington clan and finally finds the family and loving kinship he's always longed for. In this novel, *A Compromising Affair*, the Harringtons embrace Ambassador Scott Galloway, Judson's best friend, whose difficult relationship with Denise Miller engages the entire family in an effort to bring the two together. I hope you have an opportunity to read all the books in the Harringtons series.

I enjoy receiving mail, so please email me at GwynneF@aol.com. If you'd like to reach me by postal mail, contact me at P.O. Box 45, New York, NY 10044, and if you would like a reply, please enclose a self-addressed, stamped envelope. For more information, please contact my agent, Pattie Steel-Perkins, Steel-Perkins Literary Agency, email MYAGENTSPLA@aol.com.

Warmest regards,

Gwynne Forster

ACKNOWLEDGMENTS

To the memory of Walter Zacharius, founder of Kensington Publishing, whose foresight helped publish the first line of African-American romances. I shall always remember him with gratitude and affection.

I am indebted to all of the wonderful people who've helped me in any way as I've breezed through life almost undeterred. To my dear mother, who taught me how to handle the few hard knocks that came my way; to my beloved husband, who fills my life with joy; and to my Heavenly Father, who gave me wonderful talents and many opportunities in which to use them.

Prologue

Scott Galloway had one cardinal rule: he was never late. He abhorred tardiness. But owing to exceptional circumstances, he arrived at Ronald Reagan Washington National Airport with only forty minutes to spare before he needed to fasten his seat belt on flight DL7777. His secretary had already checked him in, so he made a dash for security, and then suddenly stopped.

He didn't have a second to spare, but as he hurried through the terminal he noticed an old woman sitting beside two pieces of luggage. He couldn't leave without finding out whether she needed help.

"Are you alone, ma'am?" he asked her, glancing at his watch.

"Son, I've been sitting here in this airport for forty-five minutes. The taxi driver brought my bags inside and left me, and I'm still here."

The air rushed out of him as he thought about the

possibility of missing his flight. There was no way he was going to arrive late for his first assignment as an ambassador. But he thought of his beloved grandmother back in Baltimore and her insistence upon driving alone wherever she went.

"I'll be back in a minute, ma'am." He found an airport security officer. "I'm about to miss my flight," he told the man, "but a woman sitting over there needs help."

"What's your flight number?" the man asked. Scott told him. "Come with me." They went to where the old woman sat with her bags. "Do you know your flight number, ma'am?"

"Flight DL7777. I get off in Copenhagen."

"Both of you come with me." The security officer got a wheelchair for the woman, checked her in, gave her a ticket, rushed her through security and got both of them to the gate minutes before the door to the aircraft closed.

Scott took his seat in first class, nearly out of breath but with the satisfaction one gets from having done a good deed. He enjoyed a pleasant flight and conversation with his seatmate, a Dane en route to Copenhagen, until sleep overcame him. The next morning the plane made its scheduled landing in Copenhagen, Denmark, and passengers began to disembark. He walked to the plane's exit door along with his seatmate and waited until he saw the elderly woman.

"There you are," she said with a smile that reflected her delight in seeing him. "Give me your card, please." She looked at it, and her eyes widened. "An ambassador? And you almost missed the flight helping me."

"We both made it, ma'am. I wouldn't have felt right leaving you there." He turned to the man who had been his seatmate. "Will you see that she gets a taxi?" He reached in his pocket for money to pay for the taxi.

"No, please," the Danish man said. "It will be my pleasure to see that she gets home safely."

Scott bade them goodbye and went back to his seat as the plane resumed the next leg of the flight. Late that day, he finally arrived in Vilnius, Lithuania—a city with a dreary, baroque facade—for the first time. When he stepped off the plane, the first secretary of the embassy greeted him.

"Welcome, Mr. Ambassador, and welcome to Lithuania. We have been awaiting you with great anticipation."

"Thank you." Scott shook his head. *Mr. Ambassador,* he thought. He had worked long and hard for the title, and he loved the sound of it. But as he looked around at the difference between what he saw and what he had left behind in the States, he wondered what his two-year tour would mean, personally and professionally.

Several days later, he received a personal letter, and the backward-slanted handwriting on the envelope puzzled him. He opened it and read:

Dear Ambassador Galloway,
Thank you for coming to my rescue in Reagan National Airport and for introducing me to Lars Erickson, who lives about eight blocks from me. He took me home. I think it may be time I stopped traveling around the world by myself.

But I wanted to see the States, and I'm so glad I went there.

My trip could have ended badly, but for you. However, what you did for me wasn't a surprise, because you are a charitable man. I knew you would come along, so I wasn't afraid. You'll do well in Lithuania, though you won't like the place very much.

Your happiness is in the States. You've already seen her, but your interest was elsewhere, and you didn't notice. Besides, you were a little peeved. She's very near to your older brother. I'm not a fortune-teller. I see. And I am never wrong. So enjoy your work in Vilnius and then go back home. Your happiness is there.

Yours,

Helga Wilander

P.S. You do like horses, don't you?

Scott read the letter several times. If she were a seer, why didn't she know that he didn't have an older brother? He was the eldest son. He decided to write and ask her.

Dear Mrs. Wilander,

I was glad to hear from you and to know that you arrived home safely. I liked what you said about my future, but I don't have an older brother, unless there's something that I don't know about? If you get a notion to travel again soon, why not visit me here in Vilnius?

Yours,

Scott Galloway

Six days later, Scott looked through his incoming mail and saw Helga's unusual scrawl. He slit open the envelope and read:

Dear Scott,
I knew you'd answer, but I hadn't thought I'd get your letter so soon. Of course I know you don't have an older blood brother, Scott. But you have an older buddy with whom you are closer than most blood brothers, and you have been since you were five or six years old. Trust me, Scott. You'll find her near your brother. Maybe when I get the urge to travel again, I'll pay you a visit.
Your friend,
Helga

Scott folded the letter and put it in his wallet. All the women around his friend Judson, who he had to admit was like an older brother, were married. And Heather, Judson's fiancée, didn't have a sister or any close female friends that he knew of. In fact, *he* was Heather's best buddy.

"Nobody can accurately predict the future," he said to himself. "And that includes Helga Wilander." With a dismissive shrug, he flicked on his desk lamp and settled down to the business of being a United States ambassador.

Chapter 1

Two years later...

Scott Galloway stared out of his office window into the cold sunlight of a June morning in Vilnius, Lithuania, a small country situated between Belarus and the Baltic Sea. Two years in the diplomatic outpost had gone by far more quickly than he had anticipated. He had made a difference in the lives of the people working at the embassy and in the quality of diplomatic relationships between the United States and Lithuania. But for the past two years, his personal life had been on hold.

He zipped up his leather toiletries case, put it and his laptop in his small carry-on bag and paused for a moment. He slowly perused his office and the photo of him that hung alongside those of the U.S. president and the secretary of state, which brought a smile to his face. Then, he shrugged and headed out the door and down the corridor to the exit, where the embassy staff had lined up to tell him goodbye.

"We'll miss you, sir," one of the embassy officers said. "You made this place come alive."

He didn't give the statement much credence. If he had brought life to the place, it must certainly have been dead a long time before he got there. "Thank you, Aggie. You've been of immense help." Although the comment lacked veracity, it was bound to inflate her already oversize ego. But the next ambassador would have to deal with her.

"I hate to see you go, sir," an older man, a native of Vilnius, said to him. "They said I was too old to work and they were going to fire me. I don't know what I'll do now."

"I left a letter recommending you to the next ambassador, so don't worry. You're one of the best workers here." He patted the man on the shoulder and was about to depart, when the elderly janitor, Misha, pressed something into Scott's hand. "It's from my mother. She's a hundred and one. Since you came, it was the first time she'd tasted caviar in forty years. She gave me this to give to you."

Deeply touched, he thanked the man. "Give your mother my love and my humble thanks."

A young-looking man ran toward him, seemingly out of breath. "This just came, sir." He handed Scott a letter marked personal. He recognized the handwriting of Helga Wilander, the woman he'd befriended en route to Lithuania when he'd first arrived. He put the letter inside the breast pocket of his suit jacket, waved to the staff, got into the waiting limousine and headed for the airport. His first tour as United States ambassador was behind him. He exhaled a long breath, sat back and contemplated what he imagined was his future.

Remembering the envelope that Misha had given him, he opened it and gasped when he saw the six-by-eight-inch Russian icon of Mary, painted on silver and set in an old hammered silver frame. He looked at it for a long time, put it back in the envelope, wrote the old man's name on the envelope and put it in his briefcase. It was probably the most valuable object that Misha owned, and Scott vowed to write and thank him as soon as he was settled into his new job.

An airport attendant ushered him into the VIP lounge, where a waiter immediately placed a tray with coffee and assorted sweets in front of him. He would have appreciated fruit, any kind of fruit, since that was the one thing that was hard to find during the long winter months in Vilnius. The embassy got fruit from the States for special occasions, but only rarely. He couldn't wait to sink his teeth into some blueberries. The woman who sat facing him in the lounge smiled, and asked if he would like company.

"No, thank you," he said, not sure why such a good-looking and seemingly wealthy woman would be on the make in an international airport. Just the place to find a wealthy man, to make a seemingly innocent connection or to engage in covert espionage, he thought.

He gave the woman his most rakish smile, and when she didn't back off, he said, "Nothing would be more enjoyable, but I have to hand in this report immediately after I land, so I'll be working for the next ten hours solid."

She pursed her lips in what appeared to be a pout. "Not even time out for an itsy-bitsy drink?"

He let a grin float over his face. "A guy's got to work if he wants to eat. Thanks, I'm going to get started on this work."

If she hadn't pouted, he might have thought he'd misread her, but he hadn't. She was a plant, though he couldn't imagine why. He opened his laptop and got to work. Later, when she didn't board the plane in either first or business class, he knew he'd been right in his assessment. His experiences over the past two years had been a great teacher, reinforcing his conviction that you couldn't accept women at their word, sometimes not even at their behavior and definitely not based on looks. Nowadays, sultry smiles, perfectly shaped bosoms and swinging hips barely got his attention.

He smiled to himself, though he was not amused. The last time he'd misjudged a woman's intentions, she had handed him one of the most painful lessons of his life. He'd fallen for a girl his freshman year in college, only to learn that she was very different than what she seemed—especially after she was arrested and expelled from school. But he quickly got over her. However, Louise Fiske was a different story.

For months, she'd sworn that he was the only man for her. But when he needed her, she'd let him down with a resounding thud. After agreeing to accompany him to a fraternity social where he was to receive a prestigious award in his senior year, she inexplicably disappeared. Concerned for her safety, he ended up missing the awards ceremony. How was he to know that she'd been leading him on, and was secretly dating another guy? Now, years later, he remembered those lessons and swore that he'd never make those mistakes again, and he'd kept that promise.

A heavyset middle-aged man took the seat beside him in first class, whispered a prayer and almost immediately took out some photographs from his briefcase. A smile covered his face as he gazed at the pictures.

Scott hadn't planned to initiate a conversation with the stranger, but curiosity prompted him. "Your family?" he asked the man.

"Yes. For the past year, I've been working as a construction engineer in Vilnius. I couldn't leave the job, so I've never seen my infant son. I can't wait to get home. I have twin daughters, too," the man went on as if the floodgates had opened up. "They're my life. We thought we couldn't have any more children due to my wife's age—she was thirty-five when we married, which is usually not good news if you want to start a family. But this little fellow is healthy, and I thank God all the time." The man shook his head as if amazed by the miracle of it. He handed Scott the photograph.

"I resisted getting married, but I'm happier than I ever thought I'd be. You got kids?"

Scott stared at the photograph and handed it back to the man. "Not that I know of. I've been so busy with my career that I've let some important areas of my life slide. But when I get home, I'm going to put first things first."

"You're right. I said I'd make my first million before I was thirty-five, and I put living on hold," the man said. "Money is necessary, but it won't buy any of the things that make me happy. Go for it," the man said. "Life is short."

Scott could no longer bear to look at the expression of pure joy on the man's face as he gazed at the pictures of his three children. Scott took pride in his accomplishments, since he was by any measure a success. But he needed more, a different kind of fulfillment. For two years, he had retired every evening to his personal quarters, taken off the diplomatic mask and settled into a loneliness that he couldn't escape. Sure, he was satisfied with the choices he'd made, but not with the sacrifices.

He lifted his glass to his seatmate. "Thanks. Here's to a good life."

The man took a sip after the toast, but a quizzical expression soon spread across his face. "I appreciate your goodwill, but why did you thank me?" the man asked.

Scott savored the glass of wine, held the glass up and drained it. "The people I meet in my line of work are chasing something—dreams, money, status, promotions, women, whatever," he said. "But you stuck with your values, found what you need and recognized it when you got it. That's rare. I hope to do the same."

Ten hours later, when the plane landed at Reagan National Airport, Scott had decided he was going to give himself one year in which to settle down and start a family. He realized it was a tall order, but he also knew that his bosses wouldn't give him more than a year between overseas assignments. He had no intention of spending another year wearing Brooks Brothers suits with shoes that shone like glass, working five, and sometimes seven, days a week, making certain that his face bore just the right expression as he carefully watched every word he uttered, only to be rewarded with lonely, celibate nights.

Where would he start? Of the women he knew and liked, he couldn't see himself sharing his life with any of them. A State Department chauffeur and car met him at the airport and took him to the Willard Inter-Continental hotel, where reservations had been made for him. He usually didn't require that kind of luxury, but it went with the job.

After checking in, he went to his suite. There, he dropped his bag near the door and headed for the kitchen, where he knew he'd find some fresh fruit. When his superior at the State Department had asked his preference for a hotel, he'd said he didn't care where they put him up so long as he found plenty of fresh citrus and berries in the refrigerator. He washed a handful of blueberries and savored them.

Home. How sweet it is, he thought.

He resisted the temptation to go to bed at three in the afternoon and telephoned Judson Philips-Sparkman, his closest friend since the age of five.

"Attorney Philips-Sparkman speaking."

"Man, half of that name is enough. Saying the whole thing is a damned tongue twister."

"Scott! Where the hell are you? Aren't you due back soon?"

"I am, and I'm here."

"What? When? You mean you're in D.C.?"

"I'm at the Willard in a nothing-left-to-the-imagination suite. The plane landed about two and a half hours ago. How's Heather? You two getting along all right?"

"Heather's fine, and of course we're getting along. If you mean at the office, we've easily worked that out. She has clients, and I have clients. We consult with each other, offer and give advice, but we don't interfere in each other's cases."

"That's good. Is her office as big as yours?"

Laughter seemed to roar out of Judson at the question. "Truthfully I'd give anything to say no, but they're exactly the same size. I furnished mine to suit me, and she did the same in hers. By the way, when I try to help her out, she gives me a hard time. I hope she does the same when *you* meddle in her business. How soon can you get over here?"

"I want to hand in my report the day after tomorrow, so I can probably get there late Friday afternoon."

"Why not spend the weekend with us? Check out of the hotel, and I'll pick you up, say, at three-thirty. How's that?"

"Works for me. Give Heather my love. See you Friday."

Since he didn't have any casual clothes with him, he decided to walk up to F Street, where he bought two pairs of jeans, half a dozen T-shirts and a pair of Reeboks. All he wanted was a chance to soak up some sun, be himself with his friends and leave *the ambassador* behind. After checking in with his father and younger brother, he showered and crawled into bed for a nap.

He awakened around six-thirty and called his grandmother, whom he had spoken to while en route to the hotel. "Hi, Nana. How about going out to dinner with me tonight?'

"As long as you feed me Maryland crab cakes. I love

Italian and French food, but you know I love my crab cakes."

"You're on. I'll be there in an hour."

His office had advised him not to check out, but to remain in the hotel until he could move into his condo and his belongings had arrived from Vilnius. So, when Judson arrived on Friday afternoon, Scott was leaning against the reservation desk waiting for him.

"Lord, man, you're a sight for sore eyes," Scott said as he and Judson greeted each other with a warm embrace. "Marriage agrees with you, buddy."

"You bet it does. Wait 'til you get to know my cousins and their families."

"I liked what I've seen of them already. How is Heather dealing with such a big family?"

"You'll see. Neither of us hangs around the office."

"If you'd told me otherwise, I would have thought something was wrong with your marriage. You've only been married for, let's see, eighteen months."

"Best year and a half of my life. Let's take the elevator down to the garage level."

Judson drove his Mercedes out of the hotel garage onto Wisconsin Avenue, connected to Route 270 and headed for Frederick, Maryland. "We're right in Eagle Park next to the Harrington estate, and that's less than fifteen minutes from Frederick. Everybody's expecting you. How's Nana?"

"Great. We had dinner the night I got back."

Half an hour later, Judson parked in front of a stately beige-colored brick house. The first-floor windows provided a glimpse of the cathedral ceilings and the elegant interior. "We told Russ what we wanted the house to look like," Judson explained, "and he designed it to perfection. Drake and Telford did the rest. We're so happy here."

The door opened, and Heather greeted him with open arms. "I haven't hugged a woman since I was here for your wedding eighteen months ago," Scott said, enjoying Heather's warm embrace.

"Just don't get too comfortable there, buddy," Judson told him.

The three of them went inside arm in arm. Once inside, a tall, good-looking woman in skin-tight jeans and a snug red T-shirt walked toward them. Heather grasped the woman's arm. "Adelle Smith, this is Scott Galloway. Scott's just completed a tour as ambassador to Lithuania. Scott, Adelle is one of my law associates."

They greeted each other, although she seemed a bit more enthusiastic than Scott. "How do you do, Adelle?" he said, preferring not to say that he was delighted to meet her since he wasn't so sure.

"I'm fine, Scott. Heather has told me so much about you. I couldn't wait to meet such an impressive man." Her smile bordered on an invitation, as he realized he was facing a woman who didn't mind letting a man know that she liked what she saw.

He raised an eyebrow. "Heather, you never used to exaggerate. Does marriage do that to a person?"

"Of course not. I told her you're like my big brother, and that I'm very protective of you. I also said you're a super guy."

Hmm. So he'd have to negotiate with Adelle for the remainder of the weekend, he thought. The problem was that, although she had the goods in all the right places, he did not like aggressive women who chose men on the basis of sex appeal. Besides, she'd made up her mind before she saw him.

Just play it cool, he said to himself. But how was he going to do that when he was sexually starved, and she'd let him know that nourishment was available?

"I'll show you to your room, Scott," Heather said, saving the day.

He followed her upstairs. "How far apart are these guest rooms, Heather, and does mine have a lock on the door?" Scott said.

She stopped at the top of the stairs, as her eyes widened and her jaw dropped. She stared at him, utterly speechless. Then she laughed so hard that she practically doubled over clutching her stomach. Scott slapped her on the back to help her recover.

"I'd forgotten how frank you can be," she said. "Don't tell me I struck out."

"I'm as hungry as an Alaskan wolf at the end of winter. But if I hook up with that one, I'll never find what I really want."

"What's wrong with her?"

"A gentleman never says anything bad about a woman, no matter what the circumstances."

"Chicken."

She opened the door to the guest room. He tried the doorknob to make sure that it would lock, looked at Heather and winked.

"You were serious, weren't you?" Heather said with a note of surprise in her voice.

He didn't want her to misunderstand him. "Heather,

that woman downstairs would take advantage of a drunken sailor. I'll be down shortly."

"Scott, please don't be mad. I meant well," she said, blinking rapidly, a subtle tic that appeared when she was nonplussed. "Honestly, I did. I'm remembering things about you now that I had forgotten during these past two years while you were away. You're right. I definitely didn't choose the right one."

A grin spread across his face. It was so good to be back with his two dearest friends. "Knowing you, I'm sure you've got some more lined up. See you later."

He let his gaze take in the decor of the room around him. He liked blue, and Heather had furnished the guest room in a light navy blue and rustic orange for a striking effect. He changed into black jeans and a red polo shirt, slipped on his new Reeboks and bounded down the wide, curved staircase. Russ Harrington was indeed a brilliant architect, Scott thought. He'd said as much to Judson.

"All three of them are good at what they do," said Judson. "They have a tremendous reputation as builders, and Telford, the eldest, is only forty-one. The Harringtons are coming over with their wives after dinner. And the Harrington women have taken to Heather and made her one of their own."

"So you're glad you decided to live here?"

"Absolutely! My family is here. Scott, this is where I belong."

"I'm glad for you, Judson. Say, I brought you guys something," Scott said, handing Judson a box that contained half a dozen tins of Beluga caviar.

Judson looked at the contents of the box. "Get outta

here, man. This stuff is precious. Let me see if Rosa has any crème fraîche."

Heather looked at the gift. "Crème fraîche? All I need for this is some melba toast or blinis. Scott, you always were a classy guy. Thank you."

"To tell the truth, it was caviar or vodka, unless I wanted to drag two fur coats home. Not a lot to choose from."

"I'm not complaining," Judson said. "Is this dry ice?"

"Yeah. Be careful not to let it burn you."

Adelle came downstairs after having changed into a red jersey dress that advertised her assets. The four of them sat in the den, which was cozier than the thirty-by-twenty-foot living room with cathedral ceilings.

She saw the caviar on the coffee table and slowly licked the rim of her lips with her tongue, tracing the outline of her mouth in what would have been a great Marilyn Monroe imitation. "Mmm, caviar! This is the kind of delicacy that can make you forget who you are," she said.

"In that case," Scott said, "I would avoid it."

Heather's face was flush with embarrassment. She dashed into the kitchen, and quickly returned. "Dinner's ready. Come with me," she said hastily.

Judson said grace—a habit he'd adopted from the Harringtons—and then the housekeeper, Rosa, began serving the meal, which included broiled grapefruit as an appetizer, prime roast beef, parsleyed potatoes, asparagus and artichoke hearts. A wedge of Stilton cheese, followed by lemon meringue pie, completed the dinner.

"Rosa, you and women like you are the reason why

I'm so happy to be back home," said Scott, as Rosa served the pie. Judson dropped his fork on the dessert plate, and began coughing to avoid choking as he tried to suppress his amusement.

"Mr. Ambassador, you just made my day," said Rosa, soaking up the praise. "I love to cook, and it makes me happy when I know my people enjoy what I serve them. Thank you, sir."

Scott had hoped that he'd sent the right message— that he liked simple things, and in his choice of women, he preferred the girl next door. "I just tell it like it is, Rosa. You're a wonderful cook."

"What a lovely evening for a walk," Adelle said, looking at Scott.

"Judson's cousins and their wives will be over in a few minutes," Heather said, "and the only reason they're coming is to see Scott. Maybe you can go for a walk later," she continued. Minutes later, Drake Harrington, the youngest of the three Harrington brothers, and his wife, Pamela, joined them.

"Damn!" Scott said, looking at Drake when he walked into the room. "I forgot how much alike you and Judson are. Your grandfather had some powerful genes."

"It's our private joke," Drake said, pulling out Pamela's chair and making himself comfortable. "It's a good thing we have a sense of humor, 'cause we confuse a lot of people."

"Right," Judson added, "and we're lucky that our wives have become very good friends and don't mind the resemblance."

"The first time I saw Judson, I nearly went into shock," Pamela said. "It took some getting used to."

Scott observed Adelle surreptitiously. He could have sworn she seemed to salivate, but whether it was because of him or Drake Harrington, he wasn't sure. Telford Harrington and his brother Russ arrived together, along with their wives, Alexis and Velma, who were sisters. Immediately Velma began entertaining them with her stories, and Scott leaned back in his chair, sipping piña coladas, listening to the various conversations and enjoying the good company. Like a long-lost son, Scott felt that he had come home to surroundings of warmth and love. Adelle Smith was out of her element, and her obvious discomfort showed it.

By ten-thirty, Scott felt a bit jet-lagged. He told his hosts he was tired and went to his room. He would have preferred to continue the conversation, which he had greatly enjoyed, but he reasoned that Adelle wouldn't have the nerve to follow him up the stairs in such an obvious ploy. He locked the door, and thought to himself, Safe for at least one night.

The next morning, he called Judson on his cell phone. "Say, man, what time is breakfast and who's up?"

Laughter seemed to roar out of Judson's mouth. "I had almost forgotten that you were so blunt. The reason for running off last night was obvious. But if you're hungry, why give a damn who's up?"

"Why, indeed? I like my breakfast in peace. I don't know, though. Something tells me that if Drake's around, I won't have a problem."

"What do you mean?"

"Her mouth looked like it was watering once he arrived."

He didn't need the phone to hear Judson's laughter. "Come on downstairs, man. Rosa made a fantastic breakfast."

Scott dressed for dinner that evening, since he assumed he'd be expected to drive Adelle home to Baltimore. It would also give him the opportunity to let her know in no uncertain terms that he was not interested in her.

"If you give me the keys to your Mercedes, I'll drive Adelle back to Baltimore," Scott said to Judson, in a quiet moment away from the rest of the guests, when they gathered for predinner drinks.

Judson's eyebrows shot up. "You sure you want to do that?"

"It's the best chance to disabuse her of any notion she has about me. It'll take me no longer than the half hour or so that it takes me to drive there and back."

A grin flashed across Judson's face. "That time as a bigwig didn't change you one bit. Glad to see it." He reached into his trouser pockets, took out two sets of keys and handed the smaller one to Scott. "This is the house key and this is the car key."

"Thanks, buddy."

After dinner, he tired of waiting for Adelle to announce that she was leaving, so he decided to take matters into his own hands. "Adelle, if you're going to Baltimore tonight, I'll be glad to drive you, but we'll need to leave now." He felt the tiniest inkling of guilt when he saw her face break out in the warmest smile he'd witnessed, but he quickly shook it off.

He managed to avoid saying anything personal during the drive to Baltimore. The conversation had been amicable by the time they arrived at her condominium, in what was obviously an upscale neighborhood.

"Aren't you coming in?" she asked him, when he opened the car door for her. He stood back and extended his hand for a handshake, leaving her clearly aghast.

He shook his head. "To do that would send you the wrong message. I'm not interested, Adelle, and I do not mislead women. Good night." He left her standing in front of her apartment building, walked back to the driver's side of the car and got in. When she didn't move, he started the car to let her know that he wasn't joking. Only then did she turn and enter the building. Ordinarily, he wouldn't think of being that rude, but he hadn't met many women like Adelle. He hoped that Pamela Harrington was an observant woman, and that she'd noticed the look in Adelle's eyes as she ogled Pamela's husband, Drake.

"We're having a barbecue this afternoon," Heather told Scott at breakfast the next morning, "and all the Harringtons will be here."

"What about Tara? And Henry? Is he coming?"

"Indeed, he is. Henry is the same," she said. "He's just as spry and his tongue is as tart as ever. I can't think of life without Henry."

Later that morning, Scott took his swim trunks and walked over to Telford's house. Henry opened the door for him, and he clasped the frail man in a big hug. "If you gripped me any tighter," Henry said, "I'd think you were one of those snakes that squeezes the life out of things before devouring them. Thanks for leaving my old bones intact. You look great, and I been expectin' to see you."

"You're the one who looks good. You don't think I'd come to Eagle Park and leave without seeing you, do you?"

"Some people manage to, and in most cases, I'm glad they do."

"Where's Tara? She must be a big girl by now."

"She's nine and as sweet as she ever was. Tel took her to her piano lessons. You want coffee and something to go with it?"

"Actually, I'd like to take a swim in the pool. I know it's still a bit cool for that, but I got used to swimming in water that was barely tepid."

"Looks like it did you good. You're bigger, but ya ain't fat."

He patted Henry's shoulder. "I can't afford to get fat, Henry. I'd have to buy all new clothes."

Alexis swept into the kitchen. "Scott. I thought I heard someone talking, and Henry definitely doesn't talk to himself. How are you this morning?" Her eyes twinkled with mischief, and he didn't have to guess why. "I hope you got back safely last night, and in good time." He stared at her for a minute. She didn't back down, giving the private joke free rein.

"A guy does what he has to do," Scott said, playing along. "Is the pool open?"

"Russ opened it up a few weeks back when we had a hot spell. You're welcome to swim as often as you like."

"Thanks. In Vilnius I got in the habit of swimming every day, and I miss it already."

Scott swam a few laps, and then hiked along the Monocacy River. As he walked along the trails, he wished he had a fishing rod and tackle. A profusion of spring flowers—jonquil, wild roses, lotus, morning glory, forsythia, dandelions and other wildflowers—greeted him as he strolled along the riverbank. Squirrels scampered up and down trees and across his path, ignoring him. He loved being alone in such a beautiful, natural environment. But at the moment, he longed for the company of a woman whom he deeply cared for. He made his way back to the Harrington estate, which Telford and his family occupied, and found Henry picking roses that grew beside the house.

"I never paid any attention to these here flowers," Henry said, "'til Alexis came. She loves for the place to be pretty and elegant. But these here early roses got thorns, so I pick 'em to keep her from getting pricked."

"You're a gentleman, Henry. See you at the barbecue."

Scott returned to Judson's house, and after showering and changing into a yellow polo shirt and white jeans, he went to the kitchen to find Rosa. "You've got a crowd coming," he said to her. "What can I do to help?"

She looked at him with adoring eyes, since he had become her favorite houseguest. "Maybe I shouldn't ask you, but, Mr. Ambassador, I think the food should be covered. Can you cover the food with this cotton canvas? The heat from the food will melt plastic wrap, so I bought canvas."

He took the canvas cloth from her. "For you, anything, Rosa. You've helped make my visit a really wonderful experience." As she melted, he left the kitchen grinning.

"The old boy hasn't lost his touch," he said to himself.

Pamela and Drake arrived first. Scott was leaning against a tree, with the sole of his left foot flat against the tree trunk, when he looked up and saw her walking between the couple. Now, there was a woman with grace, charm, dignity, a good measure of femininity in all the right places and beauty to boot. He straightened up, but he stayed where he was. He'd seen that woman somewhere before. But where? Who was she?

As they approached, he went to greet them. "Pamela, Drake," he said. "How are you?"

"Great," they said in unison.

"Scott Galloway, this is Denise Miller, my best friend since crib days," Pamela said.

"I'm glad to meet you," he said earnestly.

"Me, too, Scott," Denise said. "Pamela said you just returned from Lithuania. Are you glad to be home?"

"I'm happy to be with my friends, to have a steady supply of fresh produce and to soak up the sun," he said. "I haven't been home yet because my place isn't ready and my belongings haven't arrived from Lithuania." He fell into step with them as they headed toward the back patio and the barbecue.

"Is that what you missed most?" she asked.

Those were the only things he missed that he could talk about. "I missed other things, too—mainly opportunities to be just plain old Scott Galloway."

Drake walked over toward them, munching on a chicken leg. Scott appreciated—and not for the first time—that he was six feet four inches tall, and equal to Drake and his brothers in stature. Drake dwarfed most men in looks and physique, but not him. And he hoped Denise Miller was well aware of that.

"How's that barbecue?" he asked Drake, in an effort to stall for time by involving him in conversation. He was interested in Denise Miller, but wanted to go slowly, at least until he figured out why he was so sure he knew her from someplace.

Drake laughed. "It's a delicious barbecue chicken leg. But if you're not a leg man, the breasts look pretty good, too."

"I think I'll do my own investigation," Denise said, and left the two of them to enjoy Drake's joke.

Scott eyed Drake. "Is she annoyed?"

"No, but she'd rather I hadn't said that. Seems she'd prefer to make a good impression on you, and *that* surprises me."

"She didn't seem particularly interested. Why are you surprised at her wanting to make a good impression?"

"Denise is not easily impressed, but you caught her eye before we saw you. And the closer we got, the more she liked what she saw. Trust me, man, I'm right."

"She was interesting from afar, but the closer she got, the more interesting she became. Trust *me*." They both laughed.

"This is a magnificent house, Drake. Judson said that you and your brothers built it. Russ is a heck of an architect," said Scott.

"He is that, and his designs are becoming more creative. But, as an engineer, I appreciate his work even more."

"If I ever build a house, I hope you brothers are still in the business."

"Unless you plan to build it when you're ready to retire, I don't think you have much to worry about."

"Thanks for the assurance, man. But it's time I got my act together."

"Yeah," Drake said. "I thought I had to wait until I got my life exactly the way I wanted it, but Pamela's clock was ticking, and she let me know it. I realized that I didn't have to be a nationally recognized engineer in order to be happy. But I needed her for that."

"I don't regret the choices I've made, Drake," said Scott. "I regret the sacrifices."

"As long as you're ready to deal with a relationship, it's never too late."

In those few minutes, Scott realized that of the Harrington brothers, Drake was his favorite. The man gave the appearance of being a corporate executive, but he was a down-to-earth guy who had his priorities in order, and he had a great sense of humor.

"How long have you and Pamela been married?"

"Close to two wonderful years. Smartest thing I ever did. Marriage is good. Try it," he said with a grin. "You'll like it."

"I hope so. I don't have anyone in mind, but after two years in Vilnius without a companion, my antenna is up."

Drake seemed to contemplate the statement. "I can't imagine that that was easy. There must have been plenty of times you were lonely or just needed someone to talk to, and didn't have anyone with whom to share your problems. It had to be troubling."

"You nailed it on the head, Drake. In spite of all the people around to do whatever I said or asked, it was a lonely life."

"You two seem to be hitting it off," Heather said, as she approached them. "I brought you some lemonade. If you want anything stronger, it's over there in that large wooden tub."

"Thanks," Scott said. "Where'd you get that wooden tub?"

"My dad got it from his grandmother," said Heather. "You must have made quite an impression on Denise. She's asking questions about you."

Scott sipped his lemonade. "Really? Tell her I'm perfect," he said, trying to sound nonchalant. He couldn't understand Drake's sudden fit of laughter.

"I wonder if I was that scared of getting what I wanted," Drake said, amused by Scott's expression. "As I look back, I realize how lucky I really was that Pamela ignored my foolishness." He looked at Scott. "I met Adelle Smith and she isn't in Denise Miller's league by a long shot."

"I get your message loud and clear," added Scott.

Telford and Russ arrived along with their families. "Excuse me," Scott said to Drake and Heather when he saw Tara.

"You've gotten taller in the eighteen months since I last saw you," Scott said to Tara with a wide smile. "How are you?"

"I'm fine, Mr. Galloway. I'm going to finish the school year with straight As."

"That doesn't surprise me. You're as smart as you are pretty." He looked at Telford, Tara's stepfather, whose pride in his daughter shone in his eyes. "Tara is the most compelling advertisement for marriage that I can think of."

"Thank you," Telford said. "She's always a delight."

"What do they mean, Mummy?"

"Mr. Scott was congratulating your daddy on raising you properly."

"Oh. I thought he said I was lovely."

Scott suppressed a laugh. Tara was only nine years old, but already she was mature beyond her years.

The four of them walked around to the patio, where the barbecue grill, food and drinks were set up.

"It's about time you got here," Judson said. "Pamela and I want to eat. We've got pulled pork, barbecue chicken and baby back ribs, grilled new potatoes, zucchini, onions, asparagus and a green salad. Beer, wine and chilled vodka are over there." He pointed to a shaded area. "Everybody for themselves."

"Don't we have to say grace, Uncle Judson?" Tara asked.

"Yes, we do," Russ said. "I'll say it. By the time you finish it, we'll be ready to eat Christmas dinner."

Tara giggled. "Mr. Scott, my uncle Russ doesn't like the way I say grace. It really freaks him out."

Scott noticed that Denise remained on the fringe of the group. He got two empty plates, forks and napkins, and went over to her and handed her one of each.

"I'm hungry, and I haven't had any good barbecue in a couple of years. Will you join me?"

"Thanks. I was just waiting for everyone to start. Why has it been two years?"

"I've been in Vilnius, Lithuania. I only returned for Judson and Heather's wedding, but I was in the States less than seventy-two hours. I was Judson's best man."

Denise appeared reflective for a moment. "So you're close friends," she said.

"Very much so, since I was five years old. He's closer to me than my real brothers."

"Really?"

"We went from kindergarten through college and law school together." He took a pair of tongs and put some pulled pork on her plate. "Want some chicken or ribs?"

"Ribs. I love ribs, though I have to use yards of dental floss after I eat them. Where do you live, Scott?"

"Right now, I'm staying at the Willard in Washington. But my belongings should arrive from Vilnius next week. Then, I'll either move into my condo in Baltimore or sell it and move to Washington, where I work."

She accepted the plate of pulled pork, ribs and vegetables. "Thank you. I imagine you must have mixed feelings about moving."

"Of course. I'll hate not being close to my grandmother. She's getting older."

"Do you have family other than your brothers and your grandmother?"

"There's my father. My grandmother helped him raise us after our mother died in a car crash almost twenty years ago. She's very dear to me. Where do you live, Denise?" Scott said, deciding that it was time to move the focus to her.

"I have a house in Frederick and an apartment in Washington, and I divide my time between the two places."

He could see that she was deftly avoiding any details, at least about herself, so he decided to be more direct. "I work for the State Department, Denise. What do you do?"

"I know you're an ambassador, Scott. I'm a—a fundraiser." Her brow creased in a frown. "You don't remember me, do you?"

"Actually, I do. I believe I met you at a party, but I'm having trouble remembering which one."

She lowered her gaze. "Don't you remember seeing me at the party Judson gave for you when you were leaving for Lithuania? We weren't introduced, but that's where we met."

He hoped that his eagerness and excitement in preparing for his diplomatic assignment explained what must have been a testosterone malfunction. "That send-off and having everyone address me as 'Mr. Ambassador' nearly overwhelmed me. Something about that party seems to nag at me, though." He shrugged his shoulder. "My preference is for the simple life. So Denise, do you work in Washington?" he said, quickly changing the subject.

A slight smile didn't quite make it to her eyes. "I love politics, but not that much."

He wondered at her seeming reluctance to tell him where she worked. "As long as you raise money for good causes, I'd say that's a good thing." If she didn't want to open up, he'd find out what he wanted to know some other way.

"Where do your folks live, Denise?" he said, figuring the innocuous question would help continue their conversation. He had to get used to her name, since he wasn't sure that it really suited her. She had an almost aristocratic air about her that he didn't especially like, and women like that weren't usually named Denise, but rather something like Caroline, Amanda or Allison.

Maybe he'd been away from African-American women too long. He told himself to stop trying to figure her out, that if she was interested in him, she'd open up.

She hadn't answered him, so he decided to change tactics.

"Would you have dinner with me?" he said.

She looked him in the eye. "When did you have in mind?"

The heat from her fiery brown eyes seared through him. But if she could eyeball him, he could certainly do the same. "Friday, and as many times as you'd like thereafter."

"You're a bold man."

He gave a quick shrug of his shoulders. "I don't remember ever getting anything or anywhere in life by being timid, Denise. It's not my style."

"I certainly never imagined you were a man who passively accepted whatever circumstances he encountered," she replied candidly.

He stared at her, mulling over the situation. "Where will you be next Friday between five-thirty and seven?" She gave him her address in Frederick, Maryland. "I'll be there at six-thirty in jacket and tie." The brilliant smile that covered her face surged through him like an electrical charge. The woman was beautiful.

"I'm looking forward to Friday."

"So am I," he said truthfully, while hoping and praying that he wasn't shooting himself in the foot.

Chapter 2

Denise brushed her long, silky black hair until it shimmered. She curled it, brushed out the curls and let them fall softly around her shoulders. "At least it's mine and not a weave," she said to herself with a note of pride. She had inherited both her hair and her dark complexion from her maternal grandmother, who was a Shinnecock. Her father's family had been mixed since slavery.

She didn't want to overdress, but she wanted to look good. Scott Galloway was a strikingly handsome man, and she wanted to make an impression. When she'd looked into those dreamy grayish-brown eyes, half-hidden by long lashes that curled slightly at the ends, she'd felt as if a bolt of lightning had shot through her body. Leaning against a tree as if he didn't have a care in the world, he'd taken her breath away. But she didn't believe for one minute that he was as nonchalant as he appeared. The first time she'd met him, two years ago at a reception, they'd been sitting near each other at a round table. She couldn't see much more than his profile. And he'd been so thoroughly peeved with her that he barely spared her a glance, or so it seemed.

She had always been attracted to very dark-skinned men. But Scott's complexion, which was the color of shelled walnuts, gave him a polished, masculine look that got to her. And what a physique!

"Get your head on straight, sister," she told herself. "Those looks don't mean a thing if that's all there is to him."

The thought amused her. Of course, he was a man of substance and, she imagined, had plenty of it. He seemed to have it all. Nevertheless, she wondered what his Achilles' heel was. She had yet to meet a man who didn't have one.

When the doorbell rang, she was wearing a short silk chiffon dinner dress that was a goldenrod color with insets that began where the hip stopped, and a rounded bodice that revealed no cleavage. Diamond stud earrings, black patent-leather pumps, a black silk purse and a dab of perfume completed her attire.

"How do I look, Priscilla?" she asked her housekeeper. Priscilla Mallory lived in Frederick, Maryland, but she commuted to D.C. when Denise was staying in Washington.

"Like you ever look anything but great. If he isn't blind, he's gonna be when he sees you in that getup. Real sweet, ma'am."

Denise opened the door and thanked God for self-control.

"Hi. You're punctual. I like that," he said as he handed her a dozen yellow roses.

"Hi. You're both punctual and a gentleman. Thank you. You chose the right color roses. I love yellow, and I adore yellow roses. Have a seat in the living room while I put these in a vase."

She headed for the kitchen to find a vase. Decked out in a khaki-colored suit, a light shirt and burnt-orange tie, Scott Galloway was something to look at. "Go into the living room, Priscilla, and introduce yourself to Ambassador Scott Galloway," Denise said to her housekeeper.

Priscilla's eyes bulged and her lower jaw sagged. "Yes, ma'am. Yes, indeedy."

Now, when did that happen? thought Denise. She entered the living room in time to see Priscilla putting a tray with two glasses of white wine and cheese sticks on the coffee table in front of Scott, who stood and extended his hand to shake hers.

"Ambassador Galloway, this is Mrs. Priscilla Mallory. She keeps thing in order around here."

"I'm her housekeeper, Mr. Ambassador, and I take care of her like she was my own child."

"I'm delighted to meet you, Mrs. Mallory. Thank you for the wine and cheese sticks. If you have any club soda, I'd like to add it to my wine. I'm driving."

"Oh. You want a spritzer?" Priscilla asked.

"Yes, thank you."

Denise hadn't planned for them to spend time alone at her house, but it wasn't a bad idea. She had learned more about Scott since he'd come through the door than in all the time she'd spent with him the previous Sunday at Judson and Heather's barbecue. Good manners and a lack of ego came naturally to him, she surmised. She sat beside him and lifted her glass.

"Welcome to my home, Scott. Do you like these?" She pointed to the cheese sticks. "Priscilla makes them, and the house would be full of them if I encouraged her."

"I love these things. I used to buy them at Dean & DeLuca. These are the first I've had since I got back. Mrs. Mallory must have some special recipe."

"I'll tell her you enjoyed them"

"We ought to leave soon. Our reservation is for seven-thirty, and we are driving to Washington. It took me about forty minutes to get here. Do you mind if I tell Mrs. Mallory good-night?"

"Of course not."

He headed for the kitchen. "Thank you for these wonderful cheese sticks, Mrs. Mallory. I've always loved them. Good evening."

"You're welcome, and you come back soon. I've always got plenty of cheese sticks baked nice and fresh."

As if he had always done so, he grabbed Denise's hand and they left. "When did you have time to buy a car?" she asked him as he opened the door to a new luxury car

"I'm leasing it, but I'll probably end up buying it after I settle in. I've decided to live in Washington and avoid that daily commute that I had when I lived in Baltimore."

"Have you found a place yet?"

"Not yet. I have three or four places to check out."

By the time they reached Washington, he knew she

liked classic jazz—the Louis Armstrong–Duke Ellington variety. She loved Mozart and disliked Wagner. She adored Italian Renaissance art, disliked contemporary art and loved Aretha Franklin and Luther Vandross.

"I'd like a duplex apartment," Scott said, "because I like the idea of having separate levels for entertaining and my bedroom and private quarters."

"You don't want a house?" she asked.

"No. I'd have to hire a live-in housekeeper to maintain the place, and I don't want that."

At the restaurant, the maître d' seated them and beckoned the sommelier. She and Scott decided not to order cocktails.

"We'll choose the wine after we order our meal," Scott said to the sommelier. They both ordered the arugula salad, shrimp diablo, saffron rice and spinach. And for dessert, they ordered raspberries with kirsch and ice cream.

"Did you order this because I did?" he asked her.

"No. As a matter of fact, I order this every time I come here. It's one of my favorite restaurants."

Scott's eyebrow arched a bit at her comment, and she wondered what his reaction was to her preference in restaurants. She appreciated that he didn't probe, and the more she got to know him, the more she liked him.

Scott looked at the woman seated across from him. She had the elegance of a finely tuned Stradivarius, but she was, nonetheless, very approachable. He wondered how much of the latter was real and how much was for effect. They had much more in common than he would have imagined, and he found himself wanting to know her better. But something held him back, and it puzzled him. Always a man to keep his own counsel, he let his instincts guide him.

"Where did you grow up?" he asked her, opting for a safe topic of conversation.

"Waverly, Texas. My father's folks have been Texans for generations, one of the first families of African-American ranchers in the state."

"Ranchers? And did you attend one of the exclusive Seven Sisters colleges?"

"What an interesting question," Denise said, genuinely surprised. "My parents wanted me to go to Bryn Mawr, but when I found out the ratio of female to male students, I balked and went to Princeton."

He leaned forward and hoped that his anxiety didn't show. "How'd that work out?"

"That's where I developed my intolerance for snobs."

He couldn't help laughing. "Did you fall in love with or marry any of them?"

"No to both. But while I was getting my degree, I had a great time."

"Why doesn't that surprise me? I can imagine that whatever the ratio of men to women at Princeton, you probably had your pick."

She lowered her gaze. "You're too kind."

Sarcasm or humility? He wasn't certain which. The waiter brought their food, saving him the need to reply.

"You're driving, and I know you don't want to drink," she said thoughtfully when Scott offered to order a bottle of wine. "I wouldn't enjoy it if you couldn't have any. By the way," Denise said, changing the subject, "I belong to a group that's putting on a big fundraiser in Philadelphia, and Velma Harrington is catering it. She's incredible."

"Yes," he said, as something played around in the back of his mind. He knew it was important, but he couldn't put his finger on it.

They eventually finished the meal with espresso, and as they left the restaurant, he tried to remember what her mention of Velma Harrington had triggered. He shook his head in frustration.

During the drive back to Frederick, she hummed along with the songs that played on the radio. She didn't seem compelled to fill the time with idle talk, for which he was grateful. He had very little patience for meaningless chatter. He also liked the fact that, during the entire evening, she hadn't once tried to flaunt her sex appeal. And he especially appreciated that the neckline of her dress wasn't an advertisement for the milk industry.

He hated having to spend an evening with his mouth watering over a woman's cleavage. Usually if he liked her, he was tempted to hurry the evening along so that he could indulge. If he didn't like her, it invariably annoyed him.

He parked in front of the large brick house that she called home and walked her to the door. "May I have your key?" he asked. She handed it to him and stepped aside while he opened the door.

"Would you like me to see if everything is okay?" he asked her.

Her eyes widened. "Why, yes. Thank you," she said calmly.

He walked in, closed the door, locked it and handed her the key. "Stay here," he said.

It was a good-size house. Upstairs, he checked two bedrooms, a large office and three bathrooms, one of which had a big Jacuzzi and what seemed like endless closet space. He walked through the living, dining and breakfast rooms, then the kitchen and pantry, which revealed no surprises. He returned to the foyer and saw that she stood precisely where he had left her.

"Do you have a basement?"

"Yes, but do you think—"

"Denise, I never half do *anything*."

After checking the basement, he bounded up the stairs and joined her in the foyer. "Thank you for a really wonderful evening. I've enjoyed being with you," he said. He leaned down and kissed her cheek. "Good night."

He didn't laugh at her wide-eyed look of surprise. But controlling the impulse to smirk cost him plenty. However, Denise was poised, and she quickly recovered her aplomb. "This has been a wonderful evening, Scott. I've enjoyed every minute of it. Get home safely."

He got into the car and shook as the laughter he had managed to control earlier spilled out. He drove three blocks and parked so that he could safely let out peals of laughter that had him practically bursting at the seams. He didn't know what Denise had expected when he took her home. But having been celibate for so long, he'd decided to play it safe. Anything more than a peck on the cheek would have gotten him in deep trouble. He wanted her. He *really* did. But since he had managed this long, a few more weeks wouldn't kill him.

After parking in the hotel garage, he decided against taking the elevator to his floor and took the escalator to the lobby instead. As he passed the reception desk, the odor of freshly baked oatmeal-raisin cookies that the manager placed on the desk every evening tantalized his nose. He turned back around, took a couple of cookies and bit into one. The taste made him think of the dessert that Velma brought to Heather's and Judson's barbecue. He snapped his fingers. She'd served that same dessert at the going-away party Judson had given for him a couple of years ago. Suddenly, he remembered Denise Miller, and what she had said to him at that reception.

By the time he reached his hotel room, he remembered their encounter clearly. She had self-righteously taken him to task for not making environmental issues a priority as ambassador to Lithuania. "The entire region is a major industrial polluter, and you have a platform to bring about change. I am disappointed that it's not part of your mission," she'd said.

At the time, he was sure everyone at the table could see the smoke billowing from his ears. He'd answered without looking in her direction. "Our government is not sending me there to lecture the Lithuanian government about clean air." He had turned his back to her and not said another word to her until Sunday afternoon at the barbecue.

He also hadn't forgiven her for it, now that he thought about it, and he meant to let her know. A frown spread across his face. He supposed he hadn't remembered the incident because he didn't associate such a strident voice with the Denise Miller he'd just met. This Denise was much softer, more feminine and lovely. He went to the minibar, put two cubes of ice in a glass and filled it with vodka. His immediate inclination was to telephone her right then and there, but a glance at his watch disabused him of the notion. It was a quarter to one in the morning. As furious as he was, his desire to get even didn't override his sense of decency. He slept fitfully, anxious for the morning to come when he could telephone Denise Miller at last.

When his phone rang at a quarter to nine, he almost gave in to the urge to ignore it, but the ringing persisted.

"Galloway speaking."

"Hi, Scott. This is Heather. How did your date with Denise go?"

"She told you we had a date?"

"Yes. Her feet hardly touched the ground for a week in anticipation. She was so excited that we asked her why she was so eager."

"Hmm. Well, I've got a few words for that woman."

"Why? What happened?"

"Nothing," he said. "Last night, I liked her. What pissed me off was what happened two years ago at the reception Judson gave for me. It took me a while, but I finally remembered how mad she made me with her self-righteous statements about environmental consciousness."

"You mean it's over before it even got started?"

"I don't know. Maybe I just need to get this off my chest. I would appreciate it, Heather, if you wouldn't mention it."

"You like her?"

"What man wouldn't?"

After putting the receiver back in its cradle, Scott paced the length of his room and walked back to the telephone. He lifted the receiver and stood looking at it. His fingers brushed against his jawline, reminding him that he needed to shave. But he wasn't thinking about shaving. He wanted to stop procrastinating and call Denise Miller. He dialed Drake Harrington's number and asked Drake if he could get Denise's number from Pamela, his wife. Pamela came to the telephone.

"Hi, Scott. You want Denise's number?"

"Yes, please. I didn't ask her for it after our date." She gave him the telephone number. "Thanks, Pamela. I'll be in touch."

He hung up, dialed Denise's number, and when she answered, he got straight to the point. "Good morning, Denise. I hope you slept well. No wonder I didn't remember where we met. You made me mad as hell!" Scott said, barely taking a breath.

"Would you mind explaining to me why you attacked me at that dinner party? Do you remember being a smart-ass and taking me to task, someone you didn't know anything about? You embarrassed me. For days, I fumed over your indictment of me. What do you have to say about this?"

"Scott, I'm stunned," said Denise. "I had forgotten all about that. I suppose at the time I didn't think I was out of line. Two years ago, I was deeply involved in programs to improve our environment. I'm certain that I wouldn't do the same thing today."

"But why on earth did you attack *me?*"

"I don't know. For one thing, you seemed to ignore me when I tried to start a conversation with you about the environment, effectively dismissing me, and I was hurt. I guess I went for the jugular. Am I forgiven?"

"I don't know. I'm not sure."

"If you're not sure, why did you kiss me last night?"

"That certainly wasn't what I call a kiss. At the time, Denise, I hadn't figured out why I had reservations about you. And I also hadn't made up my mind."

"Not only are you brash, you're brutally honest, as well. Have you made up your mind yet?"

"Try not to ask me a question if you don't want the answer. I want a lot more, but I believe in being cautious."

"Are you planning on dropping things right now? I mean, are you still so angry with me—the me you went out to dinner with last night—now that you know me?"

"You really turned me off that night. The woman I met recently is so different that I really don't know what to make of it. Suppose we leave things as they are for the time being. Have a wonderful weekend. Goodbye."

Denise stared at the receiver in her hand. He'd hung up without waiting for her to say goodbye, and that meant he was still angry. She'd barely remembered her criticism of him, or that she'd done it because he'd ignored her. Why, he'd barely spared her a glance.

Suddenly, she started to giggle, and then she was consumed with laughter. Two years before, she was passionate about the environment. She'd believed that since men had gotten the world into its current predicament, they should step aside and allow women to correct their mistakes. That was then.

Scott probably had little patience with aggressive women, but he seemed to like women who were soft and smart.

She sat down at the kitchen table to eat her breakfast. Priscilla served the coffee and joined her. "Ma'am, how was your date with Ambassador Galloway? He's a great catch, and he knows how to treat a woman."

"I know, Priscilla. But if he isn't interested in me, nothing will happen. I may genuflect to my father, but not to any other man."

Priscilla looked at her. "You expect me to believe he didn't ask you out again? I thought it was him that called you this morning."

"It was." She related to Priscilla what had happened with Scott two years earlier. "He's still mad at me," she said. "He didn't remember what I said to him until after our date."

"What a pity! He likes you a lot."

"Or rather, he did. But I am not planning to get any gray hairs over it."

"Well, what you gon' do?"

"God didn't make just one of him. There's gotta be at least one more," said Denise.

"Well, I guess you know what you're doing," Priscilla said.

Denise finished breakfast, brushed her teeth and went to her home office, which was at the top of the stairs overlooking a small brook that fed downstream into the Monocacy River. The phone rang before she could begin recording notes that she made for her secretary, who came in twice a week.

She checked the caller ID. "Hi, Pamela."

"Hi. Can you come over Friday for the weekend? We're entertaining a client Friday evening. The brothers handed him the key to a new apartment complex a few days ago. Whenever they finish a building, they usually entertain the client. Please come. We want you to be here."

"I suppose it's a dressy affair."

"Why, yes. We'll start with cocktails at about five-thirty."

"Is Scott Galloway going to be there, too?"

"Well, I don't know whether he'll be over here for the weekend. But if he is, he is certainly welcome."

"It's not important, Pamela. Things didn't go so well with us. I thought our date was wonderful, and I think he did, too, until he remembered what I said to him at that reception."

"Yes, I know about that. But honey, if he was angry with you for two long years, then he must have been attracted to you. No man stays mad that long with a woman who means nothing to him. Trust me."

"If you say so, Pamela. But you know I don't have a lot of patience. The problem is I like Scott a heck of a lot."

"Not to worry. Drake made a date with me for the express purpose of telling me that he wanted to move on. We've been married going on two years."

"I'm very attracted to Scott, but I'm not going to prostrate myself. No way!"

"And that's a good thing, because it would probably turn him off. See you Friday afternoon. Bye"

"Right. I'll be there around four. Bye." She hung up and propped her elbow on her desk. She knew Pamela wouldn't lie to her. But Denise also knew that the minute Pamela hung up, she'd called Heather and tell her that if Scott was spending the weekend with them, have him phone her. Just the move she needed. She wasn't going to chase him, but she damn sure was not going to avoid him.

Denise knew her friend well. At that moment, Pamela was talking to Heather. "They're not getting along so well, but I've known Denise practically all of my life, and she likes Scott. But her pride won't allow her to concede to him. Will he be here this weekend?"

"He's here every weekend for as long as he's staying at the Willard. I'd better tell him about the reception and—"

"Let me call him," Pamela said. "I want to invite him personally. That way, I'll be sure he's coming." Heather gave her Scott's office number, and she dialed it.

"Hello, Scott, this is Pamela Harrington. We're having a reception for one of the Harringtons' clients this Friday at five-thirty, and we'd love you to come."

"Thanks. I'll be out there anyway. What kind of client is he...or she?" She told him. "Is the party business casual or black tie?"

"Black tie, but it's summer, so—"

"Not to worry, Pamela. I'll put together a comfortable summer monkey suit. Will Denise be there?"

Of course she'd known that he'd ask, and she had

her answer ready. "She's our houseguest. Scott, Denise is like my sister. Our families are very close, so we've been friends for a long time."

"Interesting. Thanks for the invitation. I'll see you Friday. Give Drake my regards."

"Will do. Bye."

She called Heather. "Is it all right to have dancing at a party that ends at nine o'clock?"

"Why not? Play some classics, and everyone will be dancing. Uh, why do you want dancing?"

"If other couples are dancing, how is Scott going to avoid asking Denise to dance?"

"You don't know Scott," Heather said. "Still, it's definitely worth a try. Is your guest married?"

"Yes."

"Thank God for that. He won't be in the picture. I'll be over Thursday evening to help. I won't be able to leave the office until around four, but I'll be over there as soon as I can get home and change."

Dressed in an off-white dinner jacket, white shirt, black tuxedo pants, black bow tie and black patent-leather shoes, Scott rang the doorbell on Drake Harrington's door at exactly five-thirty that Friday afternoon. Alone. He could have done without such intense heat in early July, but the prospect of seeing Denise and of meeting her on neutral ground made being dressed up in unbearable heat bearable. Drake answered the bell almost as soon as he rang.

"I'm glad you could come, Scott. It's good to have you here," Drake said. "Come with me. I want you to meet our guests. Ambassador Galloway, this is Alfred

Rimes. My brothers and I have just completed a housing complex consisting of four seventeen-story buildings for Mr. Rimes. We're celebrating. Alfred, Ambassador Galloway has just finished a tour in Lithuania with the State Department."

The two men greeted each other, and Scott did his best to concentrate on their conversation. "The Harringtons are exemplary in every respect," Rimes said. "I've hired a lot of construction companies, but none with so much integrity and professionalism and so few delays as I had working with the Harrington brothers. They're first class."

"Yes," Scott said, listening for the sound of Denise's voice. "They have an enviable reputation."

Alfred Rimes did a double take, and Scott turned his gaze in the direction of where Rimes was looking. It seemed as if she floated toward him, her body barely sheathed in a long, slightly loose, sleeveless dusty-rose silk dress with a slit that stopped above the knee. The neckline revealed enough of her bare breasts to make his mouth water.

Pamela steered her friend toward Alfred Rimes. "Denise Miller, this is Alfred Rimes, our guest. And of course, you know Ambassador Galloway.

"I'm glad to meet you, Mr. Rimes." She turned to Scott. "Hi. I was so glad when Pamela told me you were coming."

He glanced around, caught Drake's eye and signaled him to join them, since they shouldn't leave the guest of honor alone. "And I was certainly pleased when I learned that you would be here, too," Scott said.

When Drake joined them, Scott said to Rimes, "I enjoyed talking with you, Mr. Rimes. Would you excuse us, please?"

Figuring that Drake would understand, he cradled Denise's elbow and walked with her toward the dining room. "I've been here a few times, but I don't remember which door leads to the sunporch."

As if she'd done so every day for years, she took his hand and walked with him to the small hallway between the breakfast room and the dining room. At the end of the hall, she reached across him and opened the door. Fire blazed through his body when her breast grazed his right arm. He could have sworn she wasn't wearing a bra, as he felt her nipple. And it was hard. Damn!

They stood in the air-conditioned, glass-enclosed porch not saying a word, quietly watching the sunset as they continued to hold hands. He didn't want to say anything. Talk was not what he needed. He needed her.

She broke the silence. "Are you still mad at me, Scott? I really don't want you to be angry with me. I hardly know that woman who was rude to you back then. If you're still upset with me, I'm going inside."

"I'm not upset with you, and I'm not mad at you."

"Then what is it?"

He let his gaze travel from her feet to the top of her head. "You are so beautiful, so…so—"

"So what?" she asked with a twinge of apprehension in her voice.

"Listen, I told you never to ask me a question unless you want the answer."

"I want the answer."

"Desirable. When I look at you, think about you, I… Oh, hell, let's go back inside."

"Does this mean you don't want to be friends? All you have to do is make it clear, Scott, and I won't waste your time or mine."

"I like confident women…confident people, for that matter. But I'm not impressed by a woman who wants me to think she doesn't need anyone. Besides, for you, it isn't true."

"How do you know that?"

"I know when a woman wants me, and you ought to know, without being told, when a man wants you. Let's go inside. I suspect Pamela is serving the food about now." He took her hand and walked back inside holding it. He liked holding her hand, but he was also holding it to show Alfred Rimes that if he went after Denise, he'd have some serious competition.

Scott led Denise to the buffet table, took two plates, as he'd done that Sunday at the barbecue, and asked her what she would like. "Maybe I can help you avoid getting something on this lovely dress."

"Thanks. I'd love the shrimp and crab cakes, some of those little biscuits and some asparagus."

He served her plate, added several cherry tomatoes and handed it to her. *I am not being protective or possessive,* he said to himself. *Can I help it if I want to do something for her?* He put the same food on his plate and added a slice of ham. Out of the corner of his eye he saw Alfred Rimes watching him.

Too bad, buddy. You've got a ring on the third finger of your left hand. You are too old for her and, besides, she's with me. It was a mean-spirited thought, but that's the way it was.

Telford walked to the center of the room, clapped his

hands together and got everyone's attention. "Thank you all for coming to meet one of our favorite clients. The Rimes Mansions are now open, and they're dream homes. Russ outdid himself with the design of those buildings, and Drake elegantly finished them. And don't forget to patronize the businesses in the adjoining Rimes complex. Now, enjoy the food, the drinks and the music. And please dance, if the spirit so moves you."

Having been instructed by Pamela and Heather, Telford switched on the CD player, walked over to his wife, Alexis, and opened his arms. She swayed into them, and they danced like a couple of newly acquainted lovers to the sound of the Luther Vandross song "Here and Now."

Scott rested his plate on the nearby table, his appetite gone. The way Alexis looked at her husband—telling Scott and everyone who cared to see that she loved Telford and only him—shook Scott to his core. She communicated it to her husband with the look in her eyes and the yielding of her body. It reminded him of how lonely he was and how empty his life was of things that mattered so much to him. He closed his eyes and steadied himself.

"Are you all right?" Denise's soft voice penetrated his thoughts.

"I'm fine." But he wasn't, and he did not care to share his feelings with her, or with anyone. But he looked into the tender, caring eyes with which she observed him, and faced his need for her. "Dance with me, Denise?"

When she opened her arms, he brought her closer to him and stood there holding her and looking into her eyes. Uncontrollable shudders raced through his body, but he stiffened his back and began to dance, moving slowly and rhythmically, knowing at last the delight of holding her close. They moved as if the sweetness of her body in his arms had always been his to savor. The song changed, and the sound of Lester Young playing his saxophone to the tune of "(Back Home Again In) Indiana" was music to his ears. He didn't want to hear any more slow love songs, at least not then, not with a bundle of warmth in his arms. Denise seemed content, no matter what kind of music played. And when one of Laurindo Almeida's blazing Brazilian bossa nova tunes filled the room, he let himself go. To his amazement, she danced with him as if they had danced together for years. When the piece ended, he heard the applause; he hadn't noticed that they were the only ones dancing.

"You're a wonderful dancer," Denise said.

"No more so than you," he replied. "I had to learn those steps when I was in high school, or Judson would have gotten all the girls."

She winked. "Judson has his good qualities. But he can't outshine you. No way, no how."

"Something tells me you mean that."

"It's not just flattery, Scott. And while we're on the subject, you're a knockout in this tux."

"Thanks, I think. Let's go get a drink, since neither of us has to drive."

"My goodness, you're shy," she said jokingly.

"It's almost nine, and my invitation said five-thirty to nine, so I'll leave a few minutes to nine. I'd like to call you tomorrow morning, if I may."

"I'll be happy to hear from you."

"I enjoyed this time with you, Denise."

"Me, too," she said as they walked toward the bar.

"I'm having vodka and tonic. What about you?"

Her smile seemed to envelop him. "That's my favorite drink."

He ordered their cocktails from the bartender and walked with her to a corner of the living room. "Drake has a couple of riding horses. Do you ride?"

"Since I was three years old. Remember I told you my dad is a rancher."

"I'll see if we can go riding tomorrow morning. It's best to ride early before it gets hot."

"Yes, I know. I can be ready at six," she said.

"Great. You're a woman after my own heart."

"We'll see about that," she said.

"Yes. We will. It's been a lovely evening, Denise. See you at six. Good night."

He found Drake in the dining room. "Do you mind if Denise and I borrow a couple of horses tomorrow morning at six?"

"Of course not," said Drake. "I'll have the horses ready when you get there. If Heather doesn't feel like fixing an early breakfast, be here at a quarter to six, and you can eat with Denise and me."

"Thanks. And thanks for a great evening. Good night."

Once outside, Scott removed his jacket, untied his tie, put it in his pocket and strode down the hill to Judson's house. He was headed somewhere with Denise, and she seemed willing to go along. But did she want and need the same things that were so meaningful and important to him? He was willing to be patient, even wait for a while until he found them.

Chapter 3

Denise arose early that morning, did her ablutions, dressed and ambled down the circular stairs. She nearly collided with Pamela at the door to the breakfast room.

"I am so sorry. Are you all right?"

"Fine," Denise said. "If I asked why you seem so happy, I don't suppose you'd answer. Where's Drake?" she asked.

Pamela gave her a long, slow wink. "He is still in bed…in a state of happiness."

"Gotcha. You love that man."

"Oh, yes," said Pamela "Why don't you give Scott a chance? I watched the two of you last night. The man's really into you, and you're trying to show him how cool you can be. Denise, even when you really like a guy, you come off as cool. Heat it up a bit."

"You and Heather think he's interested in me, but he has yet to put it in words. I know he wants me. But after two years in Lithuania, he'd want the Wicked Witch of the West."

"Listen! Heather and Scott were best friends. They worked together for five years. He introduced her to Judson, who was like a brother to him. She said he's seriously interested in you, and I believe her."

"If you're right, I'll find out," said Denise. "But would you open your front door if nobody knocked and just stood there waiting? Of course not! If a man isn't willing to take a chance, he definitely won't win me over."

"And if you don't give him any encouragement, he'd be foolish to take a chance. Come on, let's eat. Scott will be here in a few minutes."

She scrutinized her friend. "Pamela, do you know whether Scott plans to eat before he gets here?"

"Now you're cooking with gas. I'll set a place for him. It's Saturday, so Drake may sleep until seven o'clock."

Minutes later, the doorbell rang and Denise looked at her watch. Right on time, she thought. "Hi, how are you this morning?"

"Great. This country air is bracing," Scott replied. "You look as if you've been up for hours. How are you this morning?"

"Fine. Come on in. Pamela and I are about to eat. Drake's still asleep."

His handsome face creased into a luminous smile. "Food. I was hoping that you'd save me something. I didn't want to awaken Heather and Judson so early, and I haven't found my way around in their ultramodern kitchen. Who cooked?"

"Hi," Pamela said. "I did. Our cook usually isn't here on weekends, unless we have several houseguests."

Almost as soon as they'd finished eating breakfast, the doorbell rang. Pamela drained her coffee cup and got up from the table. "That would be Miles to let us know he has the horses ready. The stallion is named Big Red, and the mare is named Sandy. They respond to their names."

After breakfast, they mounted the horses and started for the bridle path, a quarter of a mile beyond Harrington House, where Telford and his family lived. "You are an expert at this, I see. And something tells me that your horse knows it," Scott said to Denise.

She patted the horse's flank. "Horses and I get along like peaches and cream. See how Sandy looked back at me when I patted her. She practically smiled. Men could learn a lot from horses."

"Yeah. And so could women. If you caress my flanks the way you caressed hers, I'd smile at you, too. Which way is the river from here?"

"A little beyond that fork in the road," she said. "And you've never indicated that you want to be patted anywhere, not to mention your flanks. I make it a rule never to read between the lines. If you want me to know something, spell it out. Last time I took something for granted, it ended in disaster."

"How long ago was that?"

"Ten years. Ten long years," she said wistfully. "Since then, I haven't been within miles of any problems. I learn fast," she said, immediately wondering whether she'd revealed too much.

"I'm sorry, Denise. I apologize for being too protective last night, but I guess you're very adept at handling that. Are we arguing or merely getting to know each other?"

She pondered how best to respond to his question. She decided to be direct and honest with him, and slowed her mount to a trot. He did the same.

She gazed around at the perfect July morning, flowers in bloom, birds chirping and flitting around and squirrels scampering across the horse trail. "For years, Pamela has said that I don't show people who I am. She says I'm cool, even when I'm interested in something or someone. If she's right, I have misled a lot of people in my lifetime."

"So we are not arguing. Good. The day we met at Judson's barbecue, you were warm and approachable," he said. "Maybe it was because of those worn jeans. The ones you're wearing today are brand-new. Let's tether the horses and walk awhile or sit on one of those benches and look at the river."

"Okay. I love to look at the water. There's something magical about it."

He dismounted, walked over to Denise and raised his arms, and she lowered herself into them. "What would you think if I said I want you to fall in love with me?"

Her lower jaw dropped and, to her own surprise, her fingers gripped his shoulders. "Be careful, Scott. You impress me as a man who measures his words carefully."

He held her closer. "Then I'll phrase it differently. Will you give us a chance to see where we can take this relationship?"

"Is there some reason why you don't kiss me? You've had three opportunities, and you've never taken them."

"I pride myself on being a gentleman and treating women with respect. Right now, I am at the point of explosion, and I don't trust myself to get any closer to you."

She could feel the tips of her nipples tingle as her heartbeat raced. What would he be like and how would she feel if his superhuman control deserted him? Her head told her not to tempt him, but her body paid no attention.

"How will I know I want to give us a chance?" she asked him, ignoring the consequences.

He stepped back, gazed at her for a second, took her hand and walked to a wooden bench facing the river and sat down beside her. She rested her head on his shoulder and snuggled close to him. His arm eased around her and tightened. She gripped his waist with her right hand, and then mindlessly she let her hand stroke and caress him. She heard him take a sharp intake of breath, and a second later, she was sitting in his lap. The fingers of his hand pressed the side of her right breast, and his other hand clutched the back of her head.

"What kind of proof do you need in order to decide whether you'll give this relationship a shot?"

"Stop teasing me, Scott."

A hoarse groan seeped out of him, and at last she felt his mouth on her. Shivers coursed through her as he tightened his grip on her, as his tongue traced the rim of her lips and pried them open. He invaded her mouth, and like a flame doused in gasoline, heat surged through her body until she nearly exploded. She felt hot, as though her body could catch fire. His tongue sampled every crevice of her mouth, every centimeter of it. She heard herself moan and had neither the will nor the power to stop it.

His fingers stroked and teased her breasts until she cried out. "I can't stand it. Do something. Anything!"

He slipped his hand into her bra, released her left breast and rolled her nipple between his fingers, while his tongue swirled in her mouth as she inhaled it deeper into hers. As her moans escalated, she began crossing and uncrossing her legs, sought the friction she so desperately needed. He dipped his head and suckled her nipple in his mouth. Within seconds, he was hard and bulging against her. She didn't withdraw, but moved closer to him.

"Denise!"

"More," she said. "More!"

"Sweetheart! Baby. I'm on the verge of…" He abruptly pulled away from her. "Sweetheart, if we were in someplace private, we'd be making love right now. Do you realize that?"

"Yes," she whispered, shaken and still trembling with need. "I've never felt like that before, and I…I've never lost control like that."

She couldn't tell him how badly she had wanted him inside of her and how badly she still did.

"Give me a chance, Denise. I want to give you everything that a man can give a woman, and I don't mean material things, either. Are you listening to me?"

"After what just happened between us, Scott, I'd be foolish not to. I can't believe I let myself—"

He interrupted her. "Let yourself go? I'm on cloud

nine knowing that you trusted me that much." Suddenly, his face clouded in a frown. "Are you afraid to trust me?" Scott said. "Why? Have I done anything that suggests I'm not trustworthy? Talk to me!"

"No, you haven't. Quite the opposite. It was easy to… to let things move along. I thought physical attraction was the only thing I had to deal with. But now—"

"Now, you have to deal with your feelings. Don't make me pay for whatever happened in the past." He looked over his shoulder toward the horses. "Red and Sandy don't seem to be having a problem. If she's in heat, we'll have to walk home."

Thank God, she could finally laugh. How good it felt!

He asked her what was so funny. "If she was in heat, Scott, Drake wouldn't have let her get within a mile of that stallion, and she would never have been so docile when I was riding her."

He stared at her. "You're serious, aren't you?"

"You bet. Mares don't like to be denied, any more than women do." With that, she stood. "Let's ride downstream. It's beautiful down there, where the river curves."

He slowly raised his six-foot-four-inch frame from the bench. "Fortunately, I've learned to control evidence of my sexual frustrations," he said. "But as Scarlett O'Hara said, 'Tomorrow is another day.'"

She'd think about that later. Liking Scott, even making love to him, would be wonderful. But he was looking for a serious relationship, and that scared her. She'd been there and done that. She knew that a woman was a man's entire world until she gave him what he wanted.

She was not going there again. But oh, Lord, how Scott Galloway made her feel!

They mounted the horses and cantered along the path until they reached the river bend. "I want to love and to be loved," she admitted. "But I don't want to be hurt, to live in emotional pain every day."

From his vantage point atop Big Red's back, Scott looked down at the lazily flowing river. The morning breeze blew plumes from the cottonwood trees into his face. He sniffed the perfume of the wild roses that were tucked among the blooming red and white crepe myrtle trees. All was right with Mother Nature, but what he wouldn't give to say the same about himself!

So she was attracted to him. It was the thought of emotional intimacy that she couldn't handle. *I want her, and I'm going to have her. And once I get inside of her, I'll show her how a man loves a woman. I'll make her feel plenty. And when it's over, she'll remember what it was like, and she'll need me. Not just any man, but me, because I don't plan for it to be any other way.*

"How often do you ride?" he asked her, having observed the ease with which she sat in the saddle.

"Not as often as I'd like. I travel a great deal for my work."

So she was being evasive again. He stopped his horse. "Denise, if I ask you a question, and you don't want to answer it, just say you'd rather not answer. I won't be offended."

"Do you have a short fuse, or do I annoy you?"

"If I had a quick temper, the State Department would have fired me years ago. It doesn't help if you're a diplomat. You learn to hide your feelings the way a bird covers its eggs. Haven't you ever been close to a man, one with whom you shared your dreams and aspirations?"

"It's a long story, Scott, and if you'll forgive me, I'd rather not go into it now."

"It's all right. We'll get there," he said confidently.

"Why are you so certain?"

"Because I, for one, have a vivid memory. Have you forgotten what happened less than twenty minutes ago? Considering how you responded to me, do you think I won't be back for more? Trust me, I will."

"But Scott, that's not… I mean, sexual attraction doesn't guarantee anything."

"You fell for the wrong man. And one day, you'll know that for certain. It's getting warm, and the horses are becoming agitated. Perhaps we should go back."

"You're right."

"When will you be in Washington?" he asked her.

"Monday morning."

"I want to see you Monday evening."

"Scott, I…I don't know if it's such a good idea."

"Why not? You have to eat, don't you? Look, Denise, forget what I said a minute ago. You know what you want. You're just scared as hell to take it."

"That isn't true, Scott. If I'm afraid of anything, it's… I don't know that woman who kissed you back there. She's… I don't know who or what."

"Did you like her? Or are you scared of what you'll do if she makes an appearance again? Trust me, I won't let you do anything you don't want to do."

"No, but you'll make sure that I want what you want.

I know that a thirty-one-year-old woman ought to have her act together. And in most respects, I do. But I'm not willing to subject myself to disappointment. I picked up the pieces once, and that will be the last time."

Tell me about it. For every unreliable and untrustworthy man, I'll show you a woman who's the same. "Whatever it was, you're not willing to share it. Right?"

"Scott, I know I have to take chances, but right now, I am not up to taking this chance just yet."

He gave the rein a gentle tug. "Let's go. By the time we get back to the Harrington estate, the sun will be high, and Big Red will be irritable. We are not done yet. Where do you live in Washington?" She gave him an address in Chevy Chase, Maryland, a suburb of D.C. "Is it all right if I pick you up at six-fifteen Monday evening?" He didn't like the frown on her face, or that she answered him with downcast eyes.

"Okay. Will you be wearing a jacket and tie?"

"Of course. I wouldn't take you out to dinner any other way."

"Scott, I eat pizza. And when I do, I dress for pizza. But I appreciate the sentiment."

They rode back to Drake's house in silence. As much as he loved nature, and especially enjoyed its serenity, he couldn't appreciate it this morning. In another minute, he probably would have had her then and there, and damn the consequences.

The more Denise tried to distance herself, the more she intrigued him. He'd had many women in his arms, but not one as passionate and as complicated as she was. At times she seemed as if she wanted to devour him. He'd see how it went Monday evening. If nothing changed, he would move on.

Denise rang the doorbell, visibly upset from her horseback riding experience with Scott that morning. She didn't want to talk to a soul, when Pamela greeted her at the door.

"How did it go? You guys stayed out a long time."

Denise tried to force a smile, but from the expression on Pamela's face, she knew she hadn't succeeded. "It was…nice. I mean…I don't know. Pamela, how did you know that you could trust Drake? That he would always be there for you? What made you take a chance on a man like Drake Harrington, who already had everything?"

"In the first place, I didn't think about Drake's assets or his looks. If I had, I probably would have run the other way. What got me was his tenderness and caring, and the fact that he was true to his word. He was possessive, but in a way that made me feel special, and he let other men know that they'd best stay off his turf. If you don't give Scott the right, he can't do that." The doorbell rang. "That must be Heather. Join us for coffee."

"Is Heather your favorite in-law?"

"She's the one with whom I have the most in common."

"And it doesn't bother you that Judson and Drake practically look like twins?"

"Why should it? I'm never confused." She went to the door. "Hi. Coffee's ready," Pamela said, greeting Heather. They walked into the kitchen, where Denise sat on a counter-height bar stool with a brooding expression on her face.

"Hi, Denise. How was the horseback ride this morning?" Heather asked.

"It was fine, Heather. And Scott's a terrific guy—"

"But what?" said Heather. "Denise, with Scott, what you see is what you get. He has no hidden agenda. And he'll give it to you straight, which I suspect accounts for your mood right now. I've known him for years. And in all that time, you are the first woman he's been interested in. Girl, wake up. Scott Galloway is really taken with you."

"All right. All right. I believe you, I suppose."

"You suppose?" Pamela and Heather said in unison.

"You're nuts about him," Pamela said.

"Yeah," Heather said. "Seems to me you should stop pretending and be yourself."

"If he is interested in me, why doesn't he tell me?"

"Sometimes, I wonder how you can be so brilliant about some things and so clueless when it comes to relationships with men," Pamela said in exasperation. "We've been trying to tell you that if you gave Scott a chance, he'll let you know."

Heather took Denise's hand. "I see in you some of the same issues I had when I met Judson. My career was my life. I didn't have time for fun or pleasure. For a while Judson tried to change that, and then he let me know that ultimately it was my call. Scott doesn't allow anyone or anything to control him, and that includes his feelings. If he walks, he won't be back."

"Okay. I get it," Denise said. "So can we get off my case now?"

* * *

Monday evening arrived before Denise was ready for it. She had waited anxiously, but by late afternoon, she began to fear that it would be a disappointment. She dressed carefully, as if she were going to the social event of the year. She wore a modest sleeveless avocado sheath that skimmed her knees. Two strands of pearls were draped around her neck and fell past her waist, and diamond and pearl earrings adorned her earlobes.

When the doorbell rang, she opened the door, looked up at Scott and pressed her hand against her chest as if to control the fluttering of her heart. "Hi, come in."

"Hi," he said. "I can't get used to the fact that what you wear doesn't affect the way you look to me."

"Thank you. I—I…" She hated it when she stammered, but her nerves had gotten the best of her. She told herself to settle down. "Would you like a drink?" she asked him. "Priscilla sent you some of her cheese sticks. She's back in Frederick dealing with the painters. Hopefully, they will have finished by Friday evening when I get back there."

She took his hand and led him to the living room. "You remembered the club soda," he said, as he observed the bar cart. "Thanks, and please thank Mrs. Mallory for the cheese sticks."

"I will. She prepared some of them for you to take home," Denise said, handing him a small bag.

"Welcome to my home, Scott." She lifted her glass to him.

"Thanks. This is the second time that I've had the pleasure of seeing you in your home, and I've liked them both. I'm sorry that we can't spend more time here, but I have a reservation for seven-thirty, and the restaurant is in Alexandria."

The restaurant was what she had come to expect of Scott, whom she had come to learn possessed impeccable taste. She could truthfully say at the end of their evening, as he stood in her foyer, that she didn't want their date to end.

"You are an amazing man, Scott. You don't seem to take yourself too seriously. You let the couple in line behind us be seated first, and you even seemed comfortable sitting at the bar. Most men would have used their clout to demand special treatment. I admire your magnanimity, and I have ever since I introduced you to Priscilla Mallory. You were just as kind when you were meeting my housekeeper."

His gaze seemed to penetrate her. "I don't make differences between myself and other people. My dad always told us as kids that all human beings bleed the same way, and that when we die, we are equally dead."

"He is a very wise man. I had a wonderful evening, Scott." She reached up and stroked the side of his face. "Thank you." Desire suffused her like a bolt of electricity, and when his eyes darkened to obsidian, she knew he realized that she wanted him.

"Do you want me because I'm convenient?" he asked her. "Or do you need me because you care, because you feel something for me?"

"I do care. You know I do. But I'm scared, Scott. I want to—to… I want you to care for me, but I don't know how to overcome this fear." She laid her head against his shoulder and held on to him. "Help me."

He pulled her closer to him and tightened his arms around her body. "Do you believe that I care for you? Won't you let me show you?"

"In my heart, I believe it, but my head says otherwise. I want to feel what I felt with you last Saturday, only with you. I can't sleep for wanting you, needing you. I don't want you to leave me."

He crushed her body to him, and she couldn't hold back and didn't try. She raised her arms until her hands gripped the back of his head, and with a groan, his lips seared hers until she opened them and welcomed his tongue into her eager mouth. She sucked him in, wanting and needing more. Her pelvis pressed against him, and his hands went to her buttocks, melding her to him. Excited and reckless, she moaned in delight, her unspoken plea for relief as she undulated against him.

She grabbed his hand and pressed it to her aching nipple. "I need to feel your mouth on me. I ache," she moaned.

"Sweetheart, we have to stop this," he said, all the while pressing her body tightly to him and guiding his tongue into every crevice of her mouth. She rubbed her breasts against him to relieve the ache of her nipples. He dipped his fingers into the neckline of her dress, released her left breast and suckled it between his lips. She gasped as he nourished himself like the starved man that he was.

Suddenly, he released her, but not before his hard arousal grazed her belly. "Sweetheart, I don't want it to be this way. Will you go away with me next weekend? I want to give us a chance to see if we can make it."

"Yes. I'll go with you."

"I'm not seeing anyone, and I don't want another man near you."

"There isn't anyone, Scott, and there hasn't been since—"

"Shh. Don't tell me until you believe in your heart and your head that you can trust me. Understand?"

She gazed into his eyes and saw his sincerity. "Yes, I understand." She hugged him as tightly as she could, as a feeling of warmth grew inside her. "Yes. Oh, yes."

"I'd better go home before things heat up again. May I call you when I get home just to say good-night?"

"Please do. And drive carefully."

"I always do that, but you've given me added incentive." He pressed his lips to hers, then opened the door and left.

With her arms folded across her chest, she stroked her arms from her shoulders to her elbows, subconsciously trying to relieve tension. Maybe she still needed the feel of his hands somewhere on her body. "I could love that man," she said aloud. "I could love him beyond reason. And if I don't take a chance, I'll never know him."

She showered, dried off and reached in a drawer for a teddy to sleep in. She glimpsed the reflection of her nude body in the full-length mirror. Would he like her breasts, untouched by any mouth but his? Her only lover had ignored them. She knew she had a beautiful body and that her legs were shapely, but would her size 34C be enough? She laughed aloud. He certainly liked the way they tasted.

"Mr. Ambassador, we have a FedEx envelope for you," the receptionist said when he asked for his room key. "It arrived late Friday afternoon. Would you like me to send it up to you?"

"Thank you, Robin," he said, looking at the concierge's name tag. "I'll take it."

He read the message before he got out of the elevator. "This calls for a change of plans," he said to himself. His belongings had finally arrived from Lithuania, and the State Department had arranged for him to view three condominiums that met most of his requirements. If he decided to buy one of them, he'd have to move as soon as the deal was closed because the State Department's relocation housing allowance was about to end. He telephoned the office the next morning, called the real-estate agent and went to look at a condo on Sixteenth Street.

"I suggest you look at all three of them before deciding," the real-estate agent said.

"You can be sure I'll check them all," he said.

"Of course," she said.

He liked the apartment well enough, but wanted to see the others. By one o'clock, he'd decided that the condominium in Georgetown suited him perfectly. The spacious triplex had three bedrooms, one of which could serve as an office, three baths and a balcony on the top floor, a guest bathroom downstairs along with a large living room, dining room and breakfast room, a big ultramodern kitchen on the first floor and a finished basement. Of the twelve apartments in the building, three, including the one he saw, had basements and outdoor gardens. He had to sell his apartment in Baltimore, buy the triplex and move into it within ten days, which meant that he couldn't spend the upcoming weekend with Denise as he'd planned.

A soon as he reached his office, he closed the door and sat at his desk, then telephoned Denise. "Hello," he said after she answered. "How are you this afternoon?"

"I'm looking forward to the weekend."

Those words should have excited him, but instead, he felt as if a dart had zinged past his head. "I'm calling about that. First, the good news—my belongings arrived from Lithuania late Friday. Unfortunately, I have to leave the hotel in ten days. I looked at a condo this morning that I'd like to buy, but I have to sell my apartment in Baltimore. I need the weekend to get some of this done. Can we get together in, say, a couple of weeks when I've settled into my new place? If I can't sell my Baltimore apartment, I'll have to find temporary housing. Please bear with me, Denise. I want to be with you." He didn't like her silence.

Finally, she said, "Why is this move so urgent, if you don't mind my asking?"

"I can remain at the Willard in a four- or five-hundred-dollar-a-day suite as long as I can pay for it. But the State Department won't pay for my accommodations at the hotel beyond the next ten days. Now that my personal belongings are here, I have decided to move to Washington to be closer to my office and to avoid the daily commute. The department located three condos that matched my housing criteria, and I chose one of them this morning. Before I can move in, though, I have to buy it. And before I can buy it, I have to sell the one I have. I have ten days in which to do all that and move. Do you think it would be wise for me to spend this weekend with you with all I have to do?"

"No, it wouldn't. But wouldn't you expect me to be disappointed? Besides, I'm not sure I'll be free two weeks from now."

He bristled at her response. "Denise, this is not something that you can change whenever you want to. I want you, and you want me. And, unless Providence itself decides otherwise, we will be with each other. So let's not kid ourselves. You've been in my head since you strolled into Judson's barbecue. Denise, when the woman I want wants me, we're going to be together. So what'll it be?"

"I'll let you know."

"Don't wait too long."

"You don't believe in love?" she asked in a tone that had a bite to it.

"I definitely do. Once I get a chance to nurture it… that is. Have you ever seen a seedling pop out of the ground in full flower? Give it water, and it will grow. But if you want it to bloom, you have to give it tender, loving care. I'd be great at that with you, Denise. I'll take you places you've never been and didn't know existed. I'll play music for you that no one else has ever heard. I'll carry you to heaven every time you're in my arms. You'll bloom, sweetheart. And what a beautiful, magnificent flower you'll be."

"Scott, you're practically making love to me on the phone. I'd better say goodbye."

"This is nothing compared to what you'll feel, what we could have together. You said you'd let me know, so it's your call."

He said goodbye and hung up. She was going to have to stop dillydallying and make up her mind once and for all, or he'd find his future elsewhere.

Denise hung up. Her feelings ranged from being outraged to being sexually aroused by his certainty that he'd have her. She walked to the window and gazed down at the babbling brook in the hope of settling her nerves. But perspiration trickled down the side of her face. She walked back to her desk, picked up a sheet of paper and began fanning herself. If screaming would have helped she would have. By the time the telephone rang, her calm had been restored.

"Hello. Denise Miller speaking."

"Where've you been, darling? I've been calling you for days," Congresswoman Katherine Miller, from Waverly, Texas, said to her daughter.

"I spent the weekend with Pamela and Drake."

"I hope Drake invited some male friends."

"The Harrington brothers just finished building a series of buildings and a mall. The weekend was to celebrate that."

"Hmm. Your dad's after me to throw some big parties so you can meet some of the younger congressmen. I told him that the smart ones were married, and the rest aren't worth spit. This town probably has more pretenders per capita than there are potatoes in Ireland. Besides, this place is woman-rich and man-poor. I don't know why you decided to settle here."

"I'm a philanthropist, Mom, a fundraiser for worthy causes, so that means living in Washington or New York, and I'd go nuts looking at all those New York skyscrapers every day of my life." She was president of Second Chance Foundation, a charity devoted to help-ing immigrant children.

"But there aren't any eligible men in Washington. Everybody knows that."

"So they say. When are you going home, Mom? I want to send Dad some gingerbread."

"This weekend. I'll drop by late Thursday afternoon and pick it up."

"Thanks. Priscilla will be off, but I'll fix supper."

"Great. I don't know how you learned to cook so well. I certainly didn't teach you."

Denise laughed at the thought. "No, Mom, you sure didn't. You and the kitchen are barely acquainted. See you Thursday."

She hung up, wondering what her parents would think of Scott, who to her mind should be the answer to any parent's prayers. She went back to her desk and finished polishing an article about indigence among im-migrant children in urban areas. She read it over, and satisfied that it was one of her best efforts, she emailed it to her editor.

Images of Scott and her writhing in ecstasy pushed aside all other thoughts until, exasperated, she tele-phoned Pamela. "I'm going nuts. Talk to me."

"Denise, you're speaking to the wrong person. You should be talking to Scott. You've got an itch, and he's the one to scratch it, not me. As much as I love you, I'd like to wallop you for being so foolish about that man. You care a lot for him and you want him. It's mutual. What are you looking for in a man, a player who bangs every woman he sees and doesn't think about the havoc he leaves behind? Wake up."

Pamela had hit close to home. Her words were like a stab in the chest. "I don't know why I called you. He told me that it's my move, and that sounds like an ultimatum to me."

"Maybe it is, but I'm sure you brought it on yourself. What are you going to do when he looks at another woman the way he once looked at you?"

"I guess that says it. Give Drake and Heather my regards."

"Get your act together."

"I thought I was doing that when I called you. Guess I have to work harder. Love ya. Bye." After hanging up, she went to her desk and marked her calendar. *I am not going to give up without knowing what it is to come alive in Scott Galloway's arms, and that means sucking it up and calling him.*

Chapter 4

"Are you going to the fundraiser for Haiti?" Judson asked Scott, when they spoke by phone a couple of days later.

"I forgot about that. The real-estate agent told me a few minutes ago that she has two buyers for my condo. That means I'll be able to move in a few days. I'm not sure I have time to—"

"Slow down, man. You pushed for this fundraiser. You can spare one evening, can't you?"

"I guess so. I still can't get used to the fact that the State Department takes care of everything."

"So you're going. Are you bringing Denise?" Judson asked.

"She is making up her mind about us. I told her that she can call me when she decides what she wants. Funny thing is, I thought we had an understanding. In fact, we did. But with the move and selling my condo in Baltimore, I had to change plans, and she said she wasn't sure about us."

"Sounds to me like she's a bit wounded. I'd proceed with care."

"My sentiments precisely," Scott said. Chills swirled around the back of his neck.

Of course he wanted to take Denise to the fundraiser. What man wanted to go to a black-tie affair alone, while everyone else was there with a beautiful woman on their arm? Of course, none of them outshone Denise, even with little effort on her part. But damn it, why was she taking so long to make up her mind? He could ask an old flame to go with him, but he wasn't willing to deal with the consequences. Just then his phone rang. The name that appeared on the caller ID was Matt, the older—by a few minutes—of his younger twin brothers.

"Hi, Matt. What's up?"

"I hate to impose on you, Scott, but I need a favor. A girlfriend, whom I am not serious about, but whom I like, will be here Saturday en route to Costa Rica for her job. I have to be in Canada, but I'd promised to show her around. Can you help me out? She's good-looking, very fashionable and has a sharp mind. What do you say?"

"Good-looking, fashionable, a sharp mind, and you're not interested? Come on, man! Tell me some more jokes."

"At first I was interested, but then I decided I didn't want to go there. Personality clash, you know something like that."

"Yeah? Think she'd like to go to a fundraiser with me? It's formal."

"That's where she's in her element. I'll tell her to come prepared. She'll be staying at the Sheraton. Her name's Lynn Braxden."

"Okay. I'll be there at seven. We'll have dinner at the fundraiser. Hmm. I'd better call her first and put her at ease."

"Thanks, Scott. I'm proud to have you as a big brother."

"Cut it out, Matt. You're as full of it as ever. When's Doug coming back?"

"He'll be back in a few months, or so he says. Dad said that having twin sons was easier because he only had to contact one of us to know how both of us were getting along. Seems to me that you also subscribe to that notion."

"Makes sense. When he sneezes, you always manage to know it. I wish you luck in Canada, and I'll take good care of Ms. Braxden."

"Thanks. I owe you one. So long."

Hmm. Good-looking, fashionable and smart, huh? He loved his brothers. Matt and Doug were five years his junior, but accommodating his brother could get him into serious trouble. "Oh, what the hell," he said aloud. "If Denise wasn't busy making up her mind, I could have told Matt that I had a date for Saturday. Let the chips fall where they may."

When he returned to the Willard after work that day, he sent his pleated dress shirt to the laundry, phoned in a reservation for a table for two at the fundraiser, got into his new blue Mercedes and headed for Baltimore.

In less than an hour, he'd packed his personal belongings and valuables. Then he phoned his grandmother.

"Hello, Nana," he said after she answered. "I'm in Baltimore for a few hours, and I'd like to have dinner with my favorite girl."

"Oh, you," Irma Galloway said with a note of amusement in her voice. "What time do you want to eat? If I'd known you'd be here, you know I'd have made dinner for you."

"I'll be over there at six-thirty."

On his way over he saw bunches of cream- and orange-colored gazanias through the window of a florist shop as he waited for a red light. He pulled over, parked and bought a bouquet for his grandmother.

When he arrived, she opened the door instantly just as he was about to ring the doorbell. He hugged her and handed her the flowers. "Were you looking out of the window?"

"Oh, these are beautiful. Thank you so much." She looked up at him with adoring eyes. "You said six-thirty, and I know how you are about being on time. You look great. Why aren't you having dinner with a nice girl?" She put the flowers in a vase and placed them on the table.

The two of them walked out of the house. Scott closed the door behind him and locked it, handed her the keys, took her arm and started down the steps toward his car. "You can answer that now or later," she said, "because you know I'm gonna ask you again."

"Yes, Nana, I know that." He helped her into the car and walked around to the driver's side and got in. "I'm not having dinner with her tonight because she's busy deciding my future." As soon as he made the joke, he wished he'd left it unsaid, because his nana maintained that every joke carried a thread of truth.

"I thought you always boasted that you were the master of your fate. Doesn't seem that way to me, if it's *she* and not you who'll decide your future."

"A man can ask, but it's the woman who makes the final decision."

"Agreed. Do you love her?"

"I've been asking myself that a lot lately, Nana, and I have yet to come up with an answer."

"Well, if you're asking yourself whether you are in love, then you're probably pretty much there, and either scared or unwilling to admit it."

"Probably both. If I was sure that she wanted what I want, I'd be after her with guns blazing. I'm uncertain because I think she's had a bad experience and is afraid to trust herself or me. The thing is that we click on so many levels. When we're alone we're like a flint and dry grass."

"So you haven't slept with her." It was a statement, not a question.

"How do you know that?"

"Because I've lived seventy-seven years, and I know what happens to a woman when a man she cares for makes love to her. If you want her to stop pussyfooting around, you know what to do. Assuming she cares for you, that is."

"Yes, ma'am." He could always count on his nana to give it to him straight. "You want crab cakes, as usual?" he asked her.

"Son, you know crab cakes will be the last thing I

ask for before I leave this world. What does your sweet-heart do for a living?" his grandmother asked. Nana be-lieved that women should be independent and should marry for love and not because they needed a place to stay and someone to pay for it.

"She's a fundraiser, Princeton graduate and daughter of a Texas rancher and a congresswoman. She's beauti-ful and polished."

She nodded. "If she marries you, it certainly won't be as an alternative to poverty. I'd like to meet her." Scott smiled.

He took her to Mo's Fisherman's Wharf in Balti-more's Inner Harbor. "You're the delight of my life, son," she said when he took her home. "Your mother would have been so proud of you."

He hugged her and kissed her cheek. "Thanks. Un-fortunately, I'll never know."

Shortly after one o'clock Saturday afternoon, he telephoned the Sheraton Hotel. "May I speak with Ms. Braxden?"

"This is Lynn Braxden. With whom am I speaking?"

"Ms. Braxden, this is Scott Galloway."

"Ambassador Galloway. How thoughtful of you to call me. Matt told me to expect you at six-thirty, and that I'd better not keep you waiting, since you're a stick-ler for time. Thank you for inviting me out this eve-ning."

"Thank you for agreeing to accompany me to the fundraiser. It's a formal dinner, which I hope Matt told you, and there'll be entertainment. I hope you'll enjoy it."

"I'm sure I will. It will be my first opportunity to

enjoy Washington's social scene, and I'm looking forward to it."

"I'll call you from the lobby. See you then. Have a pleasant afternoon."

"Thank you. Goodbye."

"Perfect manners, at least so far," he said to himself. But, as Gershwin wrote, "It ain't necessarily so." He thought of Denise, with her perfect beauty and impeccable manners, and the feel of her red-hot body whenever he touched her.

The cover revealed practically nothing about the book.

He stood facing the elevator when the door opened, and a flawless black goddess stepped out. She glanced at him and did a double take. "Ms. Braxden." He stepped toward her with his right hand extended. "I'm Scott Galloway."

Either he was missing some testosterone or Denise had him tied up in knots, because he felt nothing for this stunning beauty. He imagined what the Harrington bunch would say when he walked into that ballroom with Lynn Braxden. He wouldn't have minded if she'd been less of a knockout, because if Denise wasn't there—and he prayed that she wouldn't be—the Harrington women would give her a detailed description of Lynn. He felt the flesh on the back of his neck prickle with anxiety. At his table—number eight—he found Pamela, Drake, Judson, Heather and two vacant chairs, and allowed himself to breathe.

He wished he'd been sitting beside Judson, but Pamela sat on his right. "What's this all about?" she whispered, ignoring Drake's high sign.

"You wouldn't expect me to get all decked out in a tux and come to a big affair like this one alone, unless I was married and my wife was out of the country," he told her without a hint of apology in his voice. "If you want to know more, ask Ms. Miller." He turned his attention to his date.

"How'd I get so lucky that you didn't have a date for a big affair like this one?" Lynn asked him.

He was not going to play cat and mouse with her. "I wasn't planning to attend."

"But these people at the table are your friends. I can tell from the way they're looking at me."

He leaned back to let the waiter put a plate of filet mignon, asparagus and roasted new potatoes in front of him. "You don't want to know the details," he said, more crisply than he'd intended.

"What's her name?"

Taken aback by her persistence, he said, "Sweetheart...or whatever else I feel like calling her in one of those moments. What's between you and my brother?"

The sharp rise of her eyebrows and the widening of her eyes told him that she'd received his remark as the dagger he'd intended. "I'm sorry, Mr. Galloway. I shouldn't have insisted."

"What will you do in Costa Rica?" he asked, changing the subject.

"I'm an agronomist, and I'm making crop inspections for the U.S. government."

"Damn. I wouldn't have guessed it in a thousand years. Congratulations!"

Her smile and sudden diffidence told him that his words had pleased her. "I grew up on a big farm, and

I love experimenting with seeds and crops. It's been a passion of mine since childhood."

"Looking at you, I'd have sworn you'd never been near dirt of any kind." It suggested that she might be more substantial than she looked. He wondered about Matt's seeming disinterest in her.

By the time the evening finally came to an end, he was somewhat relieved. He bade the Harringtons goodnight and drove Lynn Braxden back to the Sheraton.

"Would you like to come in for a nightcap?" she asked him as he walked with her to her room.

He gazed down at her, trying not to be judgmental. "You never told me what your relationship is with Matt, and I don't cheat on my girl, so we'd best say good-night right here."

"It's a pity," she said with her head held high and her shoulders back. "Thanks for a delightful and unusual evening. Goodbye."

He took the key card from her hand, inserted it, opened the door and handed the card back to her. "Good night." Normally, he would have been pleased at his gentlemanly manner. But since he hadn't been the least bit tempted, he didn't even have that satisfaction. He knew why Matt wasn't getting stuck in that honeycomb: the sweet stuff was too easy to get.

Judson's call the next morning didn't surprise him. "What was going on last night, buddy? I thought you and Denise were—"

"Butt out, Judson. Denise is enjoying a woman's right to make up her mind about me, and while she does that, I'm enjoying a single man's right to do as I please."

"Your date must have been pretty handy. Five days ago, you didn't even remember the fundraiser."

"Let Denise take care of her interests, provided she has any. I don't want to talk about it anymore."

"I don't suppose you remember how you browbeat me about Heather."

"Heather is like a sister to me. I know she and Pamela will be on my case, but they're whipping the wrong horse. If they're interested, they should talk some sense into Denise." He hung up the phone, leaned against the wall and let it take his weight. He missed Denise, and he'd promised himself that she'd have to call *him,* but keeping that promise was killing him.

"No, I don't," he said to himself. "I love her. Damn it, I need her!"

Totally out of sorts, he phoned his father and knew as soon as he'd dialed the number that he was seeking advice from the one source that never failed him. The sound of Raynor Galloway's deep baritone was all he needed to hear. "How are you, son? You're up pretty early for a Sunday morning."

"Hi, Dad. What were you planning to do today?"

"Nothing special. I was thinking about driving over to Frederick to that big antique show. They have it once a year. You can see everything from gold hairpins to handmade antique Duesenberg cars. Would you care to go with me?"

"Sure, provided you're willing to cook breakfast," he said, without giving it much thought.

"Don't I always? I know you're a pretty fair cook. If you want to fill up on my popovers, be here in an hour."

"Can I make it an hour and a half? I haven't even showered."

"All right, but don't speed."

They hadn't been at the fair thirty minutes before he saw her. In dark glasses, a wide-brimmed straw hat, a yellow T-shirt, midcalf white pants and gold flip-flops, she looked great, though her outfit seemed somewhat out of character.

"Who is she?" his father asked. "And who is she to you?"

"She's Denise Miller, and she doesn't know what I am to her." He nudged his father's elbow. "I want you to meet her."

She saw him seconds before they reached her. "Scott! What a surprise."

He tried to push back that feeling of need that tingled through his body at the mere sight of her, the vulnerability that he couldn't control. But as a career diplomat, self-control was his stock-in-trade, so his smile lit up his face. "Hi. With the decor of your houses, it wouldn't have occurred to me that you'd be interested in antiques."

From her smile, one would have thought that he was her morning sun and evening shade. "For me, antiques represent history…period."

"Denise Miller, this is my father, Dr. Raynor Galloway. Dad's the one with an interest in antiques. I'm curious about them, but that's about it." He tried not to stare at her, but his gaze refused to leave her, and he knew that his eyes told her and his father what she meant to him.

She removed her glasses, revealing the remarkable beauty of her eyes—light brown irises in a dark brown pool—and extended her right hand as she smiled. "I'm happy to meet you, sir. I hope you've been enjoying our annual fair."

Raynor shook her hand and held it for a moment as he scrutinized her. "I'm glad I decided to come, Ms. Miller. Scott hasn't mentioned one word about you, but I can see that he should have. It's a pleasure to meet you. I gather from what you said that you live in or very close to Frederick." He released her hand.

"Yes, sir. I wanted to be in commuting distance of Washington, and Baltimore isn't to my taste."

A grin slid over Raynor's face, a face that but for differences in age was mirrored in his son's. "I gather you like to step on grass occasionally and to know as many of your neighbors as possible."

"I do love the outdoors. When the two of you finish checking out the antiques, Scott, please bring your father to my house. I'll put together some lunch, and I promise it will be delicious."

Was she playing games? He had as much as told her that he wanted to know whether she was willing to work toward a committed relationship. He hadn't asked her to commit to him, only to give them a chance. He was about decline her invitation when his dad made the decision for him.

"Thank you, Denise," Raynor said. "I'd like very much to join you for lunch, and I'll bring Scott with me."

Scott glanced from his father to Denise and laughed.

The two of them had just railroaded him into doing something he wasn't sure he wanted to do, and he had let them. "Thanks for the invitation. We'll see you around one," he said. "And don't make it fancy."

"See you later." She gave him a seductive wink that he thought he'd never get used to and walked away.

"That's the slickest con job anybody ever pulled on me," he said aloud. With his fists by his sides, he stared at her departing back.

"Go ahead and kid yourself," Raynor said. "That woman's got your number. I'm looking forward to lunch."

He ignored his father, and straightened out his face. "You helped her do it," he said. He told him as much as he wanted him to know about why he hadn't seen Denise lately.

"I saw what was going on, and I wasn't about to miss an opportunity to learn as much about her as I possibly could without your coloring things to your satisfaction."

"I wouldn't have done that. Besides, there's no need. Denise is a great catch and would be to any man lucky enough to get her."

Raynor wiped his brow in what was pure mockery. "Whew! I stepped right into that one. Sorry."

This time, it was Scott who winked. "That's a great-looking little vase over there. Wonder how much it costs," he said and changed the subject.

"Anywhere from five hundred to a thousand—maybe even higher. It looks as if Louis Comfort Tiffany designed it."

"But it's glass. If I break it, that's a lot of money in broken pieces," Scott said.

His father looked at him the way he did when Scott was a teenager feeling his oats. "And you think falling for a woman isn't a gamble. If that goes wrong, it costs you one heck of a lot more than the price of a Tiffany vase. I never thought you were afraid to take chances."

"I'm not, but as you've told me all my life, when I see the potential for trouble, go the other way. I wish I had at least worn a pair of shoes."

Raynor grinned and patted him gently on the back. "Don't worry. She'll be glad to see you."

A quick stop at her favorite grocery store, and Denise had what she needed to prepare lunch. Fortunately, Priscilla kept the refrigerator, freezer and pantry well stocked. She defrosted two containers of frozen lump-crab meat, boiled some tiny green peas and put them into the freezer to cool rapidly. She made a crab salad, and mixed in the peas and some diced roasted red peppers for color, and put it in the refrigerator. She prepared a big pot of leek-and-potato soup, pureed it in the blender and put it back into the pot to stay warm. Brick-oven-baked whole wheat rolls, sliced tomatoes and peach ice cream completed the menu.

She changed into a long white cotton skirt that had tiers upon tiers of ruffles—it was the only skirt she owned that wasn't sexy-looking—a ruffled long-sleeved lavender blouse and a pair of white thong sandals. She looked good. Scott would think that she was trying to impress his father, and he'd be right. All was fair in the tug-of-war between woman and man. And at least for today, she'd established the ground rules.

The doorbell rang at exactly one o'clock. She opened

the door and looked at Scott to gauge his mood, since she knew she'd put one over on him. About an inch taller than his father, Scott stood behind him, and when she opened the door, he greeted her with a curious look.

She ignored it and smiled at seeing the two of them. "Scott's more punctual than a Swiss clock," she said to his father. "So I knew exactly what time to open the door."

"This is not the one you should be opening," Scott said, serving notice.

"I don't mind if you two fight," Raynor said. "But I'd appreciate it if you'd wait until after I enjoy the nice lunch Denise has prepared." He followed her to the living room. "What a lovely place. Attractive, comfortable and restful—that combination isn't easy to achieve."

"Thank you, sir," she said. They sat down and she passed Scott a basket of cheese sticks. She wondered what amused Scott's father as he tried to suppress his laughter.

"When I saw these cheese sticks, I figured that was the end of the fighting between the two of you. You apparently know what works, Denise."

"Dad…" Scott said.

"I sure hope you're right," Denise said, ignoring Scott's evident unease. She'd already decided to level with his father since he had taken the measure of their relationship. "I have lemonade, beer and red or white wine. Which would you like?"

"Of course I'm right," Raynor said. "I hope you've got plenty of these." He bit into a cheese stick. She loved

Raynor Galloway's sense of humor, his keen insight and his delicate way of reprimanding Scott.

"Since I'm not driving, I'll take the one that's easiest for you," Raynor said. She brought him white wine, since she hoped to serve it with their lunch, and gave Scott a tall glass of lemonade.

"How do you know I don't want wine?" Scott asked her.

"Because you don't drink when you drive, and I doubt you'd let your father chauffeur you around in *your* car."

"Thanks for the lemonade, and don't forget to hug Priscilla for these cheese sticks. They are to die for." He turned to his dad. "Priscilla is her housekeeper, and she makes these cheese sticks."

"Hmm," he said under his breath. "Surprised you haven't moved in." She heard him, but realized that the remark was only meant as a jab for Scott, so she ignored it. While they finished their drinks, she returned to the kitchen to get the food to put on the table and gasped when she noticed the all-white porcelain, the vase of white roses and the white linen tablecloth and napkins. She realized that it might have looked as if she was dropping a hint that this was something special, but she wasn't. She'd bought the white porcelain as a luncheon service. *Too late,* she thought and headed back to the living room.

"Lunch is ready." She pointed to a door. "If you'd like to wash your hands, there's the powder room." She waited for the two men at the dining room table. Raynor returned first.

"I really do like your taste," he said. "This is a fine

house." And then, in a swift change of subject, he said, "Don't be afraid to trust Scott. He hasn't a crooked bone in his body. If you're interested in him, don't let him get away. Not even *I* would dare to do that. Beautiful table. I suspect that whatever you touch becomes elegant."

"Thank you, sir, for everything."

He nodded and smiled, making it clear that he understood her meaning.

Scott walked into the dining room and took a seat opposite his father. Raynor bowed his head and waited, as Denise said grace.

Scott was a bit taken aback at the table setting. Although, he gave her the benefit of the doubt, since Denise was, if anything, well versed in etiquette.

"Thanks for this delicious lunch," Raynor said. "When did you do this? It's exactly right for a hot day like this one."

"Thank you. I did it this morning after I left you." She put the peach ice cream into individual bowls, poured a jigger of Scotch whiskey over each and served it with mini–hazelnut wafers. No one had to tell her that she was the perfect hotess, but the two men thanked her profusely.

"I'll remember this day for a long time," Raynor said as they stood at the door ready to leave. "I suspect you're a woman with many talents, and I hope to see more of you."

"Thank you, sir. I'm glad I met you." She reached up, kissed his cheek and lowered her head to avoid having him see the emotion that she knew was reflected in her face. Raynor quickly returned her affection, opened the door and walked toward the car.

Suddenly fearful and anxious, she looked up at Scott. "He…uh…I like him a lot," she stammered.

"It's obviously mutual. I didn't realize that my dad would fall so quickly for a pretty woman."

"Scott, I've been so unhappy."

"All you had to do was pick up the phone and dial my number," he said.

"I was going to, but Pamela said you took another woman to the fundraiser."

"How did Pamela know it wasn't an innocent date?"

"Because she said it didn't look like it."

He gazed down at her. "And that's all it took to convince you that I'd been cheating, right?"

"No. That's all it took to make me miserable. Is she someone you're seeing?"

He didn't see the point in lying. "No, she isn't. She's a friend of my younger brother Matt, and she was only in town for that day."

"Are we all right now?"

"Denise, you have my home phone numbers and my cell number. I'm still waiting for your call. I care a lot for you, but I won't wait indefinitely."

"Scott," Denise said as Scott was about to leave. He paused and waited. "What does your father think about me?"

"Why?"

"He's a very special man."

"Thanks. I always knew he'd like you."

She watched him walk down the stairs to the car where his father sat in the passenger seat waiting for him. He'd been nice, but that was all. Several times, when he'd thought she wasn't paying attention to him, she'd caught him looking at her, his eyes ablaze with desire. She wouldn't give up, and she appreciated his father's advice. Scott was a master of self-control and extremely stubborn. At least his father liked her. She wondered about his grandmother and the rest of his family. One thing was for certain, she was not going to listen to any more of Pamela's talk about another woman.

Around five-thirty, she put on jeans, a shirt and sneakers and went out back of the house to work in her garden, but it was still too hot. She didn't want to visit the Harringtons, she wanted…

"I'm stupid," she said aloud, then took a shower, dried off, pampered her body with perfumed lotion and fell across her bed naked. Her long hair blanketed the pillow. Her hands caressed her arms, breasts, belly and thighs until she felt a tear run down her cheek.

"I don't want to be alone. I want to be with him. I need him, and I don't want anybody else," she said to herself, fell over on her belly and wiped her eyes with the bedspread.

Don't be a fool, a voice in her head admonished. *Just call him.* She took the phone from the cradle and dialed his cell phone.

"Hello, Denise."

"Hi." She told herself that it was now or never. "Can you…can you come over?"

"I just left there."

"I know, but your dad was with you. I know I don't

want any man but you and I...I need you. I want us to
see if we can work things out. I'm terribly unhappy with
things the way they are now. You didn't even touch me."

"What are you doing right now?"

"Me? I'm lying down."

"What are you wearing?"

"Why do you ask?"

"You don't want to know," he insisted.

Like hell I don't, she thought.

"That low, sultry tenor of your voice is a giveaway.
I'll be over. It'll take me an hour and a half to dress
and then drive back to your house. Don't move 'til I get
there."

"Scott!"

"You heard me." He hung up.

If he thought she was going to answer the door
naked, he wasn't driving on four wheels. She rolled
off the bed and started dressing. *You won't get away
from me tonight,* she said to herself. But as she began
to dress, it occurred to her that she shouldn't appear as
if she was expecting to make love to him. Scott liked
a challenge. Besides, hadn't he told her that he wanted
them to have a weekend away to themselves, so that
they could give the relationship a chance?

She slipped into a pair of beige twill slacks and a
long-sleeved silk shirt that had avocado-green, tan and
beige stripes, and ran a long avocado-green silk scarf
through the belt loops of her slacks. She wore a pair
of beige sandals with three-inch heels, and gold hoops
adorned her ears. She fidgeted as she waited for him,
moving a chair, cleaning the coffee table, straighten-

ing a lamp shade, checking the ice dispenser and, in her anxiety, slowly going crazy.

At last, the doorbell rang, and she looked at her watch. He'd arrived with five minutes to spare. She rushed to open the door. "Hi. Come in."

He walked in, handed her a bunch of yellow and orange gazanias. "Oh, they're so beautiful," she said with a gasp. "I love them. You deserve a kiss for this."

He raised an eyebrow. "Unfortunately, I don't always get what I deserve. I thought I told you not to move 'til I got here."

"I know," she said, putting a tinge of sorrow in her voice, "but I couldn't figure out how to open the door for you without getting off the bed, and if I'd been able to do that, I wasn't about to open this door in the nude."

He grinned and kissed her cheek. "Chicken! I knew you wouldn't do it."

"What'll we do for dinner?" she asked him. "I can make some smoked-salmon sandwiches."

"We'll go out."

"I'm not dressed for a fancy restaurant, and you're wearing a business suit and a tie."

"Tell you what. I'll take off my jacket and tie, and let's go to Danny's and have barbecue and beer."

"I'd love it. I love barbecue, and I haven't had any since that get-together."

After parking in front of Danny's, he removed his jacket, threw it across his arm, grabbed her hand and walked her to the quaint, wood-paneled restaurant. Artificial logs crackled in the huge fireplace despite the summer heat, while air-conditioning guaranteed that patrons wished they had worn coats. They sat at a table facing a small stream, and the dull flicker of the single candle on their table made him look like a dashing hero out of the *Arabian Nights*.

She voiced her thoughts. "With this candle flickering against your skin, you're something out of a dream world."

"Thanks," he said. "I was thinking that this candle makes you look like a goddess. Not that you need the help of a candle for that. You poleaxed my dad."

"Me? Don't make jokes. Ask him how many women have been besotted with him, and I'll bet he'll tell you he can't count them. How old is he?" she asked as she softly bit her bottom lip.

"Dad's fifty-seven."

"Did he remarry?"

"No. He said he could never replace Mom."

"What a pity. He loved her."

Scott looked into the distance, and from the working of his jaw, she knew he was struggling for control. "Oh, yes. When I look back on those years, I know they shared a deep and wonderful love. I want that for myself."

She looked him in the eye. "If you can give it, you will definitely receive it."

"What'll it be tonight, folks?" the waitress said, and he wasn't sure he welcomed the interruption. Denise had just revealed something important, and he would have to wait to ask her about it.

"We've got every kind of barbecue you can imagine," the waitress continued, oblivious to the tension around her. "But I recommend the pulled pork, baby back ribs or the chicken. 'Course, if you're starved, you can order a bit of all three. You can have collards, corn bread, sweet potatoes or macaroni and cheese"

Denise didn't look at the menu. "I'll have ribs, pulled pork, collards and corn bread."

"No mac and cheese?" the waitress urged. "It's good."

Denise smiled and shook her head. She was eating three times as many calories as she normally did in one meal.

"I'll have the same and draft beer," Scott said. "What do you want to drink, Denise?"

"I'll have a beer, too. Wine doesn't go with barbecue. You're going to drink beer and drive?"

"With all the fat I'm consuming, one glass of beer isn't going to hurt."

The waitress returned with the beer. Scott took a sip, put the glass down, leaned back in his chair and looked at her. "You said a lot to me on the phone this evening. I'm with you right now because I believed you meant it. Are you going away with me next Friday? Before you answer, this is my last time to ask…unless you have a special reason to say no."

She looked him in the eye. "I'll go with you wherever you want me to. Just tell me the temperature so I'll know how to dress."

He leaned forward. "Why the sudden change?"

"Because I've been so miserable without you, and because I now realize how much I need you."

"And you trust me to take care of you in every way?"

"Yes." The word slipped out of her mouth of its own volition. "I was foolish, Scott, and I finally realized that

I would be taking no more of a chance than you would be. I don't want to live in that cocoon any longer."

He reached across the table and took both of her hands. "I care a lot for you. I'm only asking for a chance to teach you to care for me."

She squeezed his fingers. "I don't think that will cause you much of a sweat."

Chapter 5

Denise admitted to herself that she'd learned a hard lesson the previous night: when Scott said something, he meant it. She stopped trying to guess why he hadn't taken her to bed, considering how badly he wanted her. If she had opened her front door wearing a see-through negligee she would have been pushing too hard, and it would have been embarrassing for both of them. He would have teased her about it. They'd spent a pleasant evening together, and had parted on good terms, and she was glad for it.

She smelled bacon frying and made a mental note to ask Priscilla why she always served bacon for breakfast on Mondays. Her foot had barely touched the top stair when her landline rang.

"Hello. Denise speak— Mom! Hi. How are you?"

"I'm fine, darling. What about you? We should have

lunch together," Congresswoman Katherine Miller said to her daughter.

"I'd like that, but I'll be away on business for Second Chance starting tomorrow, and I'm going out of town this coming weekend. But I'll happily take a rain check."

"Denise, I'm very concerned about something that Pamela Harrington told me. She said that you're pushing a wonderful man out of your life, and that you won't listen to her. What's going on?"

"Oh, why did she bring you into this? You have enough things to think about. His name is Scott Galloway."

"You don't mean Ambassador Galloway, do you?"

"Yes. Do you know him?"

"I'm a member of the Committee on Foreign Relations. Of course I know who he is. He did a great job as ambassador to Lithuania, and I expect we'll hear a lot more from him. The man's got more than talent and finesse, too. Unless he's a serial killer, you've got to be out of your mind. I'm a good twenty-five years older than he is, but if I wasn't happily married, I'd give him a lot to think about."

"Mom!"

"I would. He's a fine man with looks to die for. Of course, he could be arrogant and conceited, but he seemed just the opposite when he appeared before the committee." Her voice softened, and she became the nurturing mother who never failed to comfort Denise. "What's the problem with him, dear? Maybe I can help."

"It isn't him, Mom. It's me. He's thoughtful, kind,

tender and caring. But until now, I haven't been able to let the past go and trust him."

"Are you sure you've let go of the past?"

"I hope so. I'll find out this weekend."

"You're going away with him, I see."

"Uh…yes."

"You've been reliving those horrible months for twelve years. Have you told him about it?"

"I don't know if I can."

"You have to tell him. I'm sorry we're having this conversation over the phone, darling. If you can't trust him with your deepest, darkest secret, if you think he won't love you unless you're perfect, I don't see how there can be deep, abiding love between you."

"But maybe I can't give him what he needs, Mom."

"Let him be the judge of that. Open up and let him see you as you are. If you need him, tell him. A man wants to know that a woman needs *him* above all else, including her family. He needs to *know* that. A man stands prouder and taller when his woman needs him and when he knows he satisfies her in bed. That's the measure of a man. If you're not prepared to give everything, don't get involved with him."

"Mom, did Daddy make love to you before you married?" Denise asked, since her mother was being so candid.

"Wh-what? Well, yes, he did. And after that, I couldn't have gotten rid of him if I'd wanted to. I hope that answers your question."

"It definitely does. If things don't work out like that for me, you and I are going to have a talk."

"All right, but first, make certain that you answer

truthfully every question that he asks *you,* and let him lead you. If you do that, you won't have any questions for me."

"I'm so glad you called, Mom. Right now, I feel great. We saw each other at a friend's barbecue, and it was hot from that minute on. I thought it was all about sex, but he played it cool."

"I see," said her mother. "It was all about sex for you, but not for him. You listen to me. A man can want you because he needs sex. But if he cares for you, he tries to lay the foundation for a good relationship. That man cares for you, and he cares a lot."

"And I care for him, too."

Then remember that he's much more precious than diamonds. I've got to get to work. Love you."

"I love you, too, Mom. Bye."

Fresh from the board meeting of Second Chance, the foundation that she was president and founder of, Denise hurried home and packed quickly in preparation for her weekend with Scott. "I have no idea where he's taking me, so I'd better bring my passport just in case." After some indecision, she packed a pair of white pants, a couple of long peasant skirts good for day and evening, an assortment of tops, three bikinis, a short sexy red dress for evening and a form-fitting evening gown, along with accessories to complement her outfits. She remembered to include supplies of cheese sticks and gingersnaps. *I assume he's taking me someplace where it's warm, since he said to bring my bathing suit,* she thought. But the one thing she couldn't figure out was what to wear on the plane, so she phoned him.

"Hi, honey. What's the temperature like where you're taking me? I'm not sure what to wear."

"Do you know this is the first time you've called me 'honey' or 'sweetheart' or any term of endearment? I'm flabbergasted."

"Well, you shouldn't be. I think of you that way all the time."

"Really?"

She dropped the bra she'd been holding onto the bed. "Are you serious? I wasn't aware of that. Oh, you should see what my dreams are like. You'd know that you're the sexiest man anywhere."

"I sure wish you'd remember about some of those dreams when I'm around," he said dryly. "A guy likes sweet talk, too."

"Please tell me what the weather's going to be like when we get where we're going."

"It'll be warm so wear something lightweight like linen, cotton—"

"Silk?" she interrupted.

"Sure, if it has short sleeves."

"Thanks. See you in two hours."

"Right on. Bye, sweetheart."

"Bye, love," she said and hung up. She pressed her short-sleeve pale green linen suit and her white handkerchief-linen blouse, polished her patent-leather sandals and headed for the bathroom, singing as she got in the shower. Half an hour later, she was ready. She paced from one end of her living room to the other, from one window to another, counting the minutes until he arrived. Finally, her nerves frayed, she sat down at the piano. The music of Chopin was guaranteed to calm her down, and soon she was lost in the composer's music. By the time she finished, the doorbell was ringing. She shook herself out of her reverie—that's what it was—pushed back the bench and raced to the door. "Hi. I'm sorry. I was trying to make the time pass. How long have you been ringing?"

"Only a minute or two. What a pianist you are! I didn't hear all of it, but I'd love for you to play for me sometime. Are these all of your bags?" He leaned down, brushed her lips with his and took a step back.

"You think I'll need more?"

"Heavens, no," he said. "I'm surprised you didn't recognize my sense of humor. Wait here while I take these to the car." She glanced out the window and saw a limousine driver coming up her walk. The driver took the bags from him and put them in the trunk.

"I want to be sure all of your windows and doors are secure." He checked them, and quickly came downstairs once he was finished. He kissed her, as both of them walked out of the house, and locked the door.

Almost as soon as the driver pulled away from the curb, he slapped his forehead. "My goodness, I didn't say goodbye to Priscilla."

"Don't worry, she's off today." His concern for her housekeeper further endeared him to her. "Since she met you and learned that you like cheese sticks, I always have a supply of them."

To her amazement, he rested his head on her shoulder and closed his eyes. "Woman after my own heart."

"Who? Priscilla or me?"

He eased an arm across her and snuggled closer. "Woman, you're queen of my heart." She stroked his hair, ran her fingers through it and smoothed the short curls back into place. "Be careful," he warned. "I spoil easily, and after two years of behaving as if I were invincible to feminine charms, I need all the spoiling I can get."

Twenty minutes later, having made it through weekend rush-hour traffic, the limousine parked at Ronald Reagan Washington National Airport. She leaned over and kissed his forehead. "Wake up, sleepyhead, we're at the airport."

He opened his eyes and gazed at her, revealing nothing of his feelings. He got out of the car, helped her out and then helped the driver with their bags.

"Do you want a porter, sir?" the driver asked him.

"Yes, of course. Thank you for such a pleasant ride." She didn't see what he handed the driver, but the man's raised eyebrows and wide smile told her that Scott had tipped him generously.

After checking in and going through security, he took her to the first-class lounge and sat with her near the window. "I love to see the planes take off," he said. "It's a joy that has survived my childhood. I'm going to have a vodka comet, what would you like?"

"What's a vodka comet?"

"Vodka over crushed ice and a twist of lime."

"Hmm. I'll have the same."

He leaned in and grasped both of her hands. "How is it that you have yet to ask me where I'm taking you?"

"I know you want me to be happy, and I will be no matter where you take me. So, what's important is that I'm with you, that we'll be someplace together."

He took a long sip of his drink. "You trust me so

much?" The eagerness in his voice told her how important it was to him.

"Yes. If I didn't, I wouldn't be here."

"You have no misgivings?" He searched her face, but she continued to look him in the eye, satisfied and glad that she'd dispelled her reservations about him and decided to give their relationship a chance.

"None."

"You won't be sorry. I won't let you be sorry." His gaze fastened on her mouth while he subconsciously rimmed his lips with his tongue. Her breathing shortened almost to a pant, and he squeezed her fingers.

"Damn! I'd give anything if we were somewhere private right now."

In hopes of reducing the tension, she tweaked his ear, but for her effort, what seemed like sparks leaped into his eyes, reflecting such blatant need.

"It's all right, hon. You've taught me the wisdom of letting…uh…things unfold naturally."

Scott knew he'd better get away quickly. He patted her knee, got up and walked around to the other side of the lounge. He walked over to the prepared food, got two plates and filled them, then got two large napkins and went back to her.

"I figured we'd be safer eating rather than drinking," he said, mostly in jest, and handed her a plate and a napkin. They'd barely finished eating when first-class boarding was announced.

Once they'd settled into their seats, the flight attendant arrived with champagne. Denise looked at him. He took the drinks, handed one to her and raised his glass.

"To the most wonderful woman!"

She grinned, but he didn't mind. Her smile and her joy were what he wanted. "Why are you smiling?" he asked.

"Because I'm getting to know me, and I realize that my public and private personalities differ. I've decided to accept that and to enjoy both of them."

The champagne hit the back of his throat before he was ready, and he broke into a coughing fit. "Are you all right, Scott?"

"May I help, ma'am?" the flight attendant asked and gave Scott a hard slap on his back.

Scott straightened up. "Thanks, man."

"No problem," the steward said. "It isn't often that I get to hit a passenger," he said jokingly. The man was back seconds later with a small bottle of cognac and gave it to Scott.

Scott winked at the man. "This is good stuff. If I find myself choking again, will I get another bottle?"

"I try to please, sir," the steward said, embarrassed.

"You have a wicked sense of humor," Denise said to Scott.

"I'd probably be just as fine if he hadn't hit me that hard." He put an arm around her shoulder. "I'm happy, Denise. And if you level with me, I'll always be that way, too. Don't ever tell me what you think I want to hear. I want to know the truth. Our relationship is important to me, and if there's anything wrong, anything at all, I'll fix it. Do you understand what I'm saying? To begin with, I got adjoining rooms with a door that locks in between. If you don't like that, tell me right now, and I'll change it."

"I'm happy, too, Scott. I feel as if I'm in some special, wonderful world." She leaned on his shoulder. "I may look and act sophisticated, but I'm not, and you... you should stop thinking that I am."

He stroked her shoulder and then tugged her closer to him. "We'll talk, sweetheart. I want you to tell me whatever you think I ought to know. If you don't want to give me details, that's okay. I'll get the message. If we're truthful with each other, we can't lose."

The waiter offered hors d'oeuvres, cocktails and non-alcoholic beverages. Scott figured that was as good a time as any to get off the subject of whatever she felt uneasy about. They needed to talk in a more intimate environment. "This guy is trying to get me buzzed before we reach cruising altitude," he said loud enough for the steward to hear.

"Yes, sir. It's my duty to keep you happy, and I believe in doing my job well. Madam, would you care for some spiced crab claws?"

"Yes," Denise said. "I love them."

He watched her chew slowly and deliberately as she closed her eyes and savored the flavor of the morsel in her mouth. Sensuous and sexy from her head to her feet, he thought. He couldn't wait to see her in something more revealing. *Straighten out your head, man, and think about your new assignment, anything except what you want to do to this woman.*

"I meant to tell you that I'm starting a new assignment. So I don't expect to spend a lot of time abroad, at least for the next eighteen months."

"I hope you're glad, because I am. Do you know what you'll be doing?"

"It isn't final, so I'll wait until it's been finalized before I tell you. I do know that my office will be in the State Department, and that's what I've wanted."

She stopped eating and turned toward him. "I'm glad for you. My mom is very impressed with you."

"Your mom? How would she know?"

"She's a member of the House Committee on Foreign Relations."

"She's... Wait a second. Katherine Miller is your mother?"

"As far as I know. She praised your work in Lithuania. I mentioned your name when we talked earlier this week, and she said she knew you. I wasn't surprised to hear her say nice things about you. I would have been shocked if she'd said anything to the contrary."

"Be careful, Denise. When a man cares for a woman, he needs to know that she respects him and appreciates who he is. Keep it up, and I may find myself trying to fly back to D.C. using my own wings."

She poked him in the side with her finger. "Really? With me on your back? I trust you, love. But that's asking a bit much of me. Don't you think?"

"It is not wise to be a smart-ass with your man," he said as he leaned over and kissed her cheek. "Wait a minute there. You called me 'love' and you called me that just before you hung up on me earlier today."

"I didn't hang up on you."

"Did so."

"Did not. I just put the receiver back into its cradle."

"Quit splitting hairs."

"Are we arguing?"

"Definitely not," he said. "We're doing what psychologists call *sublimation*. We can't do what we'd really like to do, so we're making idle small talk."

They finished their meal, and he removed the armrest between their seats. "Come closer, sweetheart," he said. And when she did, he covered her with a blanket, put his arms around her and closed his eyes. If he was lucky, this weekend would be the start to the rest of his life. Still, there was so much that he didn't know about her. Why was her mother in Congress in Washington, and her father in Waverly, Texas, running his ranch? Did she want children, and where was marriage in her list of priorities? She wanted him, but for how long? As a lawyer, he was trained to get the answers that he needed by observing people. But he knew it wouldn't work with Denise because he was in love with her.

The steward announced that the plane was preparing to land at its final destination. He awakened Denise with a kiss. "We're here," he said, surprised at the sound of his voice. He took their small carry-on bags and walked with her into the terminal.

"Welcome to Bermuda, sweetheart."

"This is wonderful." A look of consternation settled on her face, and she grabbed his forearm. "But I didn't bring my passport. I took it out, but I forgot to put it in my handbag when I changed pocketbooks."

"You only need a driver's license."

"Oh, I'm going to love this. I heard that it has mostly pink houses and even pink sand on some beaches."

"We'll be right on the ocean, and you can swim as much as you like."

She stopped walking. "Is that all I'm supposed to look forward to?"

He gave her a withering look. Surely, she didn't expect an answer. They retrieved their bags, went through customs and headed for the exit. "Here's our driver," he said when he saw a man holding a sign with his name.

"When did you plan this? I'm impressed. Evidently, you don't leave anything to chance."

"I try not to, but I took a chance this time. I had to because I knew you'd be more excited about our weekend if it had an air of mystery. You don't know how pleased I am."

"I love surprises. Like on the plane when you tucked me in that blanket and wrapped your arms around me. Every time you do something like that, a little more of you seeps into me and sticks. Scott, please don't lead me on. I couldn't bear it."

As soon as they settled into the limousine, he turned to her, grabbed both of her hands and stared into her eyes. "Don't do this, Denise. Think of the woman that you are and don't allow yourself any negative thoughts. I know there's probably a good reason, and I hope that while we're here you'll at least begin to feel that you can trust me. When you do that, everything else will come together. Believe me, nothing will come between us then."

She didn't respond to that. Indeed, she didn't seem perturbed by it, either. In the hotel lobby, she leaned against the reception desk while he checked them into the swank Hotel Fairmont Southampton on South Shore Road in Hamilton. He knew that the indifference of her body language was meant to let him know that she was okay with whatever accommodations he'd decided on.

He held her hand as they took the elevator to the third

floor. At her room door, he opened it with the key card and handed it and a second, metal key to her.

"I'm next door."

"What's this?" she asked him, looking down at the metal key in her hand.

He let a grin crawl over his face. "That's in case you miss me and want to pay me a visit. Unfortunately, I'm not entitled to one of those."

She threw the key up and caught it. "You poor baby. Boy, am I going to have fun with this!"

"What?" She went into her room, closed the door and left him gaping in her wake.

Denise surveyed her surroundings. Standing in the middle of the beautifully furnished living room, she saw in one direction a balcony with a table, chairs and plants. There was a large bathroom with a Jacuzzi on the left and next to it a full kitchen. She walked past the bathroom, saw a short hallway, turned and stopped. Fantastic! A king-size bed, chaise longue, chests of drawers and what appeared to be a fifty-inch flat-screen TV. Beside the big window was another balcony. She opened the door, walked out and looked out at the Atlantic Ocean and the pink sand beaches along the shoreline. Feeling light-headed, she made her way back into the bedroom. She picked up the telephone beside the bed.

"Operator, would you please ring Ambassador Galloway. Thank you."

"Hello. Scott speaking."

"Scott, this place is palatial. It's—it's… Look. I've never been so moved by a view in my entire life. Come over here and look at this place. It must be the royal suite. It's… I know you want me to enjoy myself and to be happy here with you and I really appreciate that. But honey, this suite must cost a mint. Maybe we should share. It's big enough for two."

"Denise, sweetheart, my suite is exactly like yours, except for the color scheme. I won't go broke over this. But I want you to know that I appreciate your being so thoughtful and considerate. Your feelings about this tell me a lot about you and that makes me happy. Now! If you want company, you have the key."

"I wasn't joking, Scott. As long as you didn't go overboard, I feel better. I'll just relax. It's almost cocktail time. What time do you want to meet?"

"How about in an hour? Is that okay with you?"

"Absolutely. I'll be in a short silk dress." She unpacked, showered, tamed her hair until it curled around her shoulders and went out on the balcony. He stood on the adjoining one, leaning with his back against the building, braced against the wall with his hands in his trouser pockets as he gazed at the ocean's frolicking waves. It was exactly how he'd been standing when she saw him at Judson and Heather's barbecue that day. He seemed so relaxed, without a care. She ducked inside before he saw her and put on the short red dress with the low neckline with a slit halfway up the right thigh.

"Why don't these designers just throw up their hands, say they don't have any more style ideas and tell us to go naked?" she said aloud, gritting her teeth. She had no idea what Scott's reaction would be to how much skin was exposed in the dress. She slipped on a pair of red patent-leather sandals that were the same color as her dress and toenails. She looked in the mirror and decided against lipstick. *What you see is what you get,* she said to herself, picked up the phone and dialed his room.

"Hello." She loved his deep, sonorous voice. It was as smooth as velvet, like the man himself.

"Hi, hon. I'm ready when you are."

"Be there in three minutes."

She remembered to dab some perfume in strategic places and was at the door seconds after he knocked. She opened the door, looked at him and gaped. Scott Galloway was one good-looking man. She was so awestruck that she failed to notice his reaction to *her*.

"Want to come in?" she asked him.

His Adam's apple bobbed as he swallowed. "Uh... thanks, but I don't—"

"But don't you want to see my suite? It's exquisite."

"Maybe another time. I'd rather not finish the day right now. Look, sweetheart, don't you have a scarf or something?"

She reached up and caressed his cheek. "I won't be cold. You look...so nice."

She'd almost told him what she really thought of his looks and what that outfit did to an already perfect man. But her father had always said, "Make a guy feel good, but don't give him the advantage."

"I wasn't thinking about the temperature in the hotel," he said dryly. "Let's go." At the elevator, he punched the button. As they waited, he gazed down at her. Suddenly, he blurted out, "You take my breath away. I don't want to think of your ever being with any man but me."

She stepped closer to him. "Why would something like that cross your mind? I'm with you, and I'm sure you know how to make certain that I stay with you."

He stared down at her, his gaze so fierce that she felt shudders dart through her body. "Denise, that comment was so loaded. I'm going to take you at your word." The elevator sounded, and with his arm around her and his hand gripping her upper arm in a possessive gesture, they entered the elevator. He didn't let go of her until they reached the lobby. He also didn't say a word.

"We're invited to the hotel manager's cocktail hour for first-time visitors," he said when they entered a room where approximately thirty people stood chatting and drinking.

"Mr. Southworth," he said when he stopped a few feet inside the room. "This is Ms. Miller."

The goateed Englishman bowed slightly. "It's a pleasure to have you with us, Ms. Miller. Enjoy your stay. If I can be of *any* assistance to you, please let me know."

"Thank you," she said, wondering whether Scott noticed that the man's gaze was not on her face, but on her cleavage.

She didn't have to wait for the answer. "If she needs any assistance, I'll see that she gets it," he said in a voice tinged with tension. Scott tightened his grip around her waist as they entered the room, a gesture that was designed to send the manager a clear signal.

She'd never been so relieved as when a smile claimed his face and he guided her through the room toward a couple he greeted warmly, one half of whom included a woman showing more cleavage than she did.

"August Jackson and Susan Andrews-Jackson, this

is Denise Miller. Denise, these people are among my best friends. August is a criminologist, and Susan is an attorney." He regarded August with a smile. "What anniversary is this for you two?"

"Man, life is one long honeymoon with this wonderful woman. She loves it here, so we come frequently, but this is our first time at this hotel. So far, it's our favorite. When did you return to the States?"

They talked for a while, as the waiters served hot hors d'oeuvres and wine and cocktails. Denise was enjoying the couple's company, but Scott seemed distracted. Finally, he said to his friends, "I see someone else that I'd like to say hello to. I hope we'll see you again later."

"I thought you said you wanted to say hello to some other people," she said to him when she realized that they had left the reception and were in the lounge. "What will your friends say when they don't see you talking with anyone else?"

"August is a partner in a top Wall Street firm. He knows I used that as an excuse to be alone with you. Do you want to eat in the grill room, in the main dining room or in a place I know on Front Street?"

"I'll be happy wherever you take me." Food wasn't her priority that evening. And if he'd paid any attention to her dress, he would have known that.

He tweaked her nose. "Then we'll go out. If you brought a wrap or a sweater, we'd better get it, because the restaurants tend to be chilly."

They went back to her room to retrieve her wrap, but he stood at the door and didn't enter. She got the black silk shawl that she'd brought, threw it across her arm and joined him. "We don't need a car," he said as they walked out into the balmy, moonlit night. "It's only two short blocks away."

"You've been here before," she said. "Alone?" she asked.

"I didn't have a woman with me, if that's what you're asking. I spent six weeks here one summer with one of my fraternity brothers, my college buddy and his parents. He lived in St. George. He's married now and lives in London."

She liked the restaurant, a charming, rustic setting at the water's edge. Their dinner began with turtle soup. "This isn't mock, sir," the waiter joked. "It's the real thing. We caught the bugger on the south shore yesterday morning." She didn't want to hear any more about the poor turtle's fate, and said as much.

"Don't worry, ma'am. We treat them good. We're very humane." His grin exposed a gold crown on one of his teeth.

She enjoyed the soup and the remainder of the dinner, which featured a dessert of flaming baked Alaska with preserved cherries on the side. They strolled back to the hotel holding hands under the moonlight and surrounded by a sky blanketed with stars. Suddenly, she stopped walking.

"What is it? Is anything wrong?" he asked, his voice laced with concern.

"Oh, no. I need to take this all in, to etch this in my memory forever. I've been many places, but I've never seen such beauty. And it's quiet and peaceful. It's so wonderful." She had never kissed a man in the street, but she wanted him to kiss her right then and there.

She stepped closer to him. "Kiss me. I…I just need to be in your arms."

He brought her to him at once, wrapped her in his arms and pressed his lips to hers. But he stepped away almost as quickly as he had initiated the embrace. "I'd like a rain check for that kiss," he said. "That was far from satisfactory."

He could have as many rain checks as he wanted, she thought. But for the time being, he needed only one. She didn't respond, but squeezed his fingers to let him know that they were on the same page.

When they returned to the hotel, he opened her room door, returned the key card to her and stepped back.

"You still haven't seen my suite," she said.

"I don't want to look at your suite. I know it's just like mine."

"Then come in and look at me," she said.

"If I go in there, you and I won't be the same when I leave."

She opened the door wider. "I don't want to be the same when you leave."

His gaze pierced her, as if trying to see inside her mind. Then, he walked past her and continued toward the balcony. "Let's sit out here for a few minutes."

She opened the minibar, got a bottle of wine, two glasses and a corkscrew and put them on the glass-top table in front of the lounge chair where he sat. He patted the empty seat beside him, inviting her to sit there.

"Denise, for the two years I spent in Lithuania, I didn't touch a woman." At her gasp, he said, "Neither virtue nor impotence had anything to do with it. The women were young, beautiful and eager for United

States citizenship and an easy life. But it didn't once occur to me to do something so stupid as sacrificing my career and my future as a diplomat.

"I've been on fire for you ever since I saw you walking toward me at Judson's barbecue, and the fire has burned hotter and hotter ever since. For weeks now, it's been far more than heat. I care deeply for you, but if all you want from me is an easing of the sexual tension that grips us every time we touch, we'll limit this to a pleasant change of scenery, go back to our respective homes and remain casual friends."

"Scott—"

"Hear me out. I need you, but I don't want a taste. I'm thirty-five years old, and I aim to get my life in order. Are you willing to see if you and I can make it together? All I'm asking is whether you want to try." He opened the wine bottle, and her eyebrows shot up at the sight of his trembling fingers.

Longing to nurture him, to soothe his concerns, she leaned over and kissed the side of his mouth. "I care deeply for you, too," she said. "I...I need to know what makes you happy, makes you laugh and what hurts you, saddens you. I want to know your hopes, dreams, joys, successes and disappointments—everything. I want to be the person you turn to when you hurt, when you want to celebrate and when you need a friend. I know I have hang-ups, but my mother said you will help me overcome them, and I believe her."

"I'll try my best."

He poured the wine into their glasses, took a sip and eased his arm around her shoulder. Suddenly her mouth became dry, and she drank the wine as if it were water.

He asked if she was nervous. "No, but I'd better tell you this because you're not leaving here the way you came in."

"No?"

"No. I...uh...I don't know much about sex. My previous experience ended in disaster and I haven't tried since. I was eighteen at the time."

"What?" He reached over, picked her up and set her in his lap. When she closed her eyes and leaned away from him, he held her closer to him. "Sweetheart, you were a kid. You weren't supposed to know anything. How old was he?"

"Nineteen," she told him, sniffing to keep away the tears. "I thought I was in love with him, but it was nothing compared to what I feel for you and with you."

He knew she wasn't telling him everything, because he could feel her body tremble. "You were both children, Denise. Animals are born knowing how to make love, but humans have to learn. Unfortunately, we learn by trial and error. I want you to forget about the past. That was child's play and has nothing to do with us." He brushed a kiss over her cheek.

"I've been staring at these things for the last four hours," he said as he surveyed her breasts. "You must think I'm made of iron."

"I don't understand what you mean," she said.

He didn't believe her. "Kiss me. I want my tongue as deep inside your mouth as I can get it. Kiss me. I need it," he said, surprised at the groan that spilled out of him. He began exploring every crevice, simulating what he'd planned to do to her later, possessing her. She brought his hand to her left breast, and he needed no urging. He put his hand inside the dress and began squeezing and massaging her nipple until she squirmed and shifted in his lap.

"What do you want, baby? Tell me," he implored. "I want this nipple in my mouth."

She freed it from her dress and held it out for his pleasure. He stared at her breast for a second, then sucked it into his mouth. Her moans excited him.

"You like it? Talk to me," he said and began sucking it in earnest.

"Yes. Yes, I love it, but I can't—" She held his head to her breast. "Why can't you take me inside and take me to bed? Scott, honey, I'm losing my mind."

He let his free hand ease into the slit in her dress and up her bare thigh until he felt the string that held her panties.

Her buttocks shifted frantically against him, but he ignored his throbbing need. He pressed his finger to her clitoris and began to rub in a circular motion.

"Honey, I can't stand it. I want you inside me. Now."

He stood with her in his arms, looked around him and thanked God for the darkness. He'd forgotten that they were on the balcony. He took her to the bed, undressed her and then took off his own clothes. She was lying on the bed before him, totally exposed. She reached for him, touched him and he jumped to full readiness. When she opened her arms and parted her legs, he climbed atop her body, wrapped her in his arms and thought he'd die from the pleasure of holding her naked form to his.

"If I can't manage to hold out long enough to satisfy

you, don't panic, sweetheart. I'll get it done before I leave this bed."

"I know it's been a long time for you," she whispered and reached for him, but he moved away. It was their first time, and he had to give it his best shot. He kissed her cheek, eyes, nose, lips and throat, gently skimming her flesh. When he got to her breasts, he told himself to enjoy them another time and sucked them only long enough to fire her up. Kissing his way down her body, he licked her belly and her thighs, and she began to undulate wildly. He stilled her, hooked her legs over his shoulder and plunged his tongue into her. Her screams split the air as she thrust her body up to him. He found that sensitive spot that would guarantee sexual satisfaction, massaged it and then twirled his tongue around her clitoris. She bucked and undulated like a snake seducing its quarry, spilling love liquid across his tongue.

He wanted to give her more, but he was afraid he wouldn't last. He kissed his way up her body, looked down into her eyes, which were nearly black with desire, and smiled. "Slip this on and take me inside," he said, handing her a condom.

Seconds later, he was storming inside of her. She braced herself between his thighs and rode with him. The tension began to build until she thought she'd die if she didn't burst wide open.

"Honey, I'm so full. I feel like I'll die if I don't explode. What's happening to me? Why do I feel like this?"

"I'm loving you. I want you to feel like that," he said. "Be still, baby, or I'll lose it."

She tried to obey him, but she needed release so badly. He began to thrust deeply, hard and fast, letting her feel his strength, his power, and she thought she would die as tremors shot through her body.

"Look at me, baby. I want you to love me. Open your eyes and look at me." She heard him, but he'd poleaxed her, and she couldn't answer.

"Don't hold back, sweetheart. Let go!" She tried hard, but it wouldn't come. "Baby, don't strain for it. Let go and trust me. I'll give you what you want."

The storm became a hurricane, twirling, tossing, shattering her. He was in her, over her, on her, under her and all around her, rocking her. Suddenly the pumping and squeezing turned into a wild throbbing, and she began to pant for relief. Her thighs quivered. She released her hold on him and flung her arms out wide, succumbing to his onslaught.

"That's it, baby. Yeah! Give yourself to me."

"Oh, Lord," she yelled as he hurtled her to the stratosphere, dropped her into sinking quicksand. And then, blessed relief, as she cried out, "Yes. Oh, yes!" But so befuddled was she by her own orgasm that she didn't know he'd splintered in her arms, as vulnerable as a baby sliding from the womb. Thoroughly shaken, she held him to her as tightly as she could and, with eyes wide open, she stared beyond him. He hadn't said he loved her.

Chapter 6

Lying on his back with his arms around Denise, Scott tried to sort out his confusion and separate it from the joy he'd just experienced in her arms. She'd been desperate to have him inside of her, and she'd welcomed him without reservation when he entered her, but he couldn't dismiss the feeling that she'd withheld something of herself. She'd wanted and needed release, but hadn't been willing—or maybe able—to let him give it to her. He'd practically had to force her to accept what was happening to her, and he couldn't imagine that they could continue for long, or that their relationship could develop much further unless she told him why. She wanted to give, and she had tried to open up to him, but some demon from her past had interfered. He'd get it out of her if he had to blackmail her.

He gathered her close to him and luxuriated in the warmth of her female body naked beside him. So long.

It had been so long, and he'd been so hungry for so many months. Yet, in spite of that, he'd been able to control his awesome need to explode the minute he entered her and to hold back and give her what she needed.

He turned on his side, braced himself on his forearm and looked down into her face. "How do you feel, sweetheart?" He knew she'd had a powerful orgasm, because he felt it along the entire length of his penis.

Her hand caressed his chest, and he bucked when it skimmed over his pectoral. "I'm lying here wondering how I lived so many years without knowing I could feel like that. Does it always happen that way, or only the first time? I can't begin to describe it. How do I feel? I don't understand it, but I know you have an important part of me. And that no matter what happens between us in the future, that part will always be with you. Physically, I feel great. Emotionally, I'm in shock."

"Shock? Why?"

"I don't know. I guess it's because you can always walk away, and I sense that I won't feel like that without you." She turned on her side, facing him, then wrapped her arms around him and whispered, "Don't be stingy. I want to feel like that again. I wonder if I'll ever get enough."

If he told her that she had to level with him, to let him know what held her back initially, preventing her from experiencing fully what they could have together, she'd probably think she hadn't satisfied him, and that would be far from the truth. There was more, much more for both of them, and he wanted it all—for him and for her.

She curled into him, stroking and caressing, not knowing that her touch would get her what she wanted. He sensed her frustration when she asked him, "Was it as good for you as it was for me?"

"I don't know how to judge that," he said, smiling to lighten the gravity of her question. "I know it was heaven on earth for me."

More assured, she wiggled against him. "I want some more."

"So do I," he said. "But you could be a little sore. It wasn't easy getting into you."

"I'm not sore, and if I am later, it will be worth it."

He fell over on his back. "Do whatever you want with me."

She leaned over him and kissed him as he'd kissed her, adoring his eyes, ears and nose before claiming his tongue into her mouth and climbing on top of him. Knowing that it could be over quickly, he restrained her.

"Don't rush it, baby," he warned.

Still imitating him, her lips went to his pectoral, and then she sucked his nipple into her mouth. He hardened and jumped to full readiness. "Baby, take it easy," he said and moved her away, but when she started to kiss his belly, he flipped her over on her back. If she ever got his penis into her mouth, he feared that he would embarrass them both. When he was once again sure of his control, he'd welcome it.

"You didn't like it?" she asked.

"I loved it, but I've been celibate for more than two and a half years, and I'm not sure of my control." He sucked a nipple into his mouth and nursed it greedily, until she began to squirm. And when his fingers touched her clitoris, she moaned as if in agony.

"Get in me. I want to feel you in me."

The liquid gushed over his hand, and he rose above her. "Don't think of anything that's ever upset you. Think about us, you and me. Think about what you know I'm going to do to you tonight and nights to come."

"I will," she said as he eased into her. He didn't bother to drive slowly. Her rhythmic gyrations threatened to bring him to climax before they'd barely begun. He found that special place in her vagina and drove fast and furiously until she screamed.

"I'm dying. Hold me. Oh, Lord. I can't stand it," she said and erupted all around him.

"Don't move. Baby, leave it right there!" he cried out, and came apart in her arms. It was the wildest, most life-affirming sex he'd ever experienced. He stared down at her and kissed the tears that dripped onto her cheeks.

With his arms around her, he asked, "Why are you crying?"

"It—it scared me. I don't know how to handle this."

"You aren't supposed to 'handle' it. You accept it and thank God for it. Some women are unable to climax."

"Really?" Suddenly she pinched his buttocks. "You stay away from them."

Proving that he could give as good as he got, he winked at her. "Keep me as happy as I am right now, sweetheart, and I'll buy my own ankle monitor and give you the key."

"I'll bet. Sounds like a pretty good idea," she said, stroking and caressing his back.

"Yeah? Don't get carried away."

For the remainder of the weekend, they explored the island, frolicked in the ocean, bought presents for friends and relatives during the day, and at night they ate scrumptious dinners, danced and made love. As they flew back to Washington, he wondered about their future. She suited him in many ways, but because she hadn't shared with him what it was that haunted her— and he was sure there was something—he didn't feel free to confide in her.

He arrived at work that Monday morning feeling *good*. In spite of his misgivings, he didn't feel conflicted about his relationship with Denise. "Good morning, sir," his secretary greeted him. "The undersecretary wants to see you at nine-fifteen. He has your file. You've got just enough time for a cup of coffee. I'll have it in a minute."

"Thank you, Midge. I didn't have time to get any this morning." He went into his inner office, brushed his hair, which had been disheveled by the wind, and straightened his tie. Midge brought the coffee and a croissant, and he enjoyed both with more speed than he would have preferred. Then he went into his bathroom, brushed his teeth and headed for the fifth floor.

The undersecretary stood and extended his hand as Scott entered the large, elegantly appointed office. "It's good to see you, Mr. Galloway. You did an impressive job in Lithuania, but I expect you're eager to spend some time here in the States."

At those words, Scott relaxed. It seemed that he wouldn't have to refuse an immediate overseas assignment. "I am indeed, sir."

"That's a tough post for a single man."

"It certainly is. I've already decided that I'd prefer to have a family if I'm sent to a similar post."

"I'll bear that in mind. I'd like you to head up our division of immigration policy. We need hard-nosed, bold initiatives to deal with our current immigration problems, both legal and illegal. How about it?"

"I appreciate your confidence, sir. You have my assurance that I'll do my best."

"Great. If you have any questions, problems or enemies—" he half smiled "—I'm here to help. Your office will be on the fifth floor, southeast corner. You begin at once, and you will continue to be officially addressed as Mr. Ambassador. I'll send out a press release this morning. Good luck."

"Thank you." They shook hands. He returned to his office on the third floor and began cleaning out his desk.

"I'm moving to the fifth floor, Midge. Do you want to come with me?"

"Oh, yes, sir. If there's anything I hate, it's breaking in a new boss." His eyebrows shot up. "I mean, getting used to a new boss," she amended. "When are we moving?"

"Now. Mark's secretary will give you the room number."

The minute he'd settled into his new office, which was twice the size of the one he'd just vacated, he telephoned his father with the news.

"I'm proud of you, son. And I'm so glad that you'll be staying in the States for a while. I hope you'll take advantage of this and Ms. Miller. I like her a lot."

He couldn't help laughing. "She likes you, too. If I didn't know any better, I'd be jealous."

"Hmm" was his dad's response.

"You'll probably read about it in tomorrow's *Washington Post*."

"I'll look forward to that."

However, MSNBC reported the news from a wire service, and when he returned from lunch, he had a call from one of its program directors.

"Mr. Ambassador, MSNBC is on the line. Do you want to take the call?"

"I'll take it."

"We'd love to have you on *Today's Issues,* our eight o'clock program tonight. I know it's short notice, but we can accommodate your schedule. You can appear by remote satellite from our Washington studio."

"I can do that. But seven is as early as I can get to the studio."

"That's fine. We'll get the information from your secretary and have a car for you at six-thirty."

So much for his date with his grandmother. He telephoned Denise first, but had to leave a message. "I have some news, but I'll wait and tell you about it when we speak. Stay sweet. Scott."

"I forget what a big shot you are," his grandmother said, after he explained to her why he couldn't keep their date. "I still think of you as my little Scottie. Knock 'em dead. You know I'll be watching."

He left voice-mail messages with his father, his

brothers Matt and Doug, and Heather, advising them of his TV appearance. After that, he prepared for a briefing on immigration issues.

By the time he reached the studio, Scott had familiarized himself with the administration's immigration policies well enough to handle any softball questions. Fortunately, the host of the program didn't assume that he was an expert on immigration issues and confined his questions to what changes he'd like to see rather than to how the changes should be brought about.

"Naturally, I hope for the time when we're no longer faced with these immigration problems. I look forward to our developing relevant policies and to their strict enforcement."

Their interview dissolved into talk of Scott's tenure as ambassador to Lithuania and his accomplishments there. "Would you go back?" his host asked.

"For a visit, yes. I left a few friends there—but not on assignment."

"Congratulations on your new assignment, sir. I hope you'll be willing to talk with us again soon."

"My pleasure. Thank you for inviting me."

He had declined the station's offer of dinner, so on the way home, he stopped at a gourmet deli and bought his dinner. He had enjoyed the interview, but the host had been previously disposed to liking him. He knew better than to expect softball questions at interviews. When he entered his apartment, he heard the phone ringing and rushed to answer it.

"Hi, Nana. How do you think it went?"

"Perfect. I'm so proud of you. I'm glad you're staying in one place."

"Thanks. Better watch that. It won't always go so smoothly."

"Maybe not, but you'll always shine, son. Just keep it between the lines."

"I'll do my best, Nana."

He wanted to talk to Denise. He couldn't enjoy his success unless he shared it with her. He hadn't realized how much he wanted her to take pride in his accomplishments. He left a message. "I need to talk with you." He didn't bother to identify himself. If she didn't recognize his voice, it wouldn't matter, anyway.

As an empty feeling began to settle over him, his cell phone rang and a glance at the caller ID raised his spirits. "Hi, buddy, what's up?" he asked Judson.

"Man, I watched that program, and you were cool enough to freeze water. Pamela, Drake, Heather and I viewed it together. You made us proud, a great excuse for a round of first-class champagne. Can you come out here this weekend? Saturday's Velma's birthday, and the Harringtons use any excuse to have a big party. Bring her a present, and if you're on good terms with Denise, bring her, too."

"I'll be there. In the meantime, see if you can't find something to do other than push me on Denise."

"I haven't been doing that. Man, you zeroed in on that woman like an eagle going after prey."

"Okay, but tell Pamela to invite her. I'm not quite ready to make a statement."

"Gotcha."

Sitting in the middle of her bed in one of Chicago's five-star hotels, Denise flipped on the television and sipped green tea. It was too early for dinner, so to soothe her empty stomach, she'd made the tea in the pot that the hotel provided.

"What the…" What on earth? It couldn't be. But there was Scott Galloway on the program *Today's Issues.* Why was he on that program, and why was he discussing immigration? It was an issue in which she and other members of Second Chance had an active interest and one in which they worked on behalf of immigrant children. At the end of the program, she applauded.

"Honey, you are one smooth brother," she said aloud, "and I liked what you had to say." She crossed her arms, hugging herself. That articulate, accomplished, gorgeous man cared for her and wanted *her.* Suddenly, she swung her feet off the bed, walked to the window, then back to the bed, and to the window again. What was this? They'd spent the weekend together in a lovers' tryst, and he hadn't mentioned a television interview. She stomped her foot, her temperature rising.

When she opened her cell phone to call and chew him out, she saw that she had four unanswered calls and decided to retrieve them. To her chagrin, each had come from Scott and said that he wanted to talk to her. On the last voice-mail message, minutes earlier, his voice had a plaintive quality. She hadn't heard the phone ring because it was in her handbag on the sofa in the living room of her suite.

"Moral of the story, kiddo," she said to herself, "is that you shouldn't jump to conclusions until you have all the facts. I should be ashamed of myself, and I am."

She dialed his number and waited, praying that he'd tell her what she wanted to hear.

"Hi, Denise. Where on earth are you? Don't you answer your phone? I've made half a dozen calls to you."

"Honey, don't you remember my telling you that I had to be in Chicago today? I took a nine-thirty flight out of Reagan. I just saw you on TV."

"Good grief, I forgot about Chicago. I've been calling you for two reasons. My boss called me in first thing this morning and promoted me to division chief in charge of immigration, and sent out a press release as soon as I agreed to take the assignment. Then, in less than two hours, a guy from MSNBC was on my line asking if I'd appear on the program. I agreed, and spent the rest of the day cramming on the hot immigration topics.

"You can't imagine what a downer it was to leave that studio feeling as if I'd done well and not being able to share it with you."

"Congratulations on your new post. You were wonderful. Your responses couldn't have been more perfect. You know what I said?"

"What?"

"I said, 'that is one smooth brother.' Honey, you looked, spoke and acted the part. I'm so proud of you. I mean, you made me feel wonderful."

"I'm sure you told me when you'd be back here, but please refresh my memory."

"I'll be back late tomorrow afternoon. I'd make it earlier, but I have to meet with my board. We have some programs for children of immigrant families in various cities, and we don't discriminate between legal and undocumented immigrants. They're here, and they need help."

"Really? We'd better get into that another time."

"Don't worry. We will. And don't be so sure that I'll be opposing you. I liked what you said on the program tonight."

"Thanks. Let me know what time your plane gets in, and I'll meet you. We can have dinner someplace."

"Great idea. Be sure and check the messages on your cell phone. See you as soon as possible."

"I'll be waiting. Bye."

She hung up, deep in thought. *Maybe I should find Oscar Jefferson and let him see who I am and what I've become. I'd like to shake up the SOB and tell him what I think of him. Until I met Scott, I had no idea what it meant to be with a man. When he made love to me, he gave me something precious.* She shook her head. *But I can't help wondering if something is still missing. Or is it my imagination that he seemed to be reaching for something else? Oh, Lord. Here we go again. Denise and her self-doubts.*

She ate dinner in her room, watched the quarter-finals of a tennis match, said her prayers and went to bed. During the night, she struggled with dreams that she was carrying Scott Galloway's child. She awoke in a sweat at five in the morning. In her dream, she awakened to discover that her child wasn't Scott's but was instead Oscar's, and that Scott had walked out on her.

She crawled out of bed and took a shower. How had she gotten tied up in a knot about Oscar Jefferson, when so many years had passed? She vowed then to find him and talk with him. He was a stumbling block in her life, an impediment to her happiness. She plugged in her laptop and began her search for Oscar Jefferson. Two hours later, she had traced several leads but was at a dead end. Still, she was not discouraged. If he was alive, she'd find him.

At her board meeting that morning, she realized that she might have a problem. The members wanted her to make demands about federal immigration policy, and she knew Scott well enough to know that their demands would get them nowhere.

"Give him a chance to settle in," she advised. "If we don't like his policies, there's time enough to bear down on him. From what he said last night, he could well be our ally." She ended the meeting in a move she considered necessary, if she were to avoid getting jammed between a rock and a hard place.

She phoned Scott minutes after she reserved her flight home. "Good," he said. "I'll meet you in the baggage area. Stay sweet."

"You, too."

Scott saw Denise walking toward him and quickened his steps. What a woman! Heads turned as she passed, and he didn't try to suppress his feelings of pride that he was the man she wanted. He opened his arms, and she dashed into them. Then, as if mindful that they were in a public place, she stepped back and grinned.

"You're teaching me all kinds of new habits," she said. "I'm glad to see you."

"I've got some more for you," he said as he took her briefcase and overnight bag, slung an arm around her and headed for the taxi stand. "I didn't drive to the airport because parking is so difficult to come by." He directed the taxi driver to a parking lot on I Street, in northwest Washington, where he'd left his car.

"Let's eat somewhere nearby," she suggested, "and then you won't have to move the car until we're ready to go home."

"Good idea. It's one of the reasons why I only date smart women." He had to touch her, so he caressed the side of her face. She looked and acted like a woman of privilege, but she was very much down-to-earth. He'd give anything to know what was behind the mask, and eventually, he would.

They settled on a Chinese restaurant, and she ordered a shrimp-and-lobster dish with snow peas and bok choy. Scott ordered Szechuan pork, and they ate family style.

"Did this assignment surprise you?" she asked.

"Actually, it did. I knew there were three open slots in which I was a good fit. But all of them were a step below this one. The problem interests me, and I'm glad to take it on. But I'm sure I'll be in the middle of some major policy conflicts and competing interests. This could be a career killer. I intend to listen for a while. Then I'll close my ears to the do-gooders, know-it-alls, protesters and bigots and do what I believe is best for the country."

"If you can find a way to get people to put aside their agendas, you will begin eradicating some of the problems. It won't be easy."

He reached across the table and covered her hand with his own. "I'm glad you're with me in this, Denise. It's important to me."

"It's important to me, too, Scott. I'm a fighter for

what I believe in, and I'm glad I won't have to work against you."

He stared at her as if he didn't believe her. "You'd do that?"

She laughed because, looking back, it seemed funny. "Do you remember how I behaved over environmental issues a few years ago?"

"Oh, yeah. I see what you mean."

"Fortunately, it will never come to that, I don't think."

"I'm with you there. What are you doing this weekend?"

She examined her broken nail and made a mental note to see a manicurist the next day. "Pamela wants me to spend the weekend with them. It seems that Velma, Russ's wife, will be thirty-five Saturday, and the family is poised for a celebratory weekend. I'll get there Friday around six-thirty or seven."

"Want to ride along with me?"

"I'd love it. Oh, Scott, they'll all be looking at the both of us to figure out what's been going on."

He leaned back and smiled. "Who among them is paying your bills?"

"Right," she said, nodding in agreement.

"Judson is the only one of them who has the nerve to ask me a direct question about it, and I have enough nerve to tell him to mind his own business. So I don't see a problem. If you're ashamed of being with me, we'd better rethink this relationship."

She narrowed both eyes. "Don't even think it."

When they arrived at the Harrington estate in Eagle Park shortly after six-thirty that Friday, Scott was already wondering at the wisdom of their arriving together, although he didn't let on to Denise. He drove her directly to Drake Harrington's house, took her bag inside, greeted Drake and Pamela and went on to Judson's house, roughly a quarter of a mile down the road.

Judson opened the door and slapped him on the back. "My hat's off to you. Only a dedicated official would willingly take on immigration policy. It looks good on you, too. Never saw you looking better."

"A dedicated public servant or a fool. I'm here to drink to celebrate Velma's birthday, and I don't want to think about Washington or immigration. There will be time for that when I get my first grilling from the Congress. Where's Heather?"

"She took some stuff to Alexis for the party tomorrow. What's with you and Denise? Is she coming?"

"She's here. Pamela invited her. See you after I shave and shower. I came directly from work. I'm assuming you haven't given my room to anyone."

"Of course not. How's Nana?"

"We had dinner together a few nights ago. She's fine. See you later."

Half an hour later he came downstairs wearing jeans, a T-shirt and sneakers. He made a vodka comet for himself and took it in the den, where he knew he'd find Judson and Heather winding down after their working day.

He sat across from them in a big, overstuffed leather chair and sipped his cocktail. "How do the two of you keep your relationship fresh when you're together at work and at home? And what happens when you disagree professionally? Does that follow you home?"

"To begin with, we consult with each other, but we each have our own cases. And that's important. We leave work where it belongs, and we don't discuss anything about it in this house. We don't bring work home. That means we can't waste time during the working hours. If one of us has to work extra hours, we stay late at the office. We don't bring it home," Judson repeated.

"That rule has forced both of us to improve our work habits," Heather said. "By the way, supper's simple tonight. We're just having broiled lobster tails, French fries, a salad and apple pie, with ice cream if you want to get fat."

"Watch your tongue, lady," Scott said. "I work out three times a week. Fat is out of the question. Warm apple pie and vanilla ice cream is an indulgence. And that is *not* a simple meal."

"My thought exactly," Judson said. They talked until after dinner. All the while, Scott's mind dwelled on the fact that Denise was only a five-minute walk from him. Finally, when he could no longer resist the urge, he excused himself, went to his room and telephoned her.

"Hi, put on a sweater and meet me in front of Drake's house. I don't want to go inside, but I need to kiss you good-night."

"Will do."

He donned a jacket, loped down the stairs and bumped into Judson, who was on his way out of the den. "Sorry about that. I'm going for a short walk. I ought to be back in about half an hour or so."

Judson grinned. "That's all the time you need?"

"It's all the time I'll take," he replied and left the house with Judson's laughter ringing in his ears.

A nip in the air announced the coming of an early fall, and he zipped up his jacket. Striding along the road, he looked up at the sky and the moon, which seemed lonely in all its luminance, as it shone through the lofty tulip trees that flanked the side of the road.

"A man shouldn't have to sleep alone on a night like this one," he heard himself say. He didn't want the feeling to get to him, so he quickened his pace and started whistling "A Change Is Gonna Come." Reflecting on the lyrics, he told himself that whistling that song meant nothing. And maybe it didn't.

She must have heard him, because he saw her when she immediately ran toward the road. "If I don't watch it, I'll fall in love with her," he said to himself. He wanted to run, but his basic stubbornness wouldn't let him. *Fight it all you want to,* a niggling voice said. *You'll have to do more than fight.*

When he reached her, he picked her up, swung her around and then hugged her. "I got lonely, and you were only a quarter of a mile away."

He bent his head, and with her arms raised and lips parted, she opened up to him the way a morning glory spreads its petals to the sun. He gripped her body and plunged into her, reveling in the passion she gave, sucking his tongue as if it were the essence of life. He needed to lay her down and get into her, wanted and needed the feeling of her exploding around him while he released the powerful sexual sediments that were building up in him at that very moment.

"Baby, you're lethal," he said, stepping back. "We'd better take a rain check on this."

"Yes," she said. "Before last weekend, making out

didn't bother me. But now that I know what comes next, I'm gonna have to watch it."

"That's not what you meant," he said, as solemn as a priest. "You're not going to make out with anybody but me. And if you want to make love, let me know. I can take a hint, and you bet I'll find a way. I'll walk with you to the door."

As they reached the steps, she stopped and looked around. "It's an awesome night, beautiful and…it seems so deserted. It isn't a night to be alone," she said.

He stared at her. "Those were my thoughts exactly as I walked along the road. I'll see you tomorrow. What do you want to do before the party?"

"Nothing. What do you want to do?"

He lifted his shoulder in successive, quick shrugs. "Nothing. Hadn't thought much about it. We could go down to the river and fish."

"Good. I'll be ready at seven."

"I'll see if I can borrow Henry's rods, reels and tackle. If it's okay with him, I'll be here at about seven. Kiss me, and no heavy stuff."

She pressed a kiss to his lips, caressed his cheek, opened the door and went inside.

No sooner had she closed the door than mixed feelings cropped up again. "This isn't working," he said aloud as he strode toward Judson's house. "I care for her, and I want her, but how the hell do you pry something out of a woman if she doesn't want to tell you about it? Right in the middle of that kiss, as soon as she realized that she'd exposed her true feelings, she put up her guard. I know I won't be satisfied with the part she wants me to have. I want the whole woman, warts and all, and I'm entitled to know what I'm getting."

Fog and drizzle the next morning meant that he and Denise couldn't go fishing. He phoned her. "Too bad," she said. "Well, at least I can sleep another hour."

He walked down to Harrington House and, as he'd hoped, Henry answered the door. "Good morning, Henry. You're the man I want to see."

"Well, yer lookin' at me. Come on in and peel the fruit while I make the biscuits. You can make biscuits, can't ya?"

"I've never tried. I was going to ask if I could borrow your fishing gear tomorrow morning so I can take Denise fishing. We wanted to fish this morning, but you see what the weather's like."

"Yer welcome to borrow me fishing gear, but there wasn't no use going fishing this morning anyway, 'cause they ain't biting."

"How do you know that, Henry?"

Henry looked toward the ceiling as if having to suffer ignorance weighed heavily on him. "'Cause I been fishing sixty-five of me seventy-one years. It's the first of the full moon, and they're busy laying eggs. You want some coffee?"

"You bet I do. What do you want me to peel?"

"A couple of oranges. Tara's going to gorge herself on it." He shook his head from side to side, and a smile crawled over his face. "She's the apple of me eye."

"I know what you mean. If I can have just one child with her manners, intelligence and self-confidence by the time she's eight—or is it nine?—I'll thank God, her mother and everybody else who contributed to it."

"Humph. You start by getting the right woman to be her mother. Tara had Alexis, all three of me boys and me. Her own daddy ain't worth the saliva in his mouth. Tara took Tel for her daddy from the minute she saw him, and it's the answer to me prayers that he was finally able to adopt her."

Scott rested the knife on the table and stared at Henry. "You're telling me that Tara's birth father is alive, and that he gave Telford permission to adopt that beautiful little girl? What's wrong with him?"

"He never wanted any children. Besides, he's a colossal ass, and he ain't worth the breath I'm spending on him."

"I should say not."

Scott looked at the clock and decided to phone Denise. "Hi. I'm at Harrington House. Henry said the fish aren't biting. But he's glad to lend me the fishing gear tomorrow morning if all we want is to sit on the edge of the river and hold the rods. Let's cancel. We can fish another time. We could drive into Frederick for lunch."

"Thanks, but Pamela said the partying will start early afternoon. We can walk in the woods, though."

He put his hand over the mouthpiece. "Henry, do you need help with the preparations?"

"All I can get."

"I think I'd like to help Henry. Want to join me?"

"That would be great. I'll be there around ten."

"Good. See you then." He hung up and turned to

Henry. "Denise and I will help you. I'm pretty good in the kitchen."

"Thanks. I'd be surprised if Denise can cook, but she can help Alexis with other things. She's got a lot going for her, though." Scott diced some pineapple, put it in a bowl and set the bowl on the table. "Very nice," Henry said. "Me boys, Tel, Russ, Drake and Judson, all brought me some fine, lovely daughters. Heather is the latest. Are you dragging yer feet with Denise?"

"Not exactly, Henry. If we're going to discuss this, it's in strict confidence."

Henry rested his hands on the bones that passed for his hips. "Nothing confidential is ever leaked from me mouth. I won't breathe a word, even to the Lord."

"Thanks. I care a lot for Denise. I mean a lot! But Henry, something's in the way. I feel in my gut that she's holding something back. I'm a lawyer and a pretty good one, and I know when I've got the whole story and when I haven't. I don't want to hurt her by pushing her to tell me whatever it is when she clearly doesn't want to. But I'll be damned if I'll take less than she can give. Maybe I'm not making myself clear, but I can't be more candid."

"It's clear as glass. The time to wheedle something out of a woman is right after you've given her some solid loving, and she knows she's everything to you."

Scott imagined that his face was the picture of confusion. "But I thought that if I used that approach, she'd take offense."

"That's the way men react. Women are different. You mark my word. She's a good woman. She just ain't sure of herself, a queen who don't know it."

"You certainly hit that one on the head. Thanks, Henry. I appreciate the advice."

"Denise won't fall for any man easily. If she falls for ya, yer lucky and ya got a prize."

Scott opened a package of bacon, laid the strips in a cold pan and turned on the gas. He looked at Henry. "She's fragile, Henry, and I have to be careful not to hurt her."

"Every one of me boys married fragile women, but all of me daughters are also tough enough to take on any problem anytime. Denise is the same, and don't make the mistake of thinking that she's not."

"I know. I just hope I remember that."

Chapter 7

Dressed in a long white ruffled peasant skirt and a scooped-neck lavender blouse with long sleeves, Denise threw a shawl across her arm and struck out for Harrington House. About halfway there, she remembered that Drake was about to make a quick errand to Frederick and called him from her cell phone.

"Drake Harrington speaking."

"Hi, Drake. This is Denise. Would you stop by my house and ask my housekeeper for a small package?"

"Sure. I'll get there around noon."

"Thanks. She'll be expecting you." Denise hung up and called Priscilla at her housekeeper's home. "Would you please go to the house, wrap all the cheese sticks you have there and give them to Mr. Harrington? He'll be there at noon."

"Noon? That gives me time to make some more. Don't you worry. They'll be ready."

She thanked Priscilla and, with the wind in her face, she walked faster and arrived at Harrington House out of breath. Alexis opened the door to greet her.

"Hi," Alexis said and opened her arms for a warm embrace. As wife of the head of the Harrington clan, Alexis nurtured them all, including her older sister, Velma, who had married Russ, the middle Harrington son. With her quiet, calm personality, the family accepted and enjoyed her role as matriarch.

"Hi. What a great morning," Denise said, letting her gaze sweep over Alexis. "You are always the epitome of poise. You seem to float through life."

"It isn't easy, Denise. I'm only happy in an environment filled with love, so I do what I can to generate that. I needed to find peace, so I became a Quaker. I don't stress about anything. It's far more productive. Henry told me that you and Scott are helping us with preparations for the party. I appreciate this, Denise, and I know Henry will."

She outlined what remained to be done. "Can you roll the silverware in napkins, and you and I can put the dishes and glassware on the buffet table. Henry will let us know what serving dishes we need. Telford will take care of the drinks, and Drake has gone into Frederick to get beverages for the children and ice cream."

"So this is really a family party," Denise said, her admiration for the idea obvious.

"We do practically everything together," Alexis said. "The brothers have always worked and played as a unit, and Judson became one of them almost instantly. I love being a part of this wonderful family. Let me know when you're ready to start."

"I'll be with you in a minute. Where's Scott? I need to let him know I'm here." She started for the kitchen and stopped. "I'd better comb my hair. That wind is fierce."

Alexis regarded her with what appeared to be amusement. "With your hair blown around like that, you look as if you just left your lover's bed. It's so sexy you'll make his mouth water. Leave it alone."

"Thanks. I…uh…thanks." She made her way to the kitchen, where Scott had assumed the task of peeling ten pounds of potatoes and was whistling as he worked. She tiptoed into the room, waved at Henry, sneaked up behind Scott, leaned over and kissed his cheek.

"Don't think you surprised me, lady," Scott said. "Your perfume announced your arrival before you reached me. How about a real kiss?"

"Honey, you know Henry is—"

Henry interrupted her. "I'm minding me own business—you take care of yours."

Scott turned to face her, parted his lips over hers, dipped into her quickly and released her. "You hold on to that mood," she whispered. "I promised to help Alexis."

"You'd leave me here peeling damned near a bucket of potatoes and run off to help somebody else? I'm wounded," Scott said, feigning injury.

She gave him a slow wink. "My poor baby. I'll help you later. I have to keep my promise to Alexis." She looked at Henry. "Are we having a birthday cake for Velma?"

"Sure as ya were born. Tel's getting it after he and

Tara leave the music school. He teaches violin and she's studying piano.

"We ought to fix somethin' for drinks," Henry said, "but I never did believe in filling up on junk just before ya eat yer real food."

"Not to worry," Denise said. "I'll come up with something." She wanted the cheese sticks to be a surprise, so she didn't mention them. "See you guys later," she said and went to find Alexis.

At about one-thirty, the quiet around him changed with the suddenness of an explosion, and Scott sat up straight and looked at Henry to gauge the man's response. Henry reacted as if he hadn't heard the door slam, a puppy bark and the sound of swift young feet coming nearer. Tara charged into the kitchen followed by Telford, the eldest Harrington brother and head of the clan. Telford placed the enormous box that he carried on the table.

"Good to see you, Scott," he said, "and thanks for the help. I tell Henry and my wife that we should have these affairs catered, because it's too much for Henry. But Henry won't hear of it."

"I don't mind, man. I'm pretty handy in the kitchen. I figured that as much as I love to eat, I ought to learn how to cook. So I bought some cookbooks and followed the instructions. What I hate is cleaning up the mess I make cooking."

"Mr. Henry, Mr. Scott, can I help?" Tara asked. "My daddy says I'll be in the way, but I promise I won't."

Scott wondered what kind of task they could give Tara, but Alexis walked in and relieved him of the need to figure that out. She took her precocious daughter by the hand. "Tara, this is a good time for you to straighten up your room."

"Yes, ma'am." She regarded Scott with a luminous smile. "When I was little, I got in the way. I'm big now, and nothing has changed." She went over to Henry. "Can we go to the movies tomorrow afternoon? I want to see that Harry Potter movie."

When Henry patted her shoulder, Scott saw the bond between them and fought off the feeling of envy. "Work on yer mother and yer daddy," Henry told her. "If they say yes, we'll go."

"Wow!" She jumped up and down, clapped her hands. "Mr. Henry is my best friend…and Grant, too, of course," she said to Scott. "I love Mr. Henry. See you later." She dashed to the door where her mother waited for her.

"Will you take her to that movie?"

Henry stopped crimping the pie crust and treated Scott to a withering look. "Son, Tara is a girl. Never lie to 'em, 'cause they'll still remember it a century later, and they'll remind ya of it five minutes before they take their last breath. If I didn't want to go, I'da said so."

"Who's Grant?"

"Grant's her friend. He'll probably be here later with his parents, Adam and Melissa Roundtree. They live in Beaver Ridge, about three miles north of here. She's crazy about that boy. Five years from now, Tel's gonna have to chain her to the house."

Scott couldn't help laughing. "I don't think so, Henry. She's a very obedient child."

"That's now. You wait 'til those hormones start causing trouble. I see ya finished with the potatoes. You ever make rosebuds out of radishes?"

"Not yet. Don't you think that's a job we can save for Denise? What are you going to do with them?"

"Decorate the meat dishes. Speakin' of meat, I wonder if Pamela and Heather got those squab roasted. What Alexis wants with those boney little things beats me."

Denise walked in. "Where's all the food?"

"I've got a pig slow-roasting in the pit out there," Henry said. "I baked a ham yesterday. Jalapeño corn bread's in the warmer, and there's asparagus, wild rice, scalloped potatoes, green salad, cheese, you name it. Can you make rosebuds out of radishes?"

"I can try. May I have a paring knife?" Henry gave her one, and twenty minutes later she'd made two dozen radishes that looked like flowers.

Scott eyed them appreciatively. "You're a talented woman. How are you planning to spend next Saturday? We could ride out to Mount Vernon. It's a fascinating place."

"I'd like that, but…Scott, I have a riding school about eighteen miles from Frederick in a little hamlet called Whispers and ten miles from Eagle Park near the Monocacy River. I have a very able manager, who's also a veterinarian. Two or three times a year, I give some underprivileged children an outing there. We teach them to ride and give them a nice picnic. Twenty of them are scheduled to visit the school this coming Saturday."

He rocked back on the chair's hind legs and pierced her with a hard stare. "You're full of surprises, sweetheart. I'm afraid to ask what other little tidbits you haven't told me."

She seemed oblivious to the bite of his words. "Who knows? By the time you and I met, we had both led full lives. Considering who and what we are, we've had a lot of experiences. It takes a while to share all of them."

His gaze darkened to an unfriendly stare. "You're kidding! I haven't heard that kind of double-talk since I finished high school. In those days, we kids did it to show off our vocabularies. What's your excuse?"

"You can be brutal," she said. "I wouldn't have thought it."

"Why not? You are well aware that I am not a man who, rather than confront an enemy, will turn tail and go meekly. Not me."

He could see her controlling the trembling of her lips, forcing herself to look him in the eye.

"Denise, if you can't give me a better reason for waiting until now to tell me you operate a riding school, especially after we've been riding together, then we're back to square one."

She stood. "I can't deal with you right now, because I'm mad enough to spit."

Some kind of metal crashed against the chrome stove top, and both Scott and Denise whirled around and saw Henry glaring at them with his hands on his hips. "Yer both acting like children, and yer both dead wrong. Scott, nobody likes to be scolded, and Denise, ya need to open up. As long as ya got secrets, ya got trouble. And the longer ya keep 'em, the harder it is to let 'em go. Ya shoulda told him about yer school the first time he took ya out. The two of ya go to my house back there and talk this out. The door's not locked. Go ahead. I'm losing me patience."

Scott stood and extended his hand to Denise, aware that she took her time accepting it. "Come on." They walked out of the door leading from the breakfast room and continued behind the garden to the two-bedroom bungalow that the Harrington brothers built for Henry. "Let's sit out on the back porch," he said. "I apologize for my behavior. But Denise, I'm getting exasperated. Don't you want anything more for us than what we have? Frankly, it's not enough for me. I want more, and I deserve more."

"Scott, I've only had one close friend in my entire life, and that's Pamela. I've never had buddies, and I'm not used to sharing things about myself. Pamela was with me when I bought my first horse. My father selected it. It's just a part of my life. I didn't keep it from you intentionally."

"From my reaction, you knew it was important, at least to me. So why did you pretend it wasn't?"

"Probably to downplay what seemed to me like an attack. I try not to let my temper surface, Scott, because it makes me say things that I may not mean, and I hate apologizing. I also don't like to say things that hurt people I care for, and I care for you."

He had more questions, but the time wasn't right. He took her hand, and when her fingers trembled, he tightened his hold on them. "I wish I could make you understand what we could have together if we truly trusted each other and embraced this relationship fully. Watch Pamela and Drake, and especially Telford and Alexis, who've been married for several years. They have good marriages. They read and understand each other without exchanging a word. We'd better go back. Russ and Velma will be over soon."

"Are we all right?"

"I want us to be." He opened his arms, and she dove into them. He turned sideways, but it was too late. He hardened to full readiness the minute he felt her nipples against his chest. "Oh, what the hell!" he said, succumbing to his needs. With one hand on her buttocks and the other at the back of her head, he pressed her to him, parted his lips over her open mouth and plunged into her. Her moans sent his libido into high gear, and when she undulated against him, he stepped back.

"Look here, baby. One more minute of that, and we'd both be indiscrete right here on this porch. I'm just as starved as you are, but this isn't the time." He wrapped his arm around her. "Let's sit here for a few minutes. Lord! Right now, I could love you to distraction." When he felt that his lust was sufficiently calm he took her hand and went back to the house.

"Yeah," she said. "Next chance I get, that's exactly what I'm going to do to you."

"What?"

"One of these days, I'm going to let it all hang out."

They'd been walking toward Telford's house. He turned her to face him. "I'd better be there when you do that."

She reached out and traced her finger along his nose. "Let that be the least of your worries, honey."

He didn't want to go back into the kitchen to face Henry's tart tongue. "I'm going over to Judson's place and freshen up. I've been in that kitchen since shortly after six this morning. What about you?"

"I'll see if I can help Alexis with anything, or maybe sit in the den until my nerves settle."

He raised an eyebrow. "Your nerves, eh? I'll be back here in about forty-five minutes." He kissed her quickly and jogged up the road. *One of these days, she was going to let it all out.* The thought was proof that either she didn't understand the meaning of true love between a man and a woman, or that she knowingly struggled with her limitations. He hoped it was the latter, because he could help her with that.

The wind pushed him into a trot, and he spread his arms and pretended to fly. About fifty feet before he reached Judson's house, he sat on one of the huge stones that lined the road and caught his breath. Nature had begun its annual display of yellow, orange, red and brown colors, and the forest surrounding him bloomed in brilliant hues. "This is the perfect place in which to be happy," he heard himself say. Children would be safe, and if he had to be away from home, he'd know that he'd left his family among caring friends.

He walked the remainder of the way and rang the bell. Judson answered the door. "You've been scarce today, buddy," Judson said.

Scott explained where he'd been and why he'd been there. "What are the chances that the brothers would sell that property down the road from Harrington House? Right now, it's just a place for animals and mosquitoes. It's a great site for a house."

Judson looked into the distance. "I considered that area when I asked them for a parcel of land. They agreed, but Heather wanted to live farther up the hill. I take it that you like it out here. Five years ago, Harrington House was the only one within a mile or so in either direction. Speak with Telford first. The rest of us usually go along with what he thinks…not always, but for the most part."

"I do like it here. I love my condo in Georgetown, but that's in the city with all of its crowds, noise and crime. This place is peaceful and beautiful. When I come here, I feel nurtured. I'd like to raise my children here."

"You know I'll be rooting for you. Are you and Denise getting on?"

He lifted his shoulders in a quick shrug. "We are, Judson. But I don't think we're there yet. I'm working on it. She's…she's wonderful, but I don't think she's sure of me."

"Is she skittish?"

"No. I can't explain it without getting too personal, and I don't want to do that."

"I don't suppose you do. I'm aware that she could use more self-confidence, but I wouldn't have thought it extended to her personal life. It will just take you longer, but you can fix that."

"I know…provided she lets me."

Denise couldn't find Alexis, so she wandered outside, where she encountered Henry, who was removing the pig from the barbecue pit. "You can't carry that by yourself," she said. "Let me help."

"I was going to put him on this here old serving cart and roll him inside. You can help me get him on the cart." He handed her a pair of tongs and a towel. "Wrap the towel around yer waist." She did, and picked up the tongs, and together they got the big pig onto the serving cart.

"You roll it," she said, "and I'll hold the door open."

They got the pig into the kitchen, and Henry covered him with aluminum foil. "That finishes me job with that one," he said as he removed his apron. "Now, I can get dressed for the party."

"Aren't you going to carve it?"

"I don't put a knife in any meat that ya can't just slice. Russ will carve it. When it comes to food, he loves to have things perfect." He looked at her for what seemed like a long time. "I hope ya got things straightened out with Scott. He ain't yer average man, and he'll make a woman a fine husband. Ya won't find another ambassador who'll spend half a day helping an old man prepare food for somebody else's birthday party. I lived a long time, Denise, and I know you're the one who's dragging this relationship. He loves ya a lot. But he's strong, and he'll walk away from ya without looking back and he won't shed a tear. If ya want him, open up to him. And ya better do it soon." He patted her arm, a rare gesture of affection coming from Henry. "You'll make me a fine daughter."

She went into the den, sat down and pondered Henry's advice. She knew she would not soon find another man who suited her as Scott did and to whom she was so strongly attracted. She had to get over the fear of letting herself love unconditionally, and she had to let him know that she might not be able to fulfill his dreams. She opened her iPad and began surfing for information about Oscar Jefferson. She'd find him if she had to get a private detective. This time, she didn't begin with Oscar, but with Jeffersons in and around Waverly, Texas. Their one-time affair happened the summer of her high school graduation when he was home after spending his freshman year at the University of Texas in Austin. She didn't know his parents. But she knew Waverly, Texas, and if he still had connections there, she'd find him.

When Alexis and Tara came into the den, Denise had to cut short her search to find Oscar Jefferson. "Miss Denise, Uncle Russ called and said he and Aunt Velma will be here in half an hour. Daddy's in the swimming pool. Where is Mr. Henry?"

"Tara has to know everything so she can tell everything," Alexis said. "My daughter has the makings of a first-class journalist."

"Yer just in time to help me put the food out."

Alexis looked toward the sound of Henry's voice. "Henry, everything's wonderful. I'll help you with it."

Denise didn't hear the doorbell, and her nerves were rattled when she looked up and saw Scott. *Will I ever get used to his eyes?* she asked herself. *He mesmerizes me almost every time he looks at me.*

"Hi. Did you get any rest?" she asked him.

"Rest? You're kidding. I made a box so that Pamela and Heather could place fifteen squabs flat and in a way that they wouldn't move."

"Did they bring them?"

"Of course not. Judson and I brought them, and Pamela insisted that we walk slowly so as not to disturb them. Imagine the two grown men carrying one five-pound box so slowly that the wind almost knocked us backward."

"You're exaggerating, Scott," Denise said.

"Not by much. Women can think up the strangest scenarios. I hope I never see a squab again."

"If ya ask me, the boney little things ain't worth the gas it took to roast 'em. Where's Drake?"

Tara looked out of the window. "He's coming now with Aunt Pamela and Aunt Heather."

"What time is Grant coming?" Henry asked Tara.

"They already left home."

"If ya want to know what's going on around here, ask Tara," Henry said. "One of you boys help me get this pig in the oven to warm it up." Judson and Scott put the pig on an oversize cookie sheet and shoved it into the double oven.

Twenty minutes later, Denise, Scott, the Roundtree family and the Harrington clan—including Henry— sang "Happy Birthday" to Velma. When Telford brought out his violin, Scott said, "I'd give anything if I had my flute."

"I didn't know you played the flute," Denise said. "How nice!"

"I play most other reed instruments, though not nearly as well."

"Will you play for me sometime?"

"Anytime you ask."

Remembering what Scott had said, Denise watched Drake and Pamela and Telford and Alexis at the party, seeing them as never before. Scott had said that both couples were so attuned to each other that nothing and no one seemed to get between them. Their attention could be diverted, but only for a short while. It's the same with Russ and Velma, she thought to herself.

Scott walked over to her. "Are you noticing what I told you about them?"

Her eyes widened. "How did you know I was watching them? Yes, I'm beginning to understand what you mean. This family is wonderful."

He seemed reflective. "Do your parents get on well?"

"Oh, yes," she said. "They still call each other every night. Between the District of Columbia and Waverly, Texas, you can imagine the size of their phone bills. My dad's very protective and mom laps it up."

"I'd like to meet your parents."

"Mom's in Washington Mondays through Thursdays, but she usually goes home to Waverly every Thursday afternoon. I could make a date for one evening this week."

"Would you have done so if I hadn't asked?"

After thinking about it for a minute, she said, "Probably not. I wouldn't presume that you wanted to meet her."

"Hmm. Interesting."

Telford had been leaning against a hutch in the dining room talking with Adam Roundtree when he suddenly walked across the room to Alexis, kissed her on the mouth, went back and resumed his conversation with Adam. Denise's lower jaw dropped, and Scott laughed.

"Get used to it, sweetheart," he said. "She's not afraid to let him know how she feels, and you saw how he responds to that."

"Did I ever!" Denise replied, before a frown creased her face. "My parents didn't do that in my presence."

Scott seemed reflexive. "I'm not sure I believe you. You were probably so used to it that you didn't pay attention. My parents were always touching and hugging each other. Dad wouldn't let Mom lift much of anything, and he taught my brothers and me to be caring and protective of her. I still miss her terribly."

She reached out to him and, unconcerned about onlookers, she wrapped her arms around him and held him close. "I don't want you to hurt," she whispered.

He stepped back and looked at her as if searching for something deep inside of her. "At moments like this, sweetheart, when you give me something so special, I hate the thought of ever being without you. Are you with me?"

"I'm working on it, Scott."

As if he needed no explanation, he hugged her. "If you need my help, I'm here for you."

The next morning, Denise crawled out of bed, got her cell phone and called her mother in Waverly. "Mom, do you know whether Oscar Jefferson's family still lives in Waverly?"

"What on earth do you want with *them?*"

She explained why she wanted to find Oscar. "I'd rather not bring Dad into this."

"Why?"

"Because I'm not going to take anybody's advice to let sleeping dogs lie. My life is a mess, and Oscar's partly to blame. I need to confront what happened with him."

"But Denise—"

"Mom, your help will be less expensive than hiring a private detective."

"All right. They live in San Antonio." She gave Denise the address of Oscar's parents. Two hours later, Denise had the information she needed. "No procrastinating, kiddo," she told herself and dialed Oscar's number in Chicago. *A professor, eh?*

"Hello." For the first time in almost thirteen years, she heard Oscar Jefferson's voice.

"Professor Jefferson, this is Denise Miller. I doubt that you've forgotten me."

"Of course I haven't." After a tense moment, he added, "My mother told me to expect a call from you. What can I do for you?"

"I need to talk with you in person. Can you meet me tomorrow at one o'clock at Farrell's Restaurant on North Michigan?"

"Yes. I suppose I can. Should I bring a gun?"

She didn't feel like joking with him. "Thank you for agreeing to meet me. You don't need to be armed."

"By the way, where are you?" he asked.

"I'm in Maryland." He didn't need to know *where* in Maryland.

"You'll fly all the way up here just to talk to me when we could talk now?"

"It's better that way. See you tomorrow."

"I'll be there."

On the drive back to Washington that evening, she hesitated to tell Scott her plan to spend Monday in Chicago. If she didn't give him a reason, he'd be suspicious and, at the moment, she didn't want to give him the details.

She let her left hand rest casually on his knee. "I have an appointment tomorrow in Chicago at one o'clock, but I plan to be back in Washington tomorrow evening. What evening will be convenient for you to have dinner with my mom and me?"

"Let me know what suits your mother, and I'll make myself available."

With a befuddled expression on her face, she shook her head. "Sometimes I think you don't realize that you're an ambassador."

"Look, sweetheart, that title doesn't give me the right to behave like an ass. What will you be doing in Chicago?"

She'd known that he wouldn't let that pass. "I have decided to collect on an old debt, and it's time I did that. I hope I'm able to tell you about it when I get back."

His silence sent chills down her back, and goose pimples popped up on her arms. After a long minute, he said, "All right. If you need me, you know how to reach me."

"Thanks. I'll call you when I get home."

"Phone me when you're about to leave Chicago, and I'll meet you at the airport."

Scott drove home slowly. During the previous forty-eight hours, Denise had handed him more than one surprise. He welcomed the domesticity and nurturing that he saw in her at Velma's party, and he appreciated the way in which she let everyone at the party know that he was special to her. But why had she not told him about her riding school when they had been horseback riding? What possible excuse could there be? He was past the stage of deciding what she meant to him, so he had decided to find out what the secret was that seemed to cloud their lovemaking. She hadn't lied about her appointment in Chicago. And from her response, he knew that whatever it was, it was important to their relationship. A sigh of frustration seeped out of him. If only they could have spent the evening together. But he didn't broach the subject, because he didn't need a fortune-teller to tell him that it wasn't the right time. She was concerned about what she'd face in Chicago, and the ache he nursed for her wouldn't be appeased with half a loaf.

He drove to his home in Georgetown and parked in the garage. It would take him a while to get used to his triplex condo. The furniture from his Baltimore apartment hadn't come yet, and only his bedroom had been furnished. Fortunately, a nook in the kitchen held a built-in table and fold-up benches, and he could eat his breakfast there. He sat on the edge of his bed and telephoned his father.

"How are you, Dad? I've got four messages from you."

"I'm fine. If you're planning to be away from home for an entire weekend, leave a message on my answering machine saying as much. I don't need to know where or with whom, only that you're not lying there burning up with a fever. I hope you were someplace with Denise Miller."

"Dad, that's a laugh. You just said you didn't want

to know with whom, and in the next breath you practically asked if I was with Denise."

"Well, were you?"

"Of course, we were together much of the time."

"No need to explain that you're dragging your feet. And don't bother to tell anybody that you're a chip off the old block, because that's definitely not my style."

"I never would have guessed it, Dad. But I think Denise read you correctly."

"How so?"

"She said in effect that you couldn't count the women who'd flipped over you."

"Did she, now? Well, there've been a few. But they did it without my encouragement."

"Hmm. I wouldn't have thought it."

"Why not? Someday you'll have this same conversation with your son, and he'll be surprised, too. Can you and Denise make a go of it? She seems so right for you."

"I think she's right for me, too." He rubbed the back of his neck and let out a long breath. "But we still have to clear a few hurdles."

"Don't forget, son. She has a biological clock, and it can't be slowed down."

"I know that, Dad, and hearing you say it is not one bit comforting."

"All right. That's it, for now. When you see her again, give her my love. I know women, and Denise is cool on the outside, and a roaring furnace inside. Handle with care."

He didn't need further evidence that his dad understood the opposite sex. He had summarized Denise in a few short words. It was what neither he nor his father could see or know that spelled troubled for Denise and him. After hanging up, he shook his head in bemusement. Raynor Galloway hadn't denied Denise's assessment of him. A grin spread over his face. He'd have to give his dad a good hard look. As a teenager, he'd thought his dad possessed rakish good looks. Evidently, at fifty-seven, the man still had it. He pulled off his shirt and dialed Denise's home phone. He waited a few long minutes while the phone rang, and her breathless "hello" told him that she'd raced to answer it.

"This is Scott. Don't tell me you were already in bed."

"Hi. No, I wasn't. I was in the shower."

He told himself to get his imagination under control. "I wanted to wish you luck tomorrow. When you get back here, I'll be waiting. Do you understand what I'm saying?"

"Yes, I think so."

"All right. I care deeply for you, and I want you to remember that every second that you're away from here."

"I...I will, and don't forget how deeply I care for you."

"Then we can't miss. Good night, sweetheart."

"'Night, hon."

Chapter 8

Denise walked into Farrell's Restaurant at three minutes past one. Oscar had already taken a table, and she saw him stand as she approached.

"I never dreamed that you would be so beautiful," he said, his expression one of awe. "How are you?"

She shook hands with him, but she didn't want to engage any pretense of friendliness. Her mission had nothing to do with friendship. "I'm well, thank you."

As if sensing that she would be all business, he said, "Shall we eat first? I'm not much on having a heavy conversation while I eat."

"If you wish." She didn't want to make small talk about the last twelve years. "Do you mind if we just listen to the music? Small talk would be dishonest."

His eyes widened. "As you wish."

When the waiter brought the coffee at the end of the meal, she leaned back in her chair and looked him in the eye. "You lied when you said you'd protect me, and you didn't use a condom. You were well aware that I wasn't experienced and wouldn't know the difference." A chuckle dripped acidly out of her mouth. "Of course, I trusted you. You swore on your knees that you would love me until the day you died. You lied on both counts. Looking at you now through the eyes of a more experienced woman, I'm glad you walked out of my life, even if you did it in a cowardly way. Have a good life." She rose to leave.

"Wait a minute! You can't leave!"

She turned but didn't sit. "Why not? You left without bothering to find out why I'd wanted to see you."

He closed his eyes. "I know I behaved like a bastard, but I've paid dearly for it."

She continued to stand, while he talked as if confessing his guilt to a priest. She doubted that he knew when she left. Still so wrapped up in himself, he didn't even ask her how she'd discovered that he hadn't used a condom. And he'd never find out from her.

Denise phoned Scott a few minutes before three o'clock, told him that she'd be on Delta's six o'clock flight, and he was there to meet her when she stepped into the terminal. He searched her face for answers, but her countenance revealed only her delight in seeing him. After taking her bag from her and dropping it on the floor, he wrapped his arms around her, bent his head and parted his lips over hers. She sucked him into her aggressively, as if she wanted to devour him. He broke the kiss, stepped back and looked at her. Tremors rolled through him when she looked him in the eye and, with a solemn expression, refused to deny what her kiss had affirmed.

"Do you want to go home now, or shall we stop at a restaurant?" he asked her, framing the question so that she'd know he wanted them to spend time together.

"Let's go home. We can order dinner from a restaurant a few blocks away."

"Are you sure? Before you answer, think about where you want us to go in this relationship." All around them, people rushed into the arms of their lovers, spouses or friends. After what seemed like forever she grabbed both his arms.

"I just kissed you. Didn't that tell you anything? Yes, I'm sure."

With one hand, he picked up her overnight bag, and with the other he held her tightly around her waist. "Let's go." He didn't want to run, yet walking seemed more like crawling.

"How was it?" he finally made himself ask.

"Fine. Just fine." He released the breath he didn't know he'd been holding and allowed himself a half smile. Maybe. Just maybe.

It was already dark when they walked into her apartment. Inside the foyer, she flicked on the light, turned and looked at him as if expecting he couldn't imagine what. But it didn't take him a minute to understand that she wanted reassurance, that she wanted evidence of his need of her. However, what his body needed wasn't his priority. He was after something to ease his mind and his heart.

"It's a bit early for dinner," he said. "Let's talk for a while."

"Okay. Would you like a glass of wine or something stronger?"

"White wine's fine if you have some."

He caught himself pacing the living room floor and sat down, taking a chair across from her so that he could observe her as she talked. She placed a tray on the coffee table with wine and a bowl of pecans. He took a glass from the tray, more to please her than because he wanted it.

He leaned forward, raising his glass to her. "How do you feel?"

She sipped the wine, and he reached into the bowl for a handful of pecans, stood and handed her a few, but she didn't extend her hand. With her lips parted, she leaned forward, and he put two of the pecan halves into her mouth. Without taking her gaze from his, she chewed them deliberately and slowly as if savoring the most delicious thing she'd ever tasted. When she finally swallowed it, she licked her lips, sending a blow to his gut and firing his libido.

"Thanks," she said. "Those were the best nuts I ever tasted." His eyebrows shot up, but she seemed unperturbed by her remark. Then she placed the glass on the coffee table, leaned back and crossed one of the shapeliest legs he'd ever seen.

"Scott, I went to Chicago to settle an old score, to get an answer to a question that has troubled me for twelve years." Just as he'd thought, so he tried to appear relaxed, though he doubted that he succeeded.

"I won't give you his name, unless you ask me to," she said.

"Go on."

"During the summer after my high school graduation, I continued seeing a boy I'd dated casually since
I was seventeen. He'd been away at college his freshman year and was home for the summer. He'd become
more mature during the year away from Waverly. He
talked of our future, what he wanted for us, and swore
on his knees of his undying love for me. We were intimate, and it was my first time. He knew that, because
it was difficult for me.

"In September, weeks before he was to go back to
school and I was to start at Princeton, I went to him
to tell him that I was almost two months pregnant. I
never got the words out, because he declared that he
was moving on. I reminded him of his vow of eternal
love. But he said he lied about that, because I was hard
to get, because I was the only *thing* he'd ever wanted
that he hadn't gotten easily.

"I squared my shoulders, and told myself that I'd deal
with it. But that meant I was left with the problem of
facing my parents, who had such high hopes for their
only child. After weeks of unbearable stress, depres-
sion, sleeplessness and lack of appetite, I had a sponta-
neous miscarriage. I forced myself to go on to Princeton
as planned and get on with my life.

"I hadn't seen him since until today. I got his phone
number from his parents and called him. He agreed to
meet me in a restaurant. That's where I met him, and
that's where I left him. He still doesn't know that I was
ever pregnant, and he never will."

"I see." He didn't, but he couldn't think of anything
else to say. It was the last thing he'd expected to hear.
He got up and went over to her, sat down and put his

arms around her. "I could break his neck. What an awful time that was for you. I don't understand how you came through it and became the woman that you are."

"You don't think I brought it on myself? You don't think I'm…that I'm not the kind of woman I seem to be?"

He grabbed her shoulders. "Look at me. You loved the man, and he swore that he loved you. Lovemaking between two consenting adults is the most natural thing in nature. He hadn't shown his colors, so you trusted him. You couldn't have known that he would be so selfish. What is he doing in Chicago?"

"He's a professor at the university. He told me that less than a month later, he married a girl whose father told him he'd either marry his pregnant daughter or take a bullet in the head. He'd treated her badly, he said. She wasn't what he wanted in a wife. He said he's made himself content with her and their two children. I felt nothing for him. And I realized at that moment that I'd rid myself of the pain he'd caused me."

"What did you hope to accomplish by contacting him after all these years?"

"I wanted to let him see the woman I've become, to see that my pride was still intact. And I admit that his frank appreciation of me as a woman when he greeted me did my soul good. I wanted especially to let him know what I thought of him, which isn't much, and I accomplished both. In retrospect, I realize that I needed to rid myself of the uncertainty I felt as a woman, and I associated that with him."

"Is that all?" He realized that the question might seem cruel, but he had to know.

She moved away from him. "You want more than *that?*"

He refused to waver. "If there is more, yes."

Her lips quivered, and he could see her struggle for control. "I've told you the truth," she said. "What else do you want? My soul?"

He knew there was more, and that what she hadn't told him was what he needed most to know. "Why can't you trust me?" he said. He'd hoped that when she returned from Chicago she would open up to him at last. Frustrated and desperate, he grabbed her and set her in his lap.

"Look at me, Denise. Why can't you trust me? I'm not that guy. I love you! Do you hear me? I love you! I've put my cards on the table. What you see is what you get. You haven't done that, and I deserve better. Talk to me!"

"I've tried. I don't... I can't give any more."

"Are you saying that it isn't enough that I love you? Is that what you're telling me, Denise?"

"No. No. You're everything to me. Love me? I need you to love me."

She turned around to try and face him, and he saw the unshed tears glistening in her warm brown eyes. It was more than he could bear, and he wrapped her close to him. "Love me. Trust me and love me. I'll show you a world that you didn't know existed."

"I do love you," she whispered.

"What? What did you say?"

Her lips grazed his neck. "I said I love you."

His heartbeat accelerated so rapidly that tremors shook him. Her hand grasped his nape, and when he parted his lips above hers, she took him in, taking his tongue as if she'd been starved for it. He couldn't let her drag him to the edge. But within seconds, he bulged against her buttocks. A harsh groan poured out of him when her hand slipped inside his shirt and rubbed his pectorals. He'd told himself that he wouldn't make love with her again until he believed she trusted him implicitly. He didn't believe that, but he needed her. His hands roamed over her body, caressing, claiming her.

Suddenly, she jerked open her blouse, popping the buttons, put his hand inside her bra and moaned from the pleasure of his touch. He released her left breast, sucked its nipple into his hot mouth and nourished himself like the starved man that he was.

She removed the last shreds of his reticence when she moaned, "It's been so long, honey, and I need you so badly. I'm so… I ache deep inside."

He stood, lifted her and carried her to her bed. An hour later, still locked inside of her, he looked down into her smiling face, and he thought his heart would run away from him. His lips brushed over hers, sampling the sweetness so dear to him.

"I know there's more, sweetheart, and I know that if I pressure you to tell me, you'll run from me. But remember this, I'm not interested in judging you. I'm only after what I know you can give me. I want all of you." When she pressed him to her and said nothing, she confirmed what he already knew. He'd wait, and eventually she would trust him enough to confide fully in him.

* * *

Denise wasn't at all nervous about her mother meeting Scott, because she knew her mother thought very highly of him. Nevertheless, she wanted them to meet on her turf and not where Congresswoman Katherine Miller had the advantage. After preparing a gourmet dinner, setting the table and giving Denise instructions as to how to serve the meal—not that Denise needed it—Priscilla went home. "There's no intimacy if you've got a housekeeper walking in and out of the dining and living rooms," Priscilla had explained. "Every time I walk in, the conversation will come to a stop."

It didn't surprise Denise that Katherine pulled no punches. "I'm glad to see you again, Mr. Ambassador, and I was delighted when I learned of my daughter's interest in you," she said to Scott while shaking his hand. "I hope the two of you are serious about this relationship."

Both women learned that Scott could be as blunt and as candid as Katherine when he said, "How are you? If you don't mind, I'd like to dispense with the titles. Call me Scott. I'm serious, and as soon as Denise finishes cleaning out her closet, we'll get down to business."

Katherine Miller laughed. "I'd forgotten how you get straight to a point. I'm not going to suggest that you call me Katherine, because I'm old enough to be your mother."

It was his turn to laugh. "How often do you broadcast that fact?"

They settled into congenial conversation, and Denise thought she would burst with pride as she observed her mother's respect for and deference to Scott. With her insight, Katherine Miller had interrogated more than one high-level politician. Her mother didn't drink, nor did Scott when he had to drive, so Denise skipped cocktails and hors d'oeuvres and served a delicious meal.

At the end of the main course, Scott stood, collected the dishes and started for the kitchen. "Who cooks shouldn't have to clean," he said.

Denise hastened to correct him. "But I didn't cook," Denise said. "Priscilla did the cooking."

"Then remind me to thank her," he said, winking at Katherine. "Did she leave me any cheese sticks?"

"Of course. I wouldn't dare let you leave here without them." Denise realized that she was happy, and then suddenly crestfallen, her whole being seemed to sag. Would he walk away from her if she told him she might not be able to have children? And did she dare continue the relationship without telling him?

Scott returned to the dining room and walked around the table to collect a serving dish. When he looked at Denise a smile froze on his face. "What is it, sweetheart? What happened while I was in the kitchen?" He looked at Katherine. "Is something wrong?"

Katherine shook her head. "I don't know."

Denise forced herself to brighten. "Sorry. My mind took a hike backward." She avoided looking at Scott, but she knew that as soon as they were alone, he'd have questions. "Let's have some of that spectacular crème Courvoisier that Priscilla made." She said it airily with a smile, but she didn't miss the studied looks that Scott and her mother gave each other. At that moment, she wished she had her piano, which she kept in her house in Frederick. Given twenty minutes at the keyboard, she could lighten her mood and anyone else's. Music was a safe topic for both her mother and Scott, so she shifted the conversation to a recent concert at the Kennedy Center.

"It's time I went home," Katherine said a little later. "I have a few things to do before I turn in. I've enjoyed getting to know you better, Scott, and I appreciate your willingness to spend time with me."

Katherine Miller was nearly two inches shorter than her five-foot-seven-inch daughter, and he had to lean down considerably in order to kiss her cheek. "It's been my pleasure, Mrs. Miller, and I'm grateful to you for agreeing to spend an evening in my company."

Katherine Miller treated Scott to a withering look. "When a woman doesn't want to spend an evening in the company of a man such as you—all things being equal—it will be cause for curiosity. I hope to see you again." She kissed Denise. "I'll call you."

After her mother left, Denise turned to face Scott. His facial expression, more solemn than she had ever seen, scattered her nerves.

"You were glowing, beaming with happiness so much so that I could hardly keep my hands off you," he said. "I was in the kitchen five minutes, and when I got back you were a different woman. Did your mother say anything to upset you?"

She grabbed his arm with her right hand and looked him in the eye. "You're right." Denise gave her head a vigorous shake. If she didn't tell him the truth, he wouldn't believe her.

"I thought about how happy I was, how full of love

and of the feeling of being loved. And then I remembered how easy it is to lose it all in a second."

He looked hard at her, as if trying to will her to follow his thoughts. "That's long passed, and you couldn't lose what you never had." He stepped closer, leaving hardly any space between them. "Don't confuse a spoiled, self-centered boy unwilling to grow up with a mature man. You can't lose what you and I have together, but you can throw it away."

She wanted to ask him what he meant by that last statement, but she didn't dare give him an opportunity to probe. "If I did that, I definitely wouldn't be aware of it. Remember, I'll be at the riding school this weekend," she said, changing the topic. "I usually get back to Frederick around six in the evening, provided I don't decide to spend the night there."

"Do you have a house there?"

"No. Just a little pied-à-terre over one of the stables."

"Why can't I join you on Saturday? I can help you with the children, and I love to ride."

"That would be wonderful. You wouldn't mind? The children can be difficult sometimes."

"Why should I mind? I love children."

She managed not to look at him. "Great." She wrote out the instructions and gave them to him. "But you can come along with me Saturday morning. I'll leave here at seven."

Still seeming to search her face, he said, "I'll be here at a few minutes to seven ready to roll."

"Morton has the horses ready before the children arrive around a quarter to ten, but I like to get there in good time. After all, they aren't his responsibility, but mine." She sensed in his good-night kiss a question mark, but said nothing, for she knew that when he was ready, he'd open up about it.

Scott drove slowly that Saturday morning. He hadn't satisfied himself with Denise's half-truth about her sudden change in mood the evening he'd spent with her and her mother. He hadn't imagined it, because Katherine's obvious alarm was more proof than he needed. *She's going to tell me. I love her, damn it, and we're dealing with the future here.* He had promised himself that he wouldn't pressure her too much. But it was becoming clear that she didn't plan to share with him the real problem.

He parked in front of her apartment building, gave the doorman a five-dollar tip and a few seconds later he rang her bell. Would his heart always dance when he knew he'd see her? She opened the door, smiled at him and he felt as if he could fly.

"Hi, hon. I'm ready. Sure you don't want some lovingly brewed coffee?"

He pulled her into his arms, covered her mouth with his and let himself relish the sweetness that she poured into him. She didn't spare him, but drew in his tongue, moaning and caressing him until he reeled beneath the onslaught of it. Shocked by encroaching arousal, he brought himself under control and stepped back.

"You're lethal. Where's that coffee?"

"Coffee? Wh— Oh, yes, the coffee. You make me forget things."

"I wish I was equally adept at making you open up," he said under his breath. "But I'll get there, and soon."

Chapter 9

"Ambassador Galloway, this is Morton Sykes, my stable manager and riding instructor." He sized up the man and extended his hand. Morton Sykes's grip was that of a man who knew who he was and didn't mind letting you know it, Scott thought with approval. Denise's stables were in good hands. She showed Scott through the stables, the tack room and the barn.

"This is certainly a well-appointed school," he told them after seeing the lavatories, kitchen and dining facilities.

"We usually give them lunch outside," Morton said, "but we have to be prepared for sudden rain, strong winds and other climate surprises."

The bus bearing twenty girls and boys from Baltimore arrived at ten o'clock and immediately Morton lined them up for hot chocolate. Scott watched in amazement as Denise mounted a mare and Morton handed a frightened girl up to her. Denise put the girl in front of her and walked the horse around the fountain in front of the stables until the child demanded to take the horse herself. Denise hugged the girl, told her that she was proud of her and dismounted.

"You think she's all right now?" he asked Denise.

"Oh, yes. She isn't looking up at the horse, but looking down from its back, and she feels her strength."

Throughout the morning, he watched her encourage and nurture the children. When one little boy cried because he didn't get the hang of it, she put the child in her lap and rocked him until he became calm, and asked if he wanted to try again.

"You don't have to mount," she told him. "Ambassador Galloway will put you up."

"You bet I will," Scott said.

Shortly after noon, the three adults gave the children lunch, after which they enjoyed another session of riding. One girl got a splinter in her leg. A boy slipped while trying to mount a horse, and another child fell into the fountain while trying to retrieve his baseball cap. There were other calamities, none critical but all of them serious to the children.

This is a different Denise, maybe the real one, Scott said to himself. He could hardly believe what he saw. She kissed a child's finger to make it better, removed her shoes, waded into the fountain to get the boy's baseball cap, held the boy who slipped while mounting the horse and told him how many times she'd done the same. She didn't scold any of them, and as they boarded the bus for the drive back to Baltimore, she hugged each one of them and gave them a bag of mints, told them how happy she was to see them and that she hoped they'd come back. Throughout the day, she had acted as if she were mother to the children and he knew she enjoyed it.

After the bus left, Morton leaned against a tree and said, "This was a good session. I'll groom the horses and feed them."

"We'll clean the kitchen and dining areas," Scott said, anxious for a chance to be alone with Denise and discern her true feelings. He felt that he'd learned a lot about her that was important to him, and he wanted to be sure that he was right. As they cleared the tables and discarded the trash, she hummed and sang, surprising him with her sense of contentment. When they finished cleaning the kitchen, she heated two meat pies in the microwave, put them on a tray along with two cans of beer, cutlery and gingersnaps and handed the tray to him.

"Where are we taking this?" he asked her.

"Over to my little pad. Don't you want to go?"

"Of course I do. After you."

He followed her up the stairs to the small room above one of the three stables and waited while she unlocked the door. "Aren't you vulnerable with only this door for protection?" he asked her.

"Oh, no. The gates are always locked and the barbed wire on top of that twelve-foot fence is electric. Besides, the cameras that scan the property are visible on a monitor in Morton's office. We're safe."

"Glad to know it," he said, increasingly less comfortable with the idea of Morton Sykes protecting her.

After they finished the light supper, Scott cleaned

their dishes while Denise disappeared for what he assumed was a chance to freshen up. "Mind if I borrow some toothpaste?" he asked when she came back wearing a peasant skirt and blouse. After she gave him the toothpaste, he brushed his teeth and freshened up, explaining that eight hours in close contact with horses was hard on his nostrils.

He took her hand and sat beside her on the sofa. "I've been enthralled with you all day. You were so tender and loving with those children, a nurturer, mothering them, and they adored you. You have many sides, and I've thought all of them incredible. But seeing you as you were today with the children touched me so deeply. You'll make a wonderful mother."

She looked away from him, and when her lips trembled, he tipped up her chin, forcing her to look at him. "What's this?" Was she about to cry? It didn't make sense. Or did it? Icy chills shot through him, and when he tried to speak, no words came. He reached for her, but the fingers of that hand shook so badly that he jammed it into his pocket.

"D-don't you want children?" he managed to ask. She nodded, but that wasn't good enough. "Yes or no," he said, sounding to himself like a drill sergeant barking at first-day recruits. "Talk to me, Denise."

"Yes," she said so softly that he barely heard her.

"Then what's the problem?" He dropped her hand and moved away from her, more miserable than he'd been since the death of his mother.

"I...I— Oh, Scott."

"You what? Either you want children or you don't, and I have a right to know!"

Tears streamed down her cheeks, alarming him. Because he loved her so deeply, he opened his arms to her and she sailed into them. So this was the real problem, the reason why she'd been holding back on him, he thought to himself. "I love children, and I want a family. Are you or aren't you willing to give me a family?" Her tears escalated into sobs. And suddenly sharp pains stabbed his gut.

"You said you miscarried. That wasn't all, was it? Tell me *now.*"

"Th-the doctor said I might not be able to have any children."

Words wouldn't come. He just stared into space. What was a man to do when the dream that had been within his grasp suddenly cracked like a crystal vase into a hundred shards? *Think, man. That was a long time ago, and every few years modern science discovers medical miracles.*

"And that's what you remembered the night when you were with your mother and me?"

"Yes."

"I knew there was more than you let on. What precisely did that gynecologist say? That you wouldn't or that you might not be able to have children?"

"He said I might not be able to bear children. I was in the emergency room, and I'm not sure he was a gynecologist."

"I see. It's been years, and you may have been worried for no reason. Monday morning, I'll contact a top guy at Hopkins and get you an appointment. That is if you're willing, and if you truly want to know…provided there *is* a problem."

"I'll do anything. But won't I have to wait for an appointment?"

"Sweetheart, the word *ambassador* means something." She hung her head and rubbed both of her forearms. "Now what's the matter?" he asked her.

"Wh-what if they can't do anything for me?" Her trembling body was all the evidence he needed that she wanted to have children.

"As my nana says, there's more than one way to skin a cat. Of course, the natural way to have a child is best, but in vitro fertilization, surrogate mothers and adoption are other ways to have a family. What we need is love, faith and trust in each other."

She looked him in the eye, and her smile was brilliant. "I love you so much that sometimes it frightens me. Medical science is wonderful, but I want to have your children myself."

He could barely contain himself. At last, she had committed to him. "It's what I want, too, love. Oh, you can't imagine what this means to me. Where will you be Monday?"

"I'll be in Frederick all day, in case you get me an appointment."

"Then it's set. I'll see this to the end," he assured her. She reached up, clasped the back of his head and urged his lips to hers. Within minutes, he had her on fire, and this time, her aggressiveness nearly undid him. She stroked and fondled him, climbed into his lap and bucked against him until he could stand it no more.

"Where do you sleep?" She motioned toward a door and he carried her over the threshold. He got her out of her clothes and put her on the bed. Standing over her and staring into her eyes, he quickly took off his own clothes. She reached out and squeezed his tumescent penis, licked her lips and spread her legs. He thought he'd die if he didn't get into her right then, but he checked himself, crawled onto the bed and sucked her left nipple into his mouth. He didn't linger there for long, but made his way down her body, kissing and nipping as he went. Her hips began to sway and undulate as she begged for completion. But this time he was charting his own course. He wanted it all, and he meant to get it. With his index finger, he teased her clitoris, rubbing and squeezing until she begged.

"Honey, please. I want you to get in me now." Ignoring her, he hooked her legs over his shoulders and kissed her. "Oh, Lord. I can't stand this."

He shoved his tongue into her, found the spot that would make her yield to him and licked it until her thighs shook and he could feel her squeeze his tongue. "You can't leave me like this," she yelled when he started up her body licking, nipping and kissing.

"Take me in, baby," he said after quickly sheathing himself. She did, and within minutes, the pumping and squeezing gripped his penis until he could hardly bear it. Screams poured out of her and she nearly pitched him out of the bed seconds before his vigorous drive brought a keening cry from her.

"Honey, I'm going to die. Why can't you give it to me?"

"I will, baby. Stay with me."

She wrapped her legs around his hips, met him stroke for stroke and raised her hips as if to give him complete access to her body. Like shooting stars, electric currents swirled in her vagina, around, under and through his penis, consuming his will and his strength until, like quicksand, she sucked him into her, squeezing his essence from him. Moaning her release, she flung her arms wide in surrender, vulnerable and helpless, totally his at last. He sank with her into mindless oblivion.

Braced on his elbows, he remained locked inside of her, lacking the strength to move, his face cradled in the curve of her shoulder. After about twenty minutes, he felt her stirring, shifting her hips as her contractions gripped him. He brushed her lips with his.

"Are you asking me for something?"

"Don't be naughty," she said. "You know what I want."

"Was it good for you? I never felt like that before in my life. It's what I wanted so badly for us."

"The first time we made love, I thought it couldn't get any better. Now I understand why you insisted that something was missing. I felt as if a tornado swept me up. And what a feeling it was when release finally came. Was it good for me? It was wonderful." She stroked his cheek and caressed his back. "Are you going to remember how we did that, so we can do it that way again?"

He gathered her closer and smiled, hoping to show her the love that burned inside of him...for her. "It wasn't so much what we did that was different, sweetheart, it was what we felt. We were open to each other. And we were more concerned with giving than with receiving. That's what love is."

The small contractions in her vagina aroused him. "You still want me?" he asked her. She tried to hide her face against his chest. "It strokes a man's ego sky-high to know that his woman wants him. Always find a way to let me know that you need me. That's all you have to do." That said, he shifted his hips and took them on a fast, torrid trip to ecstasy.

Shortly before midnight, still euphoric from love-making and making plans to find out whatever physical problems Denise might have, Scott got into his Mercedes and headed for the gate. Suddenly, he stopped, backed up and got out. In the clear, moonlit night, Morton Sykes stood with his back against a fence, smoking.

As a man who liked all of his *i*'s dotted and and his *t*'s crossed, Scott walked up to Morton. "You're a cut-and-dried, no-nonsense man who tells it like it is, so I have no qualms about asking you this. Do you have more than an employer-employee relationship with Denise?"

Morton crushed the cigarette stump, struck a match on the bottom of his boot and lit another one. "Hell, no, man. If I did, surely you don't think I'd have tolerated your being up there with her. I don't take orders from a woman I sleep with. Denise has my loyalty and respect, and if you marry her, you'll have a decent and honest woman. I wish you both the best of luck." Satisfied, Scott shook the man's hand, got back into his car and headed home.

Denise curled up and tried to come to grips with what had happened to her in that bed. She couldn't pinpoint the minute, but at a specific point in time, her life had changed. She already loved him. That wasn't new. And when they'd made love, he brought her to a shattering climax. But on this night, she hadn't remembered who or where she was; she hadn't cared about what he thought of her, whether she was a good lover or even whether she achieved an orgasm. She had wanted to satisfy him, wanted to be everything to him. And she had forgotten herself.

"I don't know that woman who went wild in this bed with Scott," she said to herself, "but I like her. I have never been so free or so…so high." She rolled over to where his body had left an imprint on the soft mattress, bearing witness to his having been there. She hugged herself, then flung her arms wide as if embracing the world. The odor of their lovemaking teased her nostrils, and when she reached for the pillow that had cradled his head and held it close to her body, the laughter and euphoria vanished, and tears streamed down her face.

What if the doctor couldn't help her? "I'll release him," she vowed, trembling at the thought. "I know I'll live in pain if he goes out of my life, but he has a right to be a father."

After a time, she got up, prepared for bed and, as she was about to turn out the light, it hit her. She no longer had any secrets that she kept from him. And for the first time, she had been honest with him in bed and had held nothing back.

"So that's what he meant. I felt as if nothing separated me from him." She got her cell phone and dialed his number.

"Denise! Sweetheart, what's up?"

She realized that she surprised him. "I hope you're home, because it's late, and maybe I shouldn't have called. But I had to. I called because it was so different tonight, and I just figured out why."

"Did you? Tell me."

"I didn't have any secrets from you, and I had nothing to hide. It was…honey, it was something wonderful. I had no idea who I was or where I was. Is that what you meant when you said there was more for us if I could… uh…level with you?"

"You got it! Baby, you were a different woman—as uninhibited as wildfire. Nothing that we experienced before prepared me for the way you were tonight. We can't miss."

"But suppose—"

"Suppose nothing! We agreed on a plan, and we'll follow that course. We love each other, and we'll work out this and every other problem we face."

All that she felt for him seemed to swell up and tumble out of her. "I love you, Scott. Right now, I think I can touch the sky. If I'm dreaming, I hope I never awaken."

"You aren't dreaming. This is real. As real as night and day. I love you, too." Those were the words she had wanted and needed to hear.

"Good night, hon." She fell across the bed and slept until the sun was high.

Scott clicked off his cell phone and walked into his apartment in Georgetown. It was well after one o'clock that Sunday morning, and the light on his answering machine drew his attention. It couldn't be Denise, he told himself, because he'd just spoken with her. He pressed the button on his answering machine.

"Where the heck are you these days?" Matt's voice asked. "Doug just got back, and we thought we'd all meet over at Dad's place. I'll pick up Nana, and we should get there around one. See you then."

That meant he wouldn't see Denise, but he hadn't seen his brother since before he went to Lithuania, and he couldn't miss their family reunion to welcome Doug home. He phoned Denise the next morning and told her of his brother's arrival.

"Of course you want to see him. Have a great time, and give your father my regards."

"Thanks, I will. I'll call you tonight."

Like a man who'd just won the lottery, Scott's face bloomed as he inserted his key into the lock of his father's front door. But before he could turn the key, the door opened and Douglas, the younger of his twin brothers, embraced him.

"Now, I feel as if I'm home," Douglas said.

"Yeah, and it's high time, too, Doug," Scott said, hugging him a second time. "It's so good to see you. It's been over two years. Hmm. You've got the look of a man who's made it big."

"I haven't done badly." They stepped back and scrutinized each other. "Well, hell, man!" Doug said. "Ambassador, and damned if you don't look like one. Matt said you came home bestriding the earth like a colossus. By damn, he was right."

They walked arm-in-arm toward the den, and Raynor met them before they reached the door. "I should have planned a feast. The three of you haven't been together here with me since I don't know when."

Scott embraced his father and let his arms rest on his

dad's shoulder. "You're the man, Dad. I never saw you looking better."

Raynor appraised his oldest son and let a grin spread over his face. "That's what happiness does for you, son. And from the looks of you, I'll bet you'd vote to make Gravel Gertie a beauty queen. Why didn't you bring your girl?"

Scott raised one eyebrow slowly and deliberately. "Do you really think I'd give Matt and Doug a chance to gang up on me? Where *is* Matt?"

"In the rec room repairing the satellite dish."

Scott bounded down the stairs to the recreation room in the basement. "Don't tell me you're doing laborious work. The Prince of Galloway down on his hands and knees getting soiled. What has this world come to?" Scott teased.

Matt jumped up and embraced Scott. "I know you're a big shot, brother, but you've got to be more respect-ful. I just got a humdinger of a raise. You're looking at one of NKL's senior managers. Genuflect, man!"

"No kidding! Congratulations. Way to go, man."

"Who's this woman dad thinks so highly of? Why didn't you bring her? Are you serious?"

Scott looked down and kicked at the carpet. He did not want to discuss Denise with anyone, not even his brothers, who he loved dearly. "Yes, I'm serious, but I'd rather not talk about her now."

"Why not? Dad says she's beautiful, well-educated, elegant and has a wonderful personality. That's more than he's ever said about one of my dates."

"She's that and more. Give me a couple of months. Okay?"

"You got it."

"Where's Nana? I thought you said she'd be here."

Matt bunched his shoulders in a shrug. "You know Nana. She changed her mind, said Doug could come to see her and that she was going to church and pray for all of us."

Throughout that Sunday, he enjoyed the camaraderie, teasing and fortifying love with his brothers and his father. Matt went out and bought barbecued pulled-pork sandwiches, stewed collards Southern style, candied yams—especially for Doug, who hadn't had any in two years—several six-packs of beer and four warm apple cobblers, plus two quarts of vanilla ice cream to top everything off.

Raynor surveyed Matt's purchases, threw up his hands and said, "Boy, when it came to food, your eyes always were bigger than your stomach. Who's going to eat all of this?"

"Don't worry, Dad," Doug said. "We'll eat it, and you'll be able to keep your svelte physique."

"Yeah," Scott drawled. "My girlfriend carried on about him so that if I was stupid, I'd be jealous."

Raynor's grin covered his entire face. "Since this is the second time you've mentioned it, I take it you're stupid."

A round of laughter and whooping filled the room, and Scott leaned back in the big barrel chair, closed his eyes and let the happiness he felt flow through him. Nothing on earth matched the love among family members. You didn't have to say it, and you rarely thought of it, but it was strong and steady. And like the lifeline for a bungee jumper, it was there for you, no matter what.

* * *

The first thing Monday morning, Scott called his friend at Johns Hopkins and within minutes, he was able to speak with the chief of the OB/GYN service. "I wouldn't put too much weight on that evaluation," the doctor said. "It happened twelve years ago. And besides, that was mainly an informed guess. We'll do some tests. Can she come in this afternoon at two?"

"Yes. I can't tell you what this means to me. Thank you so much."

"I do know what it means to you, and I'll do my very best."

Scott couldn't remember when he'd last prayed when he wasn't in church with Nana, but he said a few words of prayer and then called Denise. "Hi, sweetheart. You have an appointment with the OB/GYN chief this afternoon at two. I'll be at your place in an hour and a half. You may need to pack an overnight bag. He didn't give me any details."

"Oh, Scott! You mean… All right. I'll be ready when you get here."

"Don't be nervous, love. After speaking with him, I have a very good feeling about this. See you soon."

After hanging up, he packed his briefcase, locked his desk and stopped by his secretary's office. "I'll be away for the remainder of the day. If a call is urgent, reach me on my cell phone." He had urgent work to do, but he couldn't allow her to go to that doctor alone.

Minutes before Scott was due at her house in Frederick, Denise remembered to call her mother.

"So you finally got around to telling him. Thank

God. I want to see you married to that man, because you'll have a hard time finding his equal. Call me as soon as you know something. I'd better not mention this to your father right now. You know how impatient he is. Good luck, honey." The doorbell rang. She opened the door, walked into Scott's arms and into the next chapter of her life.

Three days later, Denise prepared to board a Delta Airlines Boeing 767 for Oakland, California, to fulfill a speaking engagement for Second Chance. She hadn't had time to prepare for the talk, so she would have to rely on her experience with the subject. Still reeling from the news that the first two tests indicated that she could bear children, she knew that her efforts to stave off premature happiness would make it impossible for her to work on the plane or even to sleep. She wouldn't know the outcome of the other tests for another week.

Shortly before boarding time, she phoned Scott, who had to attend a meeting at the Pentagon. "I just called to say I love you," she told him, remembering Stevie Wonder's song. "I hope to see you Sunday."

"I'll be at the airport. Don't worry about anything. So far, you're batting one thousand. I love you."

"Oh, Scott. It's so wonderful to be able to say that I love you. I truly do."

"Listen, sweetheart. I'm in a room full of people who can barely remember that such a thing as a libido exists. I don't think they'd be sympathetic if I let you stir me up 'til it became obvious."

She heard the amusement in his voice and wished she could see the twinkle in his mesmerizing eyes. "You wicked man. I suppose I'll have to take a rain check. Stay sweet."

"And you do the same."

Denise boarded the plane, took her business-class window seat, accepted orange juice and declined champagne from the steward, grabbed the quilted coverlet and prepared to sleep. Four hours and thirty minutes later, she awakened groggy, hungry and wishing she didn't have to make the trip back to Baltimore. She vowed that on the return trip she would at least stay awake long enough to eat. The next morning, she delivered her best lecture ever on the rights of immigrant children.

"I wonder what Scott would have thought of it," she asked herself, suddenly uncertain as to whether she was working with him or against him. Shrugging it off as unnecessary worry, she decided to spend the remainder of the day sightseeing and having fun. There was time enough to think about her future when she got back home.

Scott left his car at home that Friday morning and took a taxi to work. If the weather became any fiercer, he'd either spend the night in his office or try to make it to the nearest hotel. He wasn't easily alarmed, but the force of the wind had fear lurking in him. By three o'clock that afternoon, the wind's force had lessened well below gale strength, and he set his mind on spending the night at his home in Georgetown. However, a telephone call from his buddy Judson changed all that.

"Hi, buddy. What's up?" Scott asked Judson.

"I just got a call from Morton Sykes, Denise's stable

manager at Whispers. He said that storm knocked down trees, hedges and posts, and that Denise is in California. The brothers and I will be out there at eight tomorrow morning to clean up. If you—"

Scott interrupted him. "I'll meet you there. I know where it is."

"Good. Velma's packing a lunch for us, but you may want to eat breakfast before you get there. I hope the damage isn't bad."

"So do I. What about the horses? Are they all right?"

"So far. He said he needs to make some adjustments, but that he'd do that after we get there. I figured you'd want to know."

"Damned straight, I want to know. See you in the morning."

He arrived at Whispers a few minutes before eight, and Morton opened the gate for him. "I would have called you," Morton said, "but I didn't know how to reach you. Judson and his wife are here often, and I know them, so I called him. I didn't call Denise, because I didn't see the point in alarming her. She's two thousand miles away, and she can't do one thing about it."

"You were wise. I'll tell her when I meet her at the airport." He looked around as he drove toward the stables. "I suppose it could have been worse," he said to Morton after he got out of his car. "These trees look as if they should be cut."

"I think so. Looks like the Harringtons are here," he said as a black Buick rolled into view.

Both men went to greet Telford, Russ and Drake Harrington and Judson Philips-Sparkman. "I suppose it could have been worse," Telford said. "Let's work out a plan. Six men ought to be able to clean this up today."

They developed a plan, each man got an assignment and they went to work. By noon, they had cut the trees and begun turning them into firewood. Scott uprooted the damaged shrubs, covered the roots with burlap, tied them and stored them in the shed to be set out in early spring. Drake and Judson repaired the side of a stable, and Morton returned the horses to the stable that each normally occupied.

When they gathered to eat lunch, Scott commented on how easily the brothers and Judson worked together, taking and giving suggestions, singing, joking and supporting each other. "It's easy, man," Russ said. "You're married, and you learn pretty quickly that the best way to stay married and keep your wife happy is to be agreeable even if it kills you."

"It sounds funny, but I think you're serious," Scott said.

Telford put a fried chicken leg on his plate and reached for the potato salad. "Of course he's serious. But he wouldn't change his life for anything. There's nothing like having gone through hell all day when nothing went right, getting home and that woman opens the door and spreads her arms to you. Your children run to you, letting you know by their greeting that you're king of their world. You love your siblings and other relatives and your close friends, but your joy, your happiness is in your own home with the woman who's told the world that she belongs to you and with your children. Your family doesn't remove your problems. Hell, problems can start right there, but you gladly relinquish your arrogance, self-righteousness and even some of what you once considered as your rights in order to preserve the love you find there."

"Yeah, man," Drake said, "because you get new rights that more than compensate for what you think you lost."

Judson handed Scott a can of beer. "Now that you're sufficiently well-informed on this subject, you know what to do."

Scott finished eating a warm buttermilk biscuit. "Thanks for the advice, but having a wife who can fix a lunch like this for six men, keeping the cold stuff cold and the hot stuff hot and the dessert at room temperature and who'd actually do it is a solid recommendation for marriage."

"Yeah," Morton said, striking a match on the sole of his boot. "It's the only rational reason for marriage that I've heard yet. Been there, done that and no longer tempted. Anybody want to help me exercise the horses?"

"Sorry to hear that, Morton," Telford said. "You must have made a few missteps somewhere."

Morton pushed himself up from his lawn chair and brushed off the back of his jeans. "Missteps! Huh. An understatement if I ever heard one. From now on, I'm sticking with horses. At least, I won't be tempted to marry one of them."

When the laughter subsided, Drake dumped the remnants of his meal into the black plastic bag that Morton provided. "I'll help you exercise them after we stack this wood and clean away the brush."

"You help Morton exercise the horses," Russ said to

Drake. "I'll help stack the wood and clear away all this brush."

Seeing some of the wealthiest men in Frederick County, Maryland, cutting, sawing and stacking wood for a friend of one brother's wife told Scott a lot about the Harringtons and what it meant to have one of them as a friend. Shortly before sundown, the men packed up their tools, and Scott surveyed the results of their efforts. Whispers looked as if it had always been that way, and the horses were calm, fed and apparently happy.

Scott walked over to Morton. "The place looks great. I think it would be best if I tell her when I meet her at the airport tomorrow evening. There were six of us here, but you did a Herculean job, and I'll see that she knows it." He frowned when Morton lit another cigarette. "It's none of my business, man, but those things will kill you. Have you tried to quit?"

"I've about decided that I can't do it solo, so I've made a date with a doctor to start on it seriously. It's getting to be too damned expensive."

Scott laughed at that. "I wish you luck with it. See you."

"Come on and go with us," Drake called to Scott.

"Yeah," Judson said. "Your woman is on the other side of the country. If you go to Washington, you're subject to get into trouble. Spend the night, and leave tomorrow in time to pick her up at the airport."

"I'll leave tomorrow morning, go home and change before I meet her. You wouldn't meet Heather with two inches of mud caked to your shoes."

Both of Judson's hands went up, palms out. "I stand corrected. You coming?"

Scott wouldn't have imagined how much he'd missed being at the Harrington estate with the brothers, Judson and their families. Henry greeted him with a rebuke. "I thought you'd forgotten where we lived. I don't manage to avoid me enemies better than you avoid this place," Henry said. "You haven't come back and neither has Denise. At least I hope you've been seeing each other."

He slung an arm across the older man's shoulder. "Not to worry, Henry. We're getting on fine."

"Fine ain't good enough. Sit over there on that stool and scrape some potatoes. We're all eating at Judson's place. Heather ain't used to cooking for so many people, so I told her I'd make some gourmet potato pancakes to go with her herb-stuffed roasted chicken. Now you take Velma, me second daughter. She can plan and cook for as many people as you want. Russ got himself a real woman. Well, all of my boys did real well for themselves and brought me some wonderful daughters. What's holding *you back?*"

"I'm working on it, Henry."

"That ain't good enough. Ya making any progress?"

"Oh, yes. I don't believe in standing still, Henry. I've done my part, and the next is up to God. If I get my wish, you'll have another daughter."

Scott couldn't believe the grin he saw on Henry's face. "Yer a man like me other boys, and you'll get what yer after."

He considered hugging Henry, but decided to leave well enough alone. "Where's Tara? I haven't seen or heard her."

"Tara's visiting Grant Roundtree, her boyfriend. The two are inseparable and have been since Tara was four."

"I met his father. I hope he's a nice kid,"

"He's crazy about her, and he takes good care of her. Boys do that when they see their daddies looking after their mothers. Tara's smart. She didn't have to deal with nonsense from her own daddy, and she's not gonna take it from anybody else. I think I heard her come in."

Tara danced into the kitchen holding Grant Roundtree's hand. "Mr. Henry, do you have any more black-cherry ice cream and can Grant please have some? He loves it, too. Oh, Mr. Scott!" She came over to him, bringing Grant with her. "Mr. Scott, this is my best friend, Grant Roundtree. Grant, this is Ambassador Galloway. He works in the State Department."

Grant shook hands with Scott and turned to Tara. "If he's an ambassador, where else would he work?"

"How old are you, Grant?" Scott asked him, amused that the boy had already developed a healthy self-confidence.

"I'm nine, sir, and I'll be ten before Tara is nine."

"And if ya want black-cherry ice cream from me," Henry said, "you'll stop beating yer chest like a chimpanzee."

"Yes, sir," Grant said, then sat down beside Tara and prepared to gorge himself on Tara's favorite ice cream. Scott stared at the two of them. If only he could see his own children happily playing with their friends. He stifled a sigh, and told himself to remember the power of positive thinking.

Chapter 10

Scott did his best to enjoy the evening. He had already learned that the Harrington clan used any excuse to come together and consume food and drink and enjoy each other's company. As much as he loved being with them and sharing their camaraderie, he couldn't give in to the occasion. He'd be unhappy if the results of Denise's test didn't turn out as he hoped, and he'd have to deal with her disappointment and unhappiness. If that wasn't enough, he had to tell her how the storm had damaged Whispers, the place that she loved so much.

After dinner, Tara came over to him and sat on a leather pouf that sat beside his chair. "What's the matter, Mr. Scott? You don't seem happy. If we were at my house, I'd play something for you. Is something wrong with Miss Denise?"

She'd heard the adults talking about his relationship

with Denise. "She's fine, as far as I know, Tara. I'll talk to her sometime tonight. Thank you for asking."

Tara's face bloomed in a smile. "You don't mind that I asked? Mommy and Daddy say I'm too nosy."

He told himself not to laugh, and he decided not to tell her how right they were. "Try to be more careful about the questions you ask and of whom you ask them."

"That's what Mommy says. But Daddy says I ought to act like a child and stay in my place."

"Did he tell you how to stay in your place?"

"I'm not sure. He hugged me and told me I was the best little girl a daddy could have, so I guess I'm okay."

"Yeah," Scott said, relieved that the question had resolved itself and wondering why he was so anxious to be a parent. Any child as precious as Tara could jerk your chain.

Alexis glided over to them. Her calm demeanor always amazed him. It seemed she lived in a state of grace. "Tara, darling, you and I have to leave. You're supposed to be in bed by nine-fifteen, and it takes you forever to get ready. Tell Mr. Scott good-night."

"But Mummy, if I leave he might get lonely."

"I don't think so, Tara," Alexis said. "He's among family and friends, and they'll keep him company. Drop by before you leave, Scott. Come with me, Tara."

Tara's lips brushed his cheek. "Good night, Mr. Scott.

"If he gets lonely, Mummy, is it going to be my fault or your fault?" he heard Tara ask as she walked away from him, her hand secure in her mother's hand.

"Don't worry, darling, Daddy and your uncles will keep him company."

"I'd love to have a little girl just like that," Scott said when Drake joined him.

"She's a delight and has been since she came to us a little more than four years ago. How are things going with you and Denise, if you don't mind my asking?"

"They're coming to a head. Keep your fingers crossed and your lips sealed."

A roar of laughter erupted from Drake, who usually expressed amusement more subtly. "Way to go, man. You won't hear it from me."

"I'm going upstairs, buddy. If anybody asks where I am, tell 'em I got sleepy."

"Will do. Tell her I said hello."

Scott dashed up the stairs to his room and closed the door. He hoped Drake would waylay Heather if she started up there to inquire about his well-being. He loved Heather like a sister, but he was not in the mood for any mothering. He dialed Denise's cell phone and waited, for an eternity it seemed, before he heard her voice.

"Hi, hon. I don't get good reception in here. Could you call me on the hotel's phone?" She gave him the number. "I'm in room 921." He dialed the number.

"Hi. That's much better. I'm so glad to hear from you. I missed your call last night because I fell asleep, and I didn't check my cell. I called back, and yours wasn't on."

He had a suspicion that she was feeling down. "Are you all right? I mean, you're not worrying, are you?"

"Well, I'm trying not to. It would be easier if I were with you."

"And I'd certainly prefer to be with you right now. You…uh…you didn't get more news, did you?"

"No, sweetheart. There won't be any news until Monday, and maybe not then," Denise said.

"Try to relax. If you're in the dumps when I meet you tomorrow, I'm going to take you to my place and make love to you 'til you're too exhausted to think about anything. So—"

"Are you suggesting that making love to you won't brighten my mood?"

He imagined that, if she was standing, she'd have her hands on her hips and narrow her eyes. He'd been as tight as a ball of yarn since the previous evening when Judson called him. But the tension flew out of him then, and he laughed in a rush of pure relief.

"Never," he said when he managed to control his laughter. "I'm spending the night with Judson and Heather. The entire clan was here for dinner, and Tara decided to look after me."

"Bless her heart. That's wonderful, hon. I'll have to thank her. She's good protection from those social climbers Heather likes to invite."

"Not to worry. Every woman downstairs is married to a member of the Harrington clan."

"Why do you sound as if you've been digging trenches or splitting logs?"

He stopped himself a second before he said, "Because that's what I did all day." He hadn't realized that she was so perceptive. He liked it.

"I'm okay, love. Thanks for your concern. You know

how these guys are when they get together, buzzing around like a hive of bees. A quiet moment would be unnatural around them. Kiss me good-night. I'm sleepy. I had beer at lunch, and cocktails—which I don't like—at dinner. It's too much."

"You sure broke out of that mold."

When she said it, he imagined her right eye in an audacious wink. What a gem she was! "Woman, don't be a smart-ass. Kiss me."

"I am. Part your lips enough for me to slip my tongue between them and nibble a little bit. Now, let me have yours. More! Don't be so stingy. I'm starving, and since I can't have what I want, you can at least give me a decent kiss. Ah, that's better. Hmm. Rub your palms over my nipples. Yes. Just like that. Wouldn't you like a little taste? Ah, sweetheart. I feel like exploding."

"It serves you right, too," he said when he managed to catch his breath. "If you were within a hundred miles of me, you wouldn't have played with me like that. Take some vitamins with your breakfast tomorrow. You're going to need the energy."

"Don't be so sure of yourself."

"I'm not. I'm sure of your reaction when I get my hands on you. And, baby, you're going to think I have a dozen hands." He made the sound of a kiss. "Good night, love." He hung up, rolled over, gave up trying to stave off a full-blown erection.

Forty-five minutes before the Boeing 767 landed at BWI airport, Denise washed her face, brushed her teeth and brushed her hair until it curled in shiny waves around her shoulders. After her daring and suggestive conversation with Scott the previous night, she couldn't help being nervous. Maybe he liked that in a woman, and maybe he didn't. She didn't look her best, but she'd pass muster.

The plane made a smooth landing and, twenty minutes later, she saw him. As if their bodies were wired that way, they ran toward each other. She dropped her bag and sprang into his arms.

"I thought you'd never get here," he said, holding her so tight that the buttons on his jacket made an impression on her torso. Denise didn't care. She would have gotten even closer to him if that had been possible.

"You're like the sunrise, the most beautiful part of the day. Let me look at you. The two days since I saw you seem like…well, forever."

She gazed up at him. "You make me so happy."

Her smile, luminous and tremulous, got to him deep in his gut. She was scared, and it was not a casual fear. Scott knew that his intuition about Denise and what the outcome of the tests represented for her couldn't be far off the mark. He picked up her bag, put an arm around her and headed for his car.

"I thought you were taking me to your place," she said when he turned onto 14th Street.

"I do my best to keep my word," he said, turning left onto Wisconsin Avenue.

"You are a coward, Scott Galloway. Have you forgotten your threat?"

"Threat? What threat? Baby, that was a promise."

She settled back into the comfort of the soft leather

seat. "I'm glad to know it. I had begun to wonder if you were scared."

"Keep it up, and I'll show you what being sassy with me gets you." The note of possessiveness in his voice gave her a feeling of pride. He was hers, and he was all man.

He parked in the garage underneath his condominium building. "Pray, woman. It's your last chance," he said, grinning at her.

"I can hold my own," she said as bubbles began doing battle in her belly, and shivers raced along her spine. Excited and half-scared, she reacted as she always did when expecting a new and different experience. She squared her shoulders and pretended nonchalance. She hadn't given much thought to Scott's private life, how he lived and his preferences. Would she like his home, his style?

He ushered her into the foyer and dropped her bag beside what she supposed was a closet door. "Welcome home," he said. She knew her expression belied her confusion, but his face told her that he was as serious as he had ever been. "Yes," he said. "Welcome home."

She raised her arms to him, caressed his face and kissed his cheek. "You have a way of making me feel like a queen."

"You *are* my queen."

"Oh, Scott. I love you so much!" She clasped her hands behind his head and urged his mouth to hers.

He broke the kiss and looked down at her, his eyes telling her all that she ever wanted to know. "If you'll only trust our relationship, what seems like a problem now won't be one. Trust that I love you and that you mean everything to me."

"I do. Don't you realize that I do?"

His expression said, *we'll see,* but she was not going to leave him doubting her. She walked away from him into the living room and immediately imagined herself at home there. Her favorite colors—beige, avocado-green and burnt orange—made her feel as if she were in her own house. She sank into the beige leather chair.

"You're right. I'm home. These are my favorite colors, and I love the decor and furniture. I could live here and love it."

"Be careful what you say, Denise. Your words fuel me, even as your love fulfills me."

"Am I…staying here with you tonight? I want to, Scott. I really want to." Was he hesitating? Didn't he want her to stay with him? She bit her lips and forced a smile. "Of course, if my mom tries to reach me, she's gonna freak out and probably send the whole FBI on a wild-goose chase looking for me. I'd better—"

"Stop it, Denise. When are you going to learn to trust me? You know I want you to stay with me, and not merely tonight. Why won't you trust me?"

"I know you love me, Scott. But sometimes, the idea that, of all the women in this world, you love me boggles my mind."

He sat beside her and put her in his lap. "In response to your question, I'm a man who's worked his tail off to achieve the career he wanted, and I want so much more."

"I know, but—"

He gave her a gentle but firm shake. "You listen

to me, woman. I flipped over you before I knew your name. You were in a pair of old jeans, a T-shirt and sneakers, with your hair hanging naturally around your freshly scrubbed face. By the time I left you hours later, I had a hell of a lot more to think about than my career. I thought that when you settled the score with that guy, you would accept that I'm not like him, and—"

"I know you're not like him." *He's not your equal in any way,* she thought, but didn't say. She wasn't going to tell him that if the doctor said she couldn't have children, she had decided to end their relationship, because she knew he wouldn't want to hear it. "I watched as the people I knew fell in love. I didn't believe it would ever happen to me."

"Believe it." He tipped her chin with his finger, so that she had to look into his eyes. And the truth she saw sent ripples like a river racing throughout her body. She sucked in her breath, but not before she betrayed the heat that he had fueled in her.

He covered her mouth with his own, ran his tongue over the seams of her lips, pressed for entry and plunged into her. His rapid breathing, rising body heat and the urgency with which his tongue danced in her mouth had her reeling. Perspiration streamed from her forehead to her chin and dampened her panties. When her nipples beaded, she rubbed the left one, frantic for relief.

He brushed away her hand, dipped into her blouse, and when his hand reached her bare flesh, she jumped as if startled. "Tell me what you want, sweetheart. I want you to be able to ask me for whatever you need. I'll do it."

"My breasts ache, and I—"

"Tell me, baby."

"I want to feel my nipple in your mouth."

He waited for a long minute, and then he sucked her nipple into his mouth. She let out a loud moan. "I need you. All weekend, I've been starved for this. I want to be in your bed and get you inside of me."

He stood, picked her up and took her up the stairs to his bedroom. They got out of their clothes in a hurry. Frantically, he placed her on his bed and looked down at her. "No other woman has been in this bed, and if I'm lucky, no one else ever will be."

She raised her arms to him, and with one knee on the bed, he began to remove his boxers. "Let me do that," she said. She sat up, grabbed his buttocks and teased him while she stared at his bulging sex, licking her lips.

"For goodness' sake, Denise!"

She stripped the shorts off him, sucked him into her mouth and enjoyed him, holding his buttocks and sucking vigorously.

"Baby, stop it! Stop it!" Holding her head, he stumbled back on the bed away from her. "This is one time that you have to do as I say. That was close!" He climbed into bed, brought her closer to him and bent his head to her breast. In minutes, he had her on fire, sucking her nipples, while his talented fingers danced at the mouth of her vagina, playing her as a musician played an instrument.

"Honey, I'm on fire. I'll do what you say, but please get in me now."

"I will, but first, I want this." He spread her legs wider, bent to her and sucked her clitoris. She couldn't stand it. A keening cry erupted from her when his tongue delved deep into her as he held her undulating body still while he took his pleasure. When the rhythmic pumping began, he made his way up her body, kissing and caressing as he went.

"Take me in, sweetheart," he said, handing her a condom. She sheathed him, and he drove home. "Be still, baby. I'm beyond control."

She tried to do as he said and, for a few minutes, she succeeded, while he worked his magic. He put a hand under her hips to give him better access. With every stroke, he pressed her clitoris and massaged the most sensitive spot in her vagina. He had her on fire.

"I feel like I'm going to burst. It's killing me, Scott. Oh, Lord. Make me come." Heat settled in the soles of her feet, the pumping and swelling in her vagina intensified, while her thighs trembled like a leaf in a windstorm. Then she felt her vagina grip his penis and she screamed, "I can't hold back anymore." Her body shuddered as she gave herself to him completely.

"I love you. Oh, I love you." The words tumbled out of her of their own volition.

Seconds later, he splintered in her arms. "My love. My life. I love you!"

Her tears of joy dampened his chest.

Hours later, he awakened her. "Open your eyes, sleepyhead. I ordered dinner, and it's here."

She slowly regained consciousness, reluctant to release the rapture that still held her. "I have to put some clothes on."

He leaned over and kissed her. "If you don't want to get dressed, I can bring the food to you. Your comfort and happiness are all that I want."

* * *

The next morning, he drove Denise home before going to work. At her door, he said, "No matter what news you get, remember that I love you and I need you."

She made herself smile. "I know, and I love you for that."

Scott knew in his heart what his reaction would be. News that he couldn't father a child with the woman he loved would disappoint him, but he had accepted that. Wanting to reassure Denise, he dialed her at home, but there was no answer. He called her on her cell phone. Where could she be? He knew she'd be anxious. That was normal, but where had she gone? He called her house in Frederick, though he doubted she had gone there.

How was a man to focus on work when something so crucial was at stake? He ran his fingers through his close-cropped hair in frustration. Where could she be? He told himself to get to work, and suddenly his telephone rang.

"Mr. Ambassador, Dr. Hinds is on the phone."

He froze momentarily, but quickly recovered. "Put him through, please. How are you, Doctor? Do you… have news for Denise?"

"Yes, I do, but I can't locate Ms. Miller, and I should speak with her first. Do you know how I can reach her?"

"Yes, I do, but I just tried to call her without success. I hope the news is good."

"I expect you are as anxious as she must be. Tell her to call me."

He let out a long, harsh breath. "You can't know how I feel. Nobody can!"

"Don't be so sure. I have three children, and I can't imagine my life without them. Ask Ms. Miller to call me."

"Thank you so much. I will."

He would if he could find her. Maybe she was someplace where she couldn't be reached, perhaps because she was afraid to hear what might be bad news. At three o'clock that afternoon, she called him.

"Where on earth have you been? Your doctor and I have been trying to reach you. Please call Dr. Hinds right away."

He could almost feel her apprehensiveness. "I was a complete nervous wreck, so I went out and took a long walk. I've been walking for hours."

"And you didn't take your cell phone? Dr. Hinds said you should call him. Stop worrying, sweetheart. Call him and then call me. I love you."

After talking to Dr Hinds, Denise immediately called Scott. Her fingers shook as she dialed Scott's cell phone. "Honey, he said I'm fine," Denise said with a rush. "I'm all right! They couldn't find one thing wrong with me. I have never been so happy in my life." To her embarrassment, she began to cry, sobbing uncontrollably.

"Don't cry like that, sweetheart. It's good news, not bad. I'm happy enough to shout. We should be together right now. Let's have dinner tonight?"

"I'd love to, but my mom made a date with me. Look,

I'll call her, give her my news and reschedule. If she knows I'll be with you, she won't mind."

"I'll see you around six," he said.

Denise couldn't remember anticipating anything with so much joy. As she dressed, she sang, laughed and danced. When the doorbell finally rang, she raced to it, flung open the door and practically leaped into Scott's arms. "I'm so happy. I didn't know I could be this happy."

He wrapped her in his embrace. "Are you happy for yourself, or happy for us?"

"Both, honey. And I'm happy for you, too."

"Is this your answer to my question?"

A grin spread over her face, and then she laughed, not at him. She laughed because she couldn't contain her joy. "You're not on your knees. And I always dreamed—"

Scott immediately dropped to his knees, wrapped his arms around her waist and kissed her belly. "Will you marry me? I love you and I will be faithful to you for as long as I live. I will take care of you and our children with everything that I possibly can."

"I'd be proud to be your wife, and happy to be the mother of your three children," she said, kneeling down to face him.

His laughter warmed her, and was the most wonderful sound she'd ever heard. "You mean you'll only give me three?"

She brushed her nose against his. "You get three if the first two are the same sex."

"But if I am sweet and loving, you'll reconsider. Right?"

"You think you'll charm me into it, huh? Oh, hon, I'm so happy."

After such an emotionally draining day, they ate a dinner of soda crackers, cheddar cheese, apples and white wine, and went to sleep in each other's arms.

The next day, Denise received a call from her father. "Your mother tells me you're serious about an ambassador. Tell that young man where I live. I want to meet him."

Denise called her mother. "Mom, what's he thinking? Dad can be very bossy. Maybe I shouldn't—"

"Of course you should. If Clyde steps over the line, you can bet that Scott will put him right back in his place. They will get along like two peas in a pod."

Scott and Denise landed in San Antonio, Texas, at 4:10 p.m. that Friday. As they approached the baggage claim area, Clyde Miller—tall, handsome and a Texan to the core—walked toward them. Denise hugged her father. But as she did so, Clyde Miller's gaze locked on Scott. Although he wasn't sure what kind of reception he would get, Scott hadn't worried about it much. If the man was decent, they would get along. If he was not, he wouldn't see much of Scott Galloway.

But after Clyde Miller stared Scott down with a piercing gaze, his face broke into a smile, and he extended his hand. "I'm glad to meet you, Ambassador Galloway. Thanks for coming to visit me. Denise and my wife have kept you a secret from me because they know that I ask a lot of questions. I hope you can stay for a while."

Scott shook Clyde's hand. "I'm happy to meet you, sir. Denise issued an order. So I didn't dare not come."

After getting their bags, they drove forty miles to Waverly, Texas, in Clyde's custom Cadillac. "Did Mom come home last night?" Denise asked her father.

"You bet. Unless they have a special session, Katherine is here with me every weekend." Scott heard the pride in the man's voice and concluded that Denise grew up in a loving home. He reached for her hand, and she looked at him, her eyes shining with love. He eased an arm around her shoulder and drew her closer to him.

"My dad likes you," she whispered. "I thought he was going to be a pain in the neck, but apparently it doesn't seem so."

He caressed her cheek. "That's because you brought him a real gentleman."

She ran her fingers along his cheek and smiled. "And Mom did your work for you," she said, more than a little pleased.

Katherine Miller greeted them at the door. "Welcome, Scott. Clyde and I are glad you could visit us. Come in."

Scott knew Denise's family was well-off, but he hadn't imagined that they lived in such opulence. He loved Persian carpets, and from the foyer to the living room, elaborately patterned ones covered the floor. Velvet cushions and leather furniture in earth tones that he loved and fine walnut woods made him feel very much at home.

Nina, the family cook and housekeeper, served a meal of roast Cornish hens, saffron rice, string beans, a green salad and apple pie à la mode. Later, Scott enjoyed an after-dinner port and espresso coffee in the den with Denise and her parents. Her parents wanted to know Scott's intentions toward Denise, and he wasn't going to wait until Clyde Miller asked him and he found himself on the defensive.

He put the coffee cup on the coffee table and leaned forward. "Denise and I are in love, I've asked her to marry me and she has agreed. I want us to have your blessing. I'll be as good a son to you as I am to my father, and I'll do everything in my power to see that Denise and our children want for nothing. I'll be faithful to her, and to my family, and they will always have my love and support."

Scott stood when Clyde walked over to him and extended his hand. "Well, Scott," Clyde said, "from what my wife told me about you, I was hoping that you and Denise would make a life together. As soon as I saw you, I knew you'd do just fine."

"Welcome to our family, Scott," Katherine said. "I couldn't be happier."

"Thank you. I'd like you both to meet my father, my grandmother and my twin brothers as soon as I can arrange it. They are my family. They all live in Baltimore, of course."

"We'll definitely look forward to that," Clyde said. He left the den and a few minutes later returned with a bottle of vintage champagne. "This calls for a toast. My daughter's happiness is all that I want, Scott, and her happiness is bound with yours. If you ever need Katherine or me for anything, you have only to ask. We will always be here for you."

"Thank you." He stretched out his legs, glanced at

Denise and grinned. "Don't you think we should seal this with a kiss?"

A frown clouded her face. But that didn't surprise him since Denise was, if anything, circumspect. She looked at her mother. "I'd better warn you both. Scott has a wicked streak."

Katherine raised an eyebrow. "I don't see anything wicked about wanting a kiss. I've enjoyed quite a few." She looked at Clyde and winked. "Wouldn't you say so?"

"Mom, will you call me when you get up?" Denise said, changing the subject. "I'm ready to call it a night."

Scott pretended to pout. "And no kiss?"

She walked toward him, kissed him on the cheek. "You behave."

"There is little likelihood that I'll get a chance to do anything other than behave," he muttered. "Good night, love."

"I see she's capable of giving you a hard time," Clyde said.

"A hard time?" He thought for a minute. "Sometimes she does, but she knows how far to take it," he said pointedly and looked Clyde in the eye. "She's told me that you're a rancher," he said, "so I hope you'll show me around tomorrow. I've never been on a ranch."

"I was hoping you'd want to do that. I raise Herefords and Angus cattle, and I have ten horses and several colts. I plan to sell them."

"How do you keep the pack young if you don't keep any of them?" Scott asked.

"I keep those that are born every three years. Katherine will sleep late tomorrow, and Denise will wake up when somebody shakes her. So why don't you and I get some breakfast around six-thirty and look the place over before the sun is too high? I take it you ride. I'll take along a couple of rifles, and we can skeet shoot."

"I love to ride, but I've never been skeet shooting."

Clyde smothered a smile. "If you caught Denise, you must be pretty good at handling moving targets. I'm amazed that she stood still long enough for you to get to know her."

"This has turned into a conversation that I'm not sure is meant for me," Katherine said. "Sleep well, Scott. I'll see you in the morning, provided Clyde ever brings you back."

Scott didn't relish the idea of sleeping across the hall from Denise, but he supposed the discipline wouldn't hurt him. The following morning, reflecting on his comfortable night's sleep, he told himself that having her as close as she was must have made a difference, because a solid night's sleep had begun to elude him lately. When he walked into the kitchen, Clyde had breakfast ready.

"You can set the table for the two of us," he told Scott." We're having a fresh fruit cup, grits, waffles, sausage, bacon and coffee. For me, breakfast and grits are the same word, but I didn't know about you, so I made you some waffles."

"Great! If you've got any eggs, I'll scramble us some to go with the grits. This is what I call a real breakfast," Scott said.

Clyde shook his head slowly. "Tell me about it! Denise and Katherine will have half a grapefruit, whole-wheat toast and black coffee, and both of them will be after me if I gain half an inch in my waistline."

Unperturbed at that news, Scott put the scrambled eggs on the table, sat down and looked at the food laid out before him. "That's terrible," he said. "Thank God I know how to cook."

"Same here. And it's come in handy many times."

By the time they finished eating, they had developed an easy camaraderie, and Scott began to look forward to their morning ride. Clyde's pride in his twenty-seven thousand acres, his large herd of cattle and his horses showed in his face and in his stride. As they strolled through the barns, Scott became aware that Clyde's hands invariably rested on his shoulder in a fatherly gesture.

"I wasn't born to wealth, although my family lived very comfortably. After I finished Texas A&M University and went to work on a ranch, I quickly discovered that in order to get where I wanted to go, I needed some skill in business. I went to Harvard, got an MBA and two years later, I bought the first few acres of this ranch. Heating and cooling these barns was an enormous investment, but I never lose livestock due to extreme weather or tempertures. One steer is worth at least thirty-five hundred dollars."

My goodness, Scott said to himself. *This man is grooming me to be a rancher. He'd better live 'til he gets some able-bodied grandsons.*

"Over there beyond that grove of trees is a creek that's more like a river. It's the lifeblood of the ranch. Let's get back to our mounts," Clyde said, "and try out these rifles. I have a practice range south of here."

Clyde hit six of the ten clay disks flying through the air. "Now it's your turn," he said. Scott took aim, eventually hitting the disks three out of ten tries. "You're a quick study, son. Some fellows try it every weekend and have yet to hit the target. Denise has hit once or twice, but it was pure luck. She doesn't approve of guns, and her skeet shooting shows it. If you'd like, we can play a round of golf."

"I'm mediocre at best, mainly because I almost never play," Scott told him, "but if you're patient, I'd love to play a round with you."

Clyde glanced at his watch. "Goodness, it's a quarter to twelve. I expect they're up and already had their breakfast by now. We'd better get back."

"You think they'll be mad at us?" Scott asked him.

Clyde headed his horse toward the barn, and Scott joined him. "You bet. They want us close by while they do whatever they want to do. They'll pout, but ignore it. Put your arms around them, tell them how sweet they are and how much you love them. It works every time."

Scott couldn't help laughing. "Are you sure that won't get me into trouble?"

"Trust me, Scott. It works every time."

"I'm sure you're right, but I'm not certain I want to try it. By the way, is it all right if I swim in that creek?"

"It wouldn't be a good idea, since there might be poisonous snakes in that creek. Anyway, we have a nice pool. You'll see it when we get back."

True to Clyde's prediction, Katherine and Denise met them at the door when they returned. "Hi, sweetheart," Scott said. "Want to go for a swim? It's gotten hot."

"And it's going to get hotter. The day's almost half gone, and you haven't said beans to me."

From the corner of his eye, he could see from Katherine's expression that she was letting Clyde know of her displeasure. On the verge of asking Denise what time she got up, he remembered Clyde's advice, pulled her into his arms and kissed her.

"You could at least explain yourself," she said. "You're just like my dad. Tell him he's done something wrong, and he gets sugary sweet. It may have worked with Mom, but it has never worked with me."

Scott dropped into the nearest chair, shaking with laughter that he didn't try to control.

"What's so funny?" Denise asked him.

"You don't want to know. I can see that I'm going to love this family."

Chapter 11

That afternoon, Denise walked out to the patio, where Katherine lounged in a chair, reading legislation that she was supposed to vote on that Monday. "They've been gone since right after lunch, Mom. Where do you think they went?"

Katherine put the proposed bill aside, took a sip of the sweetened iced tea on the table beside her and looked at her daughter. "I don't know where they went, and I'm not worried about it. If you get bent out of shape whenever you're not looking at your man, pretty soon you'll look like a pretzel. Give a man his freedom, and he'll always come back."

Denise bristled at that, though she knew that her annoyance with Scott was hardly warranted. "I'm not trying to tie him down—in fact, I like my freedom, too. But he should have at least told me where he was going and asked me if I wanted to go. We're supposed to be spending the weekend together."

"I thought you wanted your father and me to get to know him, and I'm sure he wants to know what he's getting into. If Clyde didn't like Scott, you'd be furious with you father. He likes your fiancé, and you're furious with him for showing that."

"You make it sound awful, Mom. You're accustomed to the way Daddy acts, but I'm not used to not having Scott around."

"I imagine you aren't. Your father wanted a son. But after you were born, I didn't have another child. He's got one now, and he's happy. I'm going to swim. Your father's planning for us to go into San Antonio for supper. I hope you brought something lovely to wear."

"I certainly did." She went up to her room and debated joining her mother in the swimming pool. She'd always thought of her mother as an independent woman, but she had some old-fashioned ideas. She didn't mention it, but changed into a bathing suit and was about to jump into the water when she heard Scott's voice.

"Next time we come, I'm going to bring my fencing gear. Your dad used to fence, but he hasn't had anyone to spar with. We've been playing golf. I could get used to it if I had an opportunity to play more often. Your dad's a really good coach."

"I'm glad you're having so much fun."

He stared at her. "What's the matter, Denise? Are you unhappy about something?"

"Since we got here, I've rarely had time with you alone. I thought we were spending the weekend together."

A frown clouded his face. "Look, sweetheart, I'm so happy to discover that I like your father and have a lot in common with him that I didn't consider the possibility that you might feel left out. He's just as surprised and pleased that we get along so well. I thought you'd want us to like each other."

"I do, but you haven't kissed me since we got off that plane."

With a flash of white teeth, a grin illumined his handsome face. "I offered last night, but got the brush-off. Come here."

She held up both hands. "Get that look off your face. My dad's over there."

"Really?" He pulled her into his arms, wrapped them around her and covered her mouth with his. When she parted her lips, he released her and stepped back. "Did you forget where your dad is? Let's walk over to the creek or down to that pecan grove around five or five-thirty. We aren't leaving for San Antonio until seven-fifteen. What do you say?"

"I'd love it. Meet you in the foyer at five and we can be back here at six-thirty. That'll give me time to dress. I have a few things to do in my room. I'll see you at five." She kissed him quickly on the mouth and went inside. As she climbed the stairs, she met her mother.

"I've been meaning to ask you what's going on with Second Chance and what was the outcome of your meeting in Oakland?"

"There's some concern about the direction of the new immigration policies, but most board members want to wait and see what happens before we make any decisions."

"Is this going to cause a problem between you and Scott?"

"I shouldn't think so. We haven't discussed it since he got that appointment."

"Be careful, Denise. You may have to decide what's more important. Whatever you do, don't oppose him publicly. He will never forgive you."

She cared deeply about the plight of children of undocumented immigrants, but she recalled her passion for the environment and her attack on Scott. At the time she didn't know him or his views on environmental issues. She also knew that it would be hard to be quiet if the administration put forward a policy that hurt the interests of Second Chance. Why couldn't he have been given a different assignment?

"I don't usually shoot myself in the foot, Mom, and I don't intend to start doing it now. We'll find common ground. We'll have to."

"If you're stubborn, that may prove to be difficult."

In her room, Denise showered and looked at the dress she planned to wear to San Antonio. Her cell phone rang, and she dashed to answer it. "Hello."

"Hi, sweetheart. It's still very warm out here. Are you sure you want to walk?"

"We can go down in the basement. I'll play the piano for you, and that ought to let my folks know that we'd like some privacy."

"We can try that, but if I hear footsteps, I'll start kissing you. And whoever it is can turn around and go back."

"You mean you spent all that time with Clyde Miller, and you think he'd do that? Not hardly."

"Meet me at the basement door."

* * *

Scott watched Denise bounding down the stairs in front of him, and wondered when his bubble would burst. Happiness suffused him. He remembered that his grandmother hadn't met Denise, and realized that he'd better amend that at once. As soon as he could get their families together, he'd press Denise for a wedding date. But the thought gave him a peculiar sensation. What if she wanted a long engagement, or if she had some other excuse to postpone marriage? No point in dredging up doubts, he told himself just as his cell phone rang. He opened the cell phone as he reached the bottom step.

"Galloway."

"Hi, Mr. Scott. This is Tara Harrington. My piano teacher is presenting her students in recitals Friday at six-thirty, and you have to come, because Mr. Henry said you're probably going to be one of my uncles."

"Hello, Tara. I'll be glad to attend your recital. Where will it be?"

"Gee, I don't know the address, but my daddy will tell you. What? Oh. Mr. Henry said you can leave from here with us. Okay?"

"Yes. Thank you for inviting me. Let me speak with Henry.

"Hi, Henry. What time do you think the family will be leaving for that recital?"

"Tel said they'd leave here at five-thirty. If ya can't make it to the house here, ask Tel for the address. It's the same school where he teaches violin on Saturday mornings. I'm glad yer coming, Scott. Yer a member of the family, and ya oughta be there."

"Thanks. Give Tara a hug for me. I'll see you Friday."

"Is everything all right?" Denise asked him.

"Seems so. Tara wants me to go to her recital Friday. If she doesn't invite you, don't take it personally. If she doesn't call you, come with me as my date."

To his mind, Denise seemed to have difficulty warming up to that scenario. "Well, okay," she said. "You're right about Tara. She practically worships Telford, his brothers and Henry."

"Of course she does. They love her, and she knows it."

"Maybe if I don't play the piano, they won't know where we are," Denise said.

"I don't think they care, Denise. They have accepted that we'll be married, and we have their blessing. Do you think they're concerned about whether we kiss or even whether we make love? Your mother's a modern-day woman, and if she's concerned about anything, it's whether you're happy in bed with me." He grinned. "Put her at ease about that the first chance you get."

"You're not serious."

"Of course I am. That's extremely important in a marriage."

"Hmm. I'll tell her if she asks me, but I'm not going to open up about the topic."

He raised one eyebrow. "Maybe it isn't true."

She stepped closer to him. "Are you asking me to stroke your ego? If you weren't sure, you wouldn't have raised the question. Want me to brag?"

"That's up to you. I can't imagine it would hurt a man's reputation."

She stroked his cheek. "Are we talking seriously here?"

He closed his right eye in a slow wink. "About the bragging? Why not?"

"Oh, *you!*" She reached up to him and, unable to wait, he pulled her closer, covered her mouth with his and took what she gave him. When she parted her lips, bubbles danced in his stomach. Shaken, he stepped back.

"I think we'd better reserve that for when we're in your place or mine. It wouldn't do for one of your parents to see the result of what you were about to do to me."

She hugged him and rested her head on his shoulder. "I hope I never get used to feeling like this with you. It's like the whole world can go to hell and just leave us alone."

"Trust me, baby, the first time Second Chance locks horns with my office, we'll both discover how solid this relationship is."

"I know what my priorities are," she said.

And I know what my responsibilities are, he thought, but didn't say. To her he said, "I certainly hope that our feelings for each other aren't so shallow that we'd break up about immigration policy. Play something for me," he said, changing the subject. "I heard you once, and you play beautifully."

She opened the Steinway grand piano, sat down, closed her eyes and began to play Chopin's Mazurka in F. Within seconds, she was alone in the world with her music. As she played, she swept him along with her as the music reached a crescendo and then slowly declined.

"How is it that you didn't choose music as a profession? You are magnificent at that piano."

"I considered it for a short while, Scott, but there are many people who play better than I do. If I couldn't be outstanding, there was no use in pursuing a music career. I love to play, but I wouldn't do it professionally. I have degrees in music, and I can teach piano and other instruments at the university level. I could take care of my family if I had to, and I wouldn't hesitate to. In any case, I wouldn't be happy sitting at home all day and not doing anything constructive."

He sat on the piano bench beside her and put both arms around her. "I hope you never have to take care of our family." He needed to change the subject. "We'd better get dressed. I imagine your dad is a man who is somewhat impatient."

"You're right on the money."

At the top of the stairs, he brushed against her lips with his own. "I'll wait for you in the den."

Denise wore a red off-the-shoulder silk crepe dinner dress that stopped a few inches above the knee. With her hair styled with flowing curls around her shoulders and diamond studs in her earlobes, she knew she looked stunning. She didn't compete with her mother, but she was aware that when Katherine Miller stepped out with her husband she dressed to keep her husband's eyes on her alone.

"I've got the two loveliest women anywhere around here," Clyde said. He looked at Scott. "Would anyone disagree with me?"

"Certainly not any sane person with decent eyesight. If whistling wasn't bad manners, I'd definitely split the air with one."

"I might have enjoyed it," Katherine said. "It's been years since I got a wolf whistle"

Minutes after they took their seats at their table, he noticed that Denise seemed uncomfortable. Watching her from the corner of his eye, he saw her glance from time to time at a nearby table. He glanced in the direction of her line of vision. He could hardly believe his eyes when a smooth-looking man about his age, who apparently didn't have a date, smiled and winked at Denise.

"Do you know that man?" he whispered to her.

"Who's that fellow, Denise?" Clyde said, almost at the same time.

"I've never seen him before," she replied.

"Let's put an end to this. If you'd rather he didn't ogle you, you can change places with me," Scott said.

Denise stood. "That's a good idea." They exchanged places and Scott laughed at the man's obvious disappointment.

Itching to teach the guy a lesson, Scott stared at the man until he looked elsewhere. He enjoyed the meal and the evening with Denise and her parents, but one thing bothered him. He decided then and there that he was going to take the first step toward correcting it.

And on his lunch hour the following Monday, he thought about going to New York to buy an engagement ring at Tiffany's, but the opportunity to do so was nearly a month away. Impulsively, he called Denise. "Can you meet me at Mervin's at twelve-thirty today?"

"Yes, of course. But we don't have to do it today, do we?"

"Yes, we do. Before some fool hits on you again, I want him to be able to see that you're engaged. I wanted to annihilate that guy Saturday night. Can you meet me?"

"I'll be there at twelve-thirty."

He chose a four-carat diamond ring flanked by baguettes. "Do you like this one?"

She gaped at the dazzling lights in the ring. "Of course I do, hon. But that's a down payment on a house."

"Why not?" he said, laughing. "It'll last longer than a house."

"It's so beautiful. Why are you letting him put it in that box? Can't I wear it now?"

"This is not the ideal place for a man to put a ring on a woman's finger. Hell, I can't even give you a decent kiss in here."

She gave him a withering look. "Hmm. I suppose so."

He put the ring box in his shirt pocket, eased his arm around her and left the store.

"I drove, hon," she said, "so you can't take me home. Incidentally, I have to go to Wilmington, Delaware, tomorrow. Second Chance has a relatively new group there, and I need to visit with them. They're a great group of immigrant families there and I'm excited about meeting them."

"One of these days, you'll invite me to one of your groups."

"That's an idea. Can we meet for dinner?"

"Yes… Oh, no. I have a radio interview tonight. My secretary has the information on that, so I'll have to call you and tell you the time and station."

"Good. Then we can get together tomorrow night."

The week didn't go as Denise had planned. Members of the Delaware group argued over fundraising and over all of their activities. She realized then that having board members like these might not serve the purposes of a nonprofit organization such as Second Chance. While she digested that problem, a call on her cell from the secretary of Second Chance brought another.

"Hello. Denise Miller speaking."

"Denise, this is Carole Jacobs. We want you to come to Phoenix and see if you can talk our local assemblyman out of proposing a bill that would, in effect, require children of undocumented immigrants to pay tuition to attend public schools. There are so many immigrants that the people are blaming them for everything, but this is too much."

"When is he considering putting the bill up for a vote?"

"Thursday or Friday. Naturally, voting on it at the end of the week will lessen the media coverage. By Monday, it'll be old news. I can get you a meeting with him. Will you do it?"

"Of course. Make the appointment for tomorrow. I'll book a flight. Please reserve me a good hotel room for the night, and have someone meet me at the airport. See you tomorrow."

She turned her attention to the Delaware group, did her best to resolve the members' differences and got busy reserving a flight to Phoenix. An hour later, she'd booked a flight to Phoenix from BWI International Airport. She'd get a taxi from the airport to Eagle Park or Scott would come for her. *Scott!* What was he going to say about her change of plans? They had a date for tonight that she couldn't keep, a date during which he'd planned to give her the engagement ring. He was not going to take it lightly, and she didn't blame him. But what could she do about it? Nothing!

She phoned him, hoping that he would not be in a meeting or dining with colleagues. "Hello, Ambassador Galloway speaking," he said in his deep velvety voice. From the sound of it she knew that he wasn't alone.

"Scott, this is Denise. Please give me a call as soon as possible."

"Of course, I will," he said in a quiet tone.

After hanging up, it occurred to her that they should develop some shorthand or code for such occasions.

An hour later she received his call. "Sorry I couldn't talk. I was in a private conference. You caught on quickly."

"It was easy. You don't normally refer to yourself as Ambassador Galloway. Honey, I have a problem." She described it. "So I won't get home until tomorrow evening. Can we see each other then?"

She anticipated his reaction from the length of time he took to answer her, and she understood that it didn't sit well with him. "How many members does Second Chance have?" he asked her.

"Nationally, about six hundred, though only two-thirds are active." If he wanted to vent, she'd give him an opportunity. The more she learned about him, the better for both of them.

"And of those four hundred members, you're the only one capable of discussing your organization's goals with the legislator? Seems like the structure is pretty weak. I'm not happy, Denise. I've been counting the minutes until I see you this evening, and I've made dinner reservations. With your change of plans, what am I supposed to do?"

"I'm sorry, honey. If that legislation should pass, other states could soon follow with similar laws."

"He's not the first elected official to promote that idea, and he won't be the last."

"But will you forgive me and meet me at BWI tomorrow?"

"I would, but I'll be at the Pentagon tomorrow afternoon until at least four-thirty. Denise...I hope this doesn't happen again. If at all possible, try to discuss your change of plans with me before they're a fait accompli. Whenever possible, I'll pay you the same courtesy."

"All right. I apologize, and I want you to know that I consider myself the loser, because I won't be able to flash my brand-new diamond at those Harrington women."

That brought a laugh from him, and she relaxed. He wasn't pleased, but he understood. She could definitely live with that.

"Sweetheart, they'll flash their engagement rings right back. I hope you don't plan to compete with them."

"Heavens, no! I've always walked to the beat of my own drummer, but I can see that you and I are going to have to get a drummer with whom we can both stay in step."

"That's what I like to hear. We're going to have to spend some private time working on that."

"I agree, but we are not going to spend it in Waverly, Texas."

"Why not? I promised your dad we'd come back in a couple of weeks."

"You did not! Look. Let's not discuss that, because I don't want us to fight. I hardly saw you when we were at my parents. No way!"

"You liked my dad. Why don't you want me to like yours? Denise, this is silly. I have to get back to work, so we'll have to continue this another time. I'll call you at nine-fifteen tonight.

"I'll be waiting for you. Love you. Bye."

"I love you, too. Bye."

Whew! She'd have to get used to being a couple and remember that she'd have to make decisions with her future husband. *Husband...* Scott Galloway was going to be *her* husband. She flung out her arms and laughed. Life couldn't get any better.

Sitting in the backseat of the limousine that was taking her to Eagle Park that Friday, she wondered if the twelve minutes she'd spent with that state representative was worth the time she'd spent away from Scott. When she arrived at Drake's house, the sun was still fairly high, and Pamela and Heather were in the sun-room drinking coffee and wrapping toys for children.

"Put your bag down and help us," Pamela said after greeting her friend. "We've got a couple of boxes of toys downstairs waiting to be wrapped. How's Scott?"

She sat down, crossed her knees, picked up a Miss Piggy doll and began to wrap her in red-and-gold paper. "Scott was fine when I last spoke with him."

"You'd better shape up, Denise," Heather said. "That man's nuts about you. And you act as if guys like Scott Galloway are standing on every corner waiting for you. I know you're attracted to him, so why are you playing hard to get?"

"Who said I was playing hard to get?"

"You are," Pamela intoned, swinging her right foot rhythmically. "And you're going to be sorry."

What a perfect moment to display her engagement ring. Unfortunately, she didn't have it, and if she told them she was engaged to Scott, they probably wouldn't believe her.

"I'm not going to be sorry," she said. "And I wish you'd stop lecturing to me as if I'm a teenager who doesn't know a man when she sees one." She looked at Pamela. "Do you know what Tara's playing at her recital?" she asked, hoping to change the topic.

"No, I don't. I didn't think to ask."

"She left a message on my cell phone inviting me to come. If I'm lucky enough to have a child, I'll be happy with one who's half as delightful as Tara."

Pamela nodded. "So will I. But Henry says that for a child to be like Tara, it would have to grow up as Tara did with five adults showering her with love daily and a mother who disciplines her."

"There's a good bit of advice in there somewhere," Heather said, "and I hope I find it."

The phone rang, and Pamela rushed to answer it. "Hello. Scott! How nice to hear from you. Are you coming today?"

"Yes. If Denise is there, may I please speak with her?"

"Yes, of course. Denise, Scott wants to speak with you."

"Thanks. Tell him just a minute. I'll take it in my room." She quickly ran up the stairs to one of the guest rooms.

"Hi. I'm glad you got there safely," Scott said, when Denise picked up. "I should be there in about forty-five minutes. I just got a call from your dad. He wants us to come back next weekend, and I'd like that a lot. I told him I'd have to check with you and call him back."

"Next weekend? But we were just there this past weekend. What's with him? I don't want to go back so soon. I only saw you at mealtime."

"That isn't true, and you know it."

"Well, it seemed that way. He completely monopolized you. You hardly got to say two words to my mom."

"Your mom knows me. Are you saying we won't go? He'll be very disappointed, and so will I."

"Let's talk about it later."

"I told him I'd call him back. How much later?"

"Oh, Scott. I didn't enjoy last weekend because I hardly spent any time with you."

"I don't fudge the truth, sweetheart, and I keep my word. I'll call him and tell him that you're not sure."

"Please don't... Okay, we'll go. Otherwise, I'll be in the doghouse."

"Interesting. I'll see you shortly."

It seemed to Scott that Denise should have been overjoyed that her future husband got along so well with her parents. Granted, she had been an only child and hadn't had to share her parents with a sibling. But now it seemed like she didn't want to share *him* with her father. He parked in Judson's garage, got out and knocked on the kitchen door. The kitchen was connected to the garage by an enclosed walkway.

Rosa opened the door for him. "You're just in time to get a little bite before we leave to hear Tara play. I made you a couple of smoked-salmon sandwiches, and I've got some good leek soup. I'll set the table."

"Set the table? Don't go to that trouble. After I run upstairs and freshen up, I'll eat it right here in the kitchen."

"Mr. Ambassador, I'm not feeding you in this kitchen."

He put an arm around her shoulder. "Yes, you are, and stop calling me that. My name is Scott, and that's what you're to call me."

"You can't be serious. It's not every day one of us gets to be an ambassador. I'm as proud of you as I can be."

He kissed her cheek. "Thanks. I appreciate that, but I'll eat right here in this kitchen. Be back in a few minutes."

Twenty minutes later, he drained his coffee and patted Rosa on her shoulder. "That smoked-salmon sandwich was just what I needed." He met Judson in the hallway leading from the den to the living room.

"Where's Heather? Isn't she coming?"

"Of course she's coming. She's at Drake's house with Pamela. I'll pick her up there, and we'll go on down to Harrington House."

"Good. Denise is there, too."

"I know you play it close to the chest, buddy. But isn't it time something happened between you and Denise? How's it going?"

"Stop worrying about that. What will be will be. And you'd be the first to know." His anger flashed as he thought about the reason why he couldn't tell his best friend that the woman he loved had agreed to marry him. He wanted the proof on her left hand. Instead, the ring was in the inside pocket of his jacket.

"Are you ready?" Judson called to Rosa. "Tara will be climbing the walls if we're a minute late, and we have to make a stop at Drake's place."

"I'm 'bout ready as I'll ever be."

When Drake opened the door, Pamela and Heather stood with Denise just behind them. Denise appeared crestfallen, and he knew it was because she thought she wouldn't get a kiss. To hell with it! A grin spread over his face as he delighted in the shock he was about to give them. His amusement increased when—divining his motive—Denise suddenly appeared petrified as he headed toward her. Like a man who had established his rights, he pulled Denise into his arms, brushed her lips with his own and when she parted them, he went into her. Drake's sharp whistle told him that he might have overdone it, but he didn't care. He rubbed Denise's nose with his right index finger, winked at Drake and said, "Let's go."

"Since you were never prone to public displays of affection," Judson said to Scott, "not even as a teenager, I'm drawing my own conclusion about that scene at the door."

"Why doesn't that surprise me?"

They joined the rest of the Harrington clan and headed for the school. When Tara walked ahead of them holding Henry's hand, he experienced a pang of jealousy. How many years would it be before he could hold his child's hand, go to their recital or watch them play football or baseball? He told himself to snap out of it and that he should be thankful because he finally had the wind at his back.

"Do you think we can start our family within two years?" he whispered to Denise.

"I hope so," she said after what he considered a lengthy pause.

"I'd like you to have lunch with me and my family on Sunday," he whispered.

"Okay. I think that's a very good idea, but, honey, let's discuss these things when we don't have to whisper."

They took their seats in the auditorium in a section reserved for guests of the students performing. The first four of the five students, all in Tara's age group, played well and without mistakes. Wearing a long rose-colored chiffon dress and silver slippers, Tara walked to the piano, sat down, folded her hands and closed her eyes. Scott sat forward, thinking that she might have a temporary lapse of memory, but she placed her fingers on the piano keys and played a flawless "Au Claire de Lune" by Claude Debussy, for which the audience gave her a standing ovation. She bowed first to her family and then to the audience.

"I played last, because I'm the best student," she told them at the reception.

"You aren't supposed to brag," Alexis said, beaming at her precocious daughter.

"But Mummy, I wasn't bragging. I'm the best student. I play better than anyone, don't I, Daddy?"

"Yes, you do," Telford said, smiling proudly, "but your mother is right. You're not supposed to brag about it."

"Gee, Mr. Henry. Why do I practice so hard, if I can't tell anybody how well I play?"

"You can tell me," he said.

She turned to Grant, her playmate. "Didn't I play well, Grant?"

"Yeah. It was da bomb. Wanna go biking tomorrow? Daddy will go with us, and my mom says she'll pack us a lunch. Want to?"

"Sure, but I have to ask my parents first."

"I know that. Ask them now."

Scott shook his head. "Nine years old and already behaving as if he's a young man." He got two glasses of fruit punch and strolled over to where Denise talked to a woman he hadn't met.

She turned to him at once. "Ambassador Galloway, this is Ms. Bridges, a member of Second Chance. Her daughter played the Chopin Waltz in A-flat Major this evening."

He let himself smile. "Congratulations, Ms. Bridges. You must be very proud." He remembered that the little girl had not played well. But he refused to lie. Besides, the woman had to know that her child hadn't performed well. "Excuse me," he said and handed Denise the cup of fruit punch. When the woman continued to look at him, he asked her, "May I bring you some of this punch?"

Embarrassed at having been caught ogling him, the woman excused herself and left them alone. "Thanks," Denise said. "Now that she knows I hang out in this part of the country, she'll make a nuisance of herself."

He took her arm, because he had to touch her somewhere. "If you ever need to get rid of her, I'm very good at that. Are we going to my dad's place on Sunday?"

"Does your family know you're planning this?"

"No, but they will in the next hour. They'll drop whatever they've planned and be there."

"Are you sure?" she asked, wrinkling her brow.

"Sweetheart, I'm the eldest son, and when I growl, the other two bite. You bet they'll be there. They wouldn't miss an opportunity to give me grief."

"You mean the twins?"

"Who else? But don't worry. My grandmother will keep them in their place." He walked with her to a far corner of the reception hall, his arm loosely around her waist. "I'd better warn you. My grandmother thinks I walk on air."

"She does not, though I expect she thinks you're

wonderful. And I do, too. Will I have my ring when I meet them?"

"I wanted you to have it earlier this week, and I'm still smarting over having to change the elaborate plans I made. But we'll talk about that when we leave here. I take it you're going to Washington with me tonight."

"That's what I'd planned." She was quiet for a minute. "Scott, why did you give me a such a passionate kiss in front of the Harringtons? Wasn't that a little over the line?"

"Probably was. But I was still vexed at not seeing you this week, and when I started to give you a polite kiss on the side of your mouth, you seemed terrified. So I said what the hell and went for broke. Incidentally, I couldn't have given you that kiss if you hadn't parted your lips. With that invitation, what did you think I was going to do?"

"I did not part my lips."

"I suppose they open automatically."

"When your mouth gets close to them, they definitely do."

"Glad to know it. Nothing like a guaranteed welcome."

"Guaranteed for as long as you don't mess up. You've heard of lockjaw, haven't you?"

He had to laugh. "Honey, that's a bit far-fetched, but I get the message. How long before you think we can make our excuses and leave?"

"We can't. My bag is at Pamela's place, and I need stuff that's in it."

"Wait here." He went to Drake and told him that he wanted to leave.

"I imagine you do, considering what you started at my house. Tell Tara good-night, and I'll run you and Denise home to get her bag. In this crowd, no one will notice."

"Where are we stopping for dinner?" she asked him as he turned out of John Brown Lane and headed for Washington. "I don't feel like snacking tonight."

"But it was wonderful the other night," he said. "When I awakened with you snug in my arms, it slowly dawned on me that I was going to spend my life waking up like that, and no one can imagine how good it felt. I wanted to shelter you from everything and everyone who could ever harm you, and from anything that didn't make you smile and laugh."

"Oh, Scott. What a sweet and loving thing for you to say. You always make me so happy," she said, her eyes glistening with unshed tears. "And I want to make you happy, to give you everything you need in a woman." She tried, but failed, to prevent a sniffle.

"What is it?" he asked when her hand tightened around his.

"Scott, is your grandmother going to like me?"

"Why wouldn't she?" He thought for a moment. "If she doesn't, we'll both know it at once. But don't worry about that. Any parent would want their son to have you for his wife, and my nana is no different. I know it—maybe now she'll stop nagging me about finding a nice girl and settling down so she can have some great-grandchildren."

"I sure hope she's not looking for more than three, at least not from me."

* * *

Dressing to meet a man's brothers for the first time was a simple matter of looking your feminine best. But meeting his grandmother called for a different mindset *and skirt length.* After an hour during which she rejected three blouses and two sweaters—the necklines of which she deemed too low—and skirts that were either too short or had a long slit up the side, she settled on a simple sheath that had a jewel neckline, a matching soft dressmaker jacket and three long strands of eight-millimeter white pearls. "That takes care of grandmother," she said to herself. "The guys will just have to trust their brother's judgment."

When Scott rang her bell a few minutes before noon on Sunday, she walked to the door on rubber legs, opened it and looked up at him. He bent down to kiss her and stopped before he reached his target.

"What's wrong, honey?" he asked her. "Don't you want to go?"

"I do." She rubbed her right hand back and forth across the back of her left one. "It's…I've never been so nervous in my life. Suppose your grandmother decides you've lost your mind? I couldn't find anything decent to wear, and—"

"But you look wonderful. I like you in red. In fact, you look good to me no matter what you wear. A beautiful woman can wear anything." He grinned as if reflecting on a private thought. "Or nothing." He handed her a bunch of yellow roses. "You can give these to my grandmother. She loves them. Since I just planned this last evening, I knew you didn't have a chance to get any."

She stared up at him. "I don't know why I was so nervous. You always make sure that everything's right. Thanks so much for getting these."

His smile, so filled with love and affection, got to her and warmed her heart. She reached out to him and stroked his arm. She had to touch him, to feel herself a part of him.

As if he read her mind and gauged her emotions, he opened his arms. She dropped the roses on the table beside her and hugged him, receiving him with open arms and her lips parted for his kiss. He lifted her off her feet and held her close as he invaded her with his tongue. Holding him as tightly as she could, she sucked him into her mouth, taking and giving, loving and adoring him. His hand stroked her buttocks, and she hooked her ankles behind his back. Pressed against his chest, her nipples beaded, and when they began to itch, she rubbed one vigorously. But he hugged her and eased her to her feet.

"Be thankful that you're wearing a high-neckline dress. I can almost taste them. If I'd gotten my mouth on one of them, I doubt we'd leave here for Baltimore anytime soon."

"I know. I'd already forgotten about meeting your family. I need some water, and then let's get going." She rushed to the kitchen, ran water from the tap and sipped it. She couldn't leave her house with her nerves frayed and her body perspiring from every pore. She took a deep breath, started back to him and smothered a laugh when she saw him standing beside a window he'd opened, taking long, deep breaths.

During most of the ride from Washington to Baltimore, where Scott's family lived, she sang along with the music coming from the radio station. Music had always chased away any tension or stress, and it served the same purpose that Sunday. Scott put his key in the door at about the same time as the door opened. She gazed up at a man who resembled Scott.

"I see you made it," he said in a voice similar to Scott's. And though he spoke to Scott, he looked past him to her and smiled. "Come on in, Denise. I'm Matthew, but you should call me Matt." He stepped around Scott, took her by the arm and started in the house with her.

She looked from Matt to Scott, lifted her right shoulder in a quick shrug and told herself to play along with whatever game they started. But Matt bumped into his father, who was followed by a man who had to be Matt's twin.

"Welcome to my home, Denise," Raynor said as he leaned over and kissed her cheek. "My sons are pranksters, and Matt and Doug are obviously planning to trip Scott's trigger. Denise Miller, this is my son Douglas. As you've no doubt guessed, he and Matt are twins."

"Thank you, Mr. Galloway. I'm happy to see you again and to meet Scott's brothers."

"What is this?" Scott said, pretending to be annoyed. "I didn't even get a chance to introduce my girl. Where's Nana?" He looked at Matt. "The two of you had better not introduce Denise to Nana. That's my prerogative."

"All right, already!" Doug said with his hands extended. "We know not to get between you and Nana."

"Mom's in the den," Raynor said. He looked at Denise, grinned and whispered, "Don't be nervous. The two of you will get on beautifully. I've already told her that you hit a home run with me."

At least he liked her. She patted his hand. "Thank you, but I can't help it. Scott loves her so much."

He nodded, and in his face she saw a knowing expression. "You love him. Good," he whispered and stepped away from her.

With an arm firmly around her waist, Scott walked with her into the den where, to her amazement, his grandmother stood, waiting for them. Denise relaxed when the woman smiled and took a step forward. Scott's arm tightened as they both stepped closer to the older woman.

"Nana, this is Denise Miller, my sweetheart. Denise, this is my nana, Irma Galloway."

"How do you do, ma'am? I'm honored to meet you. I...brought you some flowers." She handed the flowers to Irma, but the woman took the flowers with one hand and, with the other, she hugged Denise to her.

"I knew I was going to like you, Denise, because my boy was always such a good judge of people. Thank you for these lovely flowers. I see he's told you that I love yellow roses."

"Yes, ma'am."

"I'll put them in a vase with some water," Matt said. "Yellow roses are beautiful, but they wilt the first chance they get."

"Scott told me that you play the piano beautifully," Irma said. "I hope you'll play something for me before you leave."

"I'll be glad to." She looked at Raynor, her surprise obvious to all of them. "You have a piano? Who plays?"

"All of us to one degree or another. Doug and Mom play much better than Scott, Matt and I." He looked at his mother. "Lunch will be here in about five minutes. I know it's the middle of the day and you look askance at noonday drinking, but this is a special occasion. The vodka and tonics will be mild, especially since I'm going to fill the glasses with ice."

"Before you do that, I have something to say," Scott told them. He took the ring out of his inside pocket and lifted Denise's left hand. "I've asked Denise to marry me, and she has agreed." He slipped the ring on her finger. She stared at him with her eyes wide as her lower jaw dropped. She was speechless. She hadn't dreamed that he'd give her the ring in the presence of his family. But her recovery came swiftly, and she flung both arms around his neck and kissed him passionately. Then, clearly flummoxed, she looked at Scott's grandmother as if to apologize.

"I'd say you used considerable restraint," Irma said. "Let's see it. This is wonderful."

Beginning with Irma, Denise walked to each of them with her left hand extended and the diamonds sparkling. When she reached Raynor, he took both of her hands and held them. "This is the answer to my prayers. An hour after I met you, I knew that you and Scott were perfect for each other, and I wanted you for him." Still holding her hand, he looked at Matt. "Where'd you put that champagne?"

"In the refrigerator downstairs. I'll get it."

"This calls for a genuine celebration," Raynor said.

Irma patted Scott on his shoulder. "Absolutely, even if it means drinking alcohol in the middle of the day."

Matt brought a bottle of champagne and six crystal flutes. With about an inch of the wine in her glass, Irma put one arm around Denise. "Welcome to our family. May you and Scott love well and happily for as long as you both live."

Scott walked over to Denise, kissed her and clicked her glass with his own. Shaken, since she had not expected to be received so warmly, she tried to blink back the tears, but when she saw the tears glistening in Scott's eyes, her own tears rolled down her cheeks. She reached out to him, and he opened his arms.

"I didn't know I could be so happy," he said.

"Me neither," she replied, wiping her eyes. "I'm overwhelmed."

Oddly, she welcomed the ringing of the doorbell and the reprieve from such an emotionally charged atmosphere. She needed to be alone with Scott to share her feelings with him. Still, she was grateful for the love that Scott's family showered on her.

"Lunch is here," Doug said, "and not a minute too soon. I was half-starved before I drank that champagne. And it went straight to the bottom of my stomach. Come on, Matt. I know Scott usually sets the table, but let's give the lovers a break."

"You're kidding. A kindergartner wouldn't feel that little bit of champagne you drank," Matt said.

"Do they fool around like that all the time?" Denise asked Scott.

"All three of us do. They usually gang up on me."

A sigh escaped her. "It must have been wonderful growing up with siblings."

"I guess it was," Scott said, "provided the little devils weren't your responsibility when your parents couldn't keep an eye on them."

Chapter 12

Scott's father hadn't planned for the event to be a feast, but to her, it seemed like one. "Imagine having two brothers," she said to Scott after Matt and Doug declared that she could count on them as she would a blood brother.

"I'm getting more out of this deal than you are," she said to Scott as they drove back to Washington shortly after sundown.

"Don't be so sure of that. My dad's love of the outdoors ends with water. Except for boating, Matt and Doug are strictly city slickers, and the bigger the city the better. But your dad loves the country and the outdoor activities that I love. That's why we got on so well. I can't wait to get back to Waverly."

She hoped he didn't notice how quiet she was, because she didn't want to spoil one of the most wonderful days of her life with an argument over his eagerness for her father's company, which didn't make one bit of sense. She opened her cell phone and saw that she had three missed calls, all of them from Pamela. She dialed her friend's number.

"Hi, Pamela, you called me?"

"You bet I did—three times. Haven't you missed your wallet? You left it on your night table."

"Good grief. No, I haven't missed it. Thanks. I have to go to Whispers Tuesday morning to close up the school for the winter, so I can stop by when I leave there, maybe around five."

"Okay. I'll be home about five-thirty. See you then."

Denise hung up, looked at Scott and pursed her lips in self-mockery. "Before I fell in love with you, I didn't misplace things. Pamela found my wallet."

A smile radiated on his face. "I had no idea that I possessed such power. Where are we headed, your place or mine? We have to eat something, and I haven't kissed you enough today."

"You didn't kiss me in my apartment this morning?"

"Yeah, but that was more of a promise than a real kiss."

"In that case, let me at the real thing."

Shortly after eleven that night, Scott rolled onto his back and pulled Denise on top of him. "Nana told me that she thinks you're wonderful. I'm glad my family likes you and that they're prepared to love you. But if they hadn't received you so graciously, I'd still love you. Their embracing you makes our path that much easier. I hope you won't feel badly if I leave you tonight. My briefcase and papers are in my apartment, and I have a meeting with the chief at nine-thirty tomorrow morning. I'll see how much autonomy he plans to give me."

As he sat in the elegant office the next morning, he remembered that only fifteen years earlier, the chief had been an ambassador to a middle-level country, when he told Scott to make every minute count. "A number of organizations are promoting immigration policies. But the trouble is coming from outside the immigrant community. Groups like Upward and Onward, Halfway There, Second Chance and Americans for Liberty aren't immigrant groups. They're wealthy liberals, and they also contribute to members of the Congress. They have a voice."

"I'm aware of them," Scott said, "and I believe our program is sound."

"So do I," the chief said. "If you have any problems, and especially if you're short of resources, come straight to me. I want this plan to succeed, and if I find that anyone responsible for implementing it drags his or her feet, that person will be out. A lot is hanging on this. We have a good team, and we ought to be able to make it work."

He'd have to have a talk to Denise about Second Chance. He'd postponed doing so, because he didn't think she'd give in, and he was concerned about where the discussion would lead. But when they met that evening, he'd decided that he'd bite the bullet and tell her that her group was at odds with his policies. However, news traveled fast in the nation's capital, and Congresswoman Katherine Miller got to Denise first.

Denise was surprised to receive a call from her mother at two o'clock in the afternoon. Katherine usually didn't socialize during working hours. "I'm going to make this snappy," she said, after greeting her daughter. "The secretary served notice to Scott and some of his aides that the failure of his immigration policy would not be tolerated. He promised that heads would roll. Second Chance was one of four groups mentioned as causing some problems, so watch it. He loves you, but he won't tolerate your undermining him."

While Katherine talked, Denise paced from her desk to the limits of the phone cord and back. "Who told you this?"

"I have my sources."

"I see."

"I hope you do. A public fight between a man of Scott's status and his fiancée won't be good for either of you. Incidentally, Clyde wants us to announce your engagement this weekend. Chew on that. I have to go. Love you."

Denise dropped into the chair. Hadn't she told officers of local Second Chance chapters to be less vocal about the issue until the administration spelled out its policies and goals? But they hadn't heeded her and would nonetheless expect her support. She imagined that Scott left that meeting incensed with her. In fact, she was sure of it, because he hadn't called her to complain about it.

Her cell phone rang, and the temptation not to answer it weighed heavily on her. "Hi," she said to Scott after the sixth ring.

"Hi. I have to overhaul a report I just received. So I have to cancel our date this evening. Can we get together tomorrow evening?"

Hmm. Not hi, sweetheart. Just plain hi. He was sore, all right. "Fine, but I'll be at Whispers tomorrow afternoon, and I planned to spend the night at my house in Frederick."

"How is six-thirty in Frederick?"

"Okay." She thought for a minute. It might be reckless, but she wasn't afraid to test the water. "Is everything all right with you?"

"Not entirely, Denise. But I expect it will be...one way or the other. See you tomorrow. Love you."

She hung up and stared into space. One way or the other! He was furious with her or with somebody. Maybe he's disappointed, her nagging conscience suggested.

What was she to do? Second Chance had its agenda before she knew Scott. Still, he had a right to expect her to support him. And at the very least, to refrain from undermining him. She telephoned Priscilla. "I'll be spending tomorrow night in Frederick. Think of something real nice in case I have a dinner guest."

"Yes, ma'am. You bet."

Denise telephoned Carole Jacobs, the Second Chance national secretary. She suspected that the woman had her own agenda, and that she didn't enjoy following her leadership. "Hello, Carole, this is Denise. We don't know the government's policy on immigrant children, so let's not make an issue it."

"But if we can get ahead by promoting our own plan, we're more likely to succeed," Carole said. "I have contacted Upward and Onward, and they are ready to join us. I'll bet some others will, too."

Denise tamped down her anger, which threatened to

spill over in harsh words. "Carole, we'll abide by the board's decision. That's why we had a meeting."

"Whatever you say!"

Denise hung up. The crack in Second Chance had to become a fissure. *Too bad,* she thought

At Whispers the next morning, Denise closed the riding-school section of her stables and called Morton Sykes to her office.

"Morton, I'll come here occasionally to ride, but as manager, I think it's best that you take care of supplies and the operations, in addition to training and caring for the horses. How much more per month will you need for the added duties?"

"A few hundred will do it. I'll send you the monthly receipts, and you pay the bills. I don't need to handle anybody's money but my own."

"Perfect. I'll add five hundred to your monthly salary."

"I hope that's Galloway's ring on your finger. He's solid."

"Thanks. We've been engaged a little over a week, but we may never marry."

He put a cigarette in his mouth, removed it, put it in his pocket and let out a deep sigh. "Why do you say that?"

She gave him an overview of the conflict between Second Chance and Scott's job in the administration. Morton's keen whistle split the air. "You're damn right, you won't. If you don't drop that business right now, he'll be long gone. That's a no-nonsense man. If I was in his place, I'd be walking this minute. Don't you love him?"

"Of course I love him."

"Then, that should be your answer. You're doing volunteer work, but he's making a living, and there's a hell of a difference. Denise, I married the daughter of one of this country's wealthiest men. I was CEO of a multibillion-dollar company. I fired a female employee for insolence, and she said I fired her because she wouldn't sleep with me. The media and the women's groups loved it. It was an absolute lie. My in-laws were mortified, and so my wife didn't support me. The minute I knew she wasn't with me, I walked and never looked back. After six years, she's still sorry, but I barely remember what she looks like."

"I get the message."

"Do you? He loves you, and if you two don't marry, I'll know you let him down." He took the cigarette from his pocket and was about to put it into his mouth. "Funny thing. He asked me to stop smoking and, for the first time, I'm trying. I like the guy. Be careful, Ms. Miller."

"Thank you, Morton. I will."

Between Carole's insolence, her mother's warning and Morton's prediction, Denise had plenty to think about. Somehow, she hadn't foreseen a problem. They would work it out. They had to!

She left Whispers, arrived at Pamela and Drake's home and approached Pamela, who was accompanied by Heather. "I came for my wallet. My driver's license is in it. Lord help me if I'd been pulled over."

She hugged the two women. "I can't stay but a few minutes."

"I hope you're rushing off to meet Scott," Heather said.

"Well, I'm not. I'm headed home."

"What's wrong with you, girl?" Pamela said. "How many times do you have to be told that you're not going to find another man like Scott Galloway?"

"Besides, he's crazy in love with you," Heather added. "You're going to lose him to somebody who isn't half the woman that you are."

"Not hardly," Denise said, running up the stairs to get her wallet. "Why do you two think you know Scott better than I do?" she asked when she got back to them.

"Because—"

"Because nothing," Denise said and extended her left hand.

"Holy cow!" Pamela screamed. "Look at this rock!"

Heather grabbed Denise's hand. "Well, I'll be!"

Denise's grinned. "And all this time, you thought I'd need to make Scott look good to me." She threw up her hands and laughed aloud. "You thought we were fussing when we were buzzing."

"We've got to drink to this. When did it happen?" Pamela asked.

"I said yes a few weeks ago and I got the ring Sunday."

"I'm so happy for you," her friends said in unison.

"Thanks. I love you both, but I have to go. I'll call."

"You're coming to Russ's birthday party, aren't you?"

"You bet I'll be there."

* * *

Scott left the office at four, went to his house in Georgetown and got a book of poems that had belonged to his mother. He had loved the poems, when as a small child, his mother recited the lyrical lines that he didn't understand. But he remembered the words of her favorite poems. He bought a dozen roses for Denise and, for the first time, he mixed white with the yellow. If that conveyed a meaning, he didn't know what it was, but he liked the mix.

The door to Denise's house at 271 Henderson Street, in Frederick, Maryland, opened in response to his ring. Denise faced him with her arms open, eyes wide and a look of vulnerablity. Unable to resist, he drew her into his arms, parted her lips with his tongue and sipped the nectar that she gave him. When he released her, she asked him, "Do you mean that?"

"Mostly," he said, honestly.

"I planned for us to have dinner here, because something is wrong, and I know what it is."

"What is it?"

"Mom called me shortly before you did. She has spies, and it seems she's heard something. I'm not sure what you should do with that information."

"I'll keep it to myself."

Priscilla came into the den, where they were about to sit down. "Hi, Mr. Ambassador. I brought you some of my cheese sticks. Think you'd like a vodka collins to go with them? I'll make it nice and weak, and I'm bringing you some hot snacks. Sure is good to see you."

"I'm glad to see you, Mrs. Mallory. Make that drink very weak, please."

"Yes, sir."

Priscilla returned with the drinks and hors d'oeuvres. "Dinner will be ready about seven-fifteen, ma'am."

"That's fine, Priscilla."

Scott sipped his cocktail and put it aside. "Where do you want to start?"

"I'm not the one who put pressure on your office about immigrant issues, and I called Second Chance's national secretary this afternoon to reprimand her. The board decided to do nothing until the federal policy was announced. And I had pushed for that."

"So far, so good. But suppose your group doesn't approve of it? Then what?"

"I don't intend to work against you."

"What about supporting me? That's what I need from you, Denise. I respect your desire to help bring about the changes that you would like to see, and your willingness to work toward that end. But that's why we have government policies—to manage the bigger picture. If every citizen or group tried to implement its own policy, we would have chaos. My goals aren't so different from yours. Why can't you find a way to help me? This is your avocation, but it's my career. It's our life."

"Were you angry with me?" she said.

"If only it was that simple. I was mad, but I was also hurt. Deeply hurt."

"I'm sorry. If Second Chance won't change tactics, it will have to have a new president."

"Denise, a portion of our policy involves ensuring that all foreign-born immigrants have an opportunity to learn English. You could help in that and in other ways."

"Yes, I can."

He took the book of poems from his jacket pocket. "When I was little, my mother read poetry to us. I still remember several of the poems. From Marlowe, she especially loved these lines, 'Come live with me and be my love, and we will all the pleasures prove.' When I read it, I need you close to me." She moved closer to him, and he read the entire poem to her.

"But Denise, these lines from Oscar Wilde also apply to us. He said that men kill what they love and, 'A coward does it with a kiss.' I've been down that road, sweetheart, and the experience was a lesson I have tried never to repeat again." With his right hand covering hers, he said, "Love is fragile, sweetheart, but affection, loyalty, fidelity and genuine caring strengthen it. I'm offering you that and so much more."

"And I'll give you the same and as much love as you can tolerate."

He leaned forward and kissed her on the mouth.

When Priscilla served dessert, she put a bag of cheese sticks beside his plate. He kissed her on the cheek in a gesture of thanks.

"You know, I'm always gon' remember what you like," she said, referring to the bag of cheese sticks. She patted her hair. "Good night, ma'am. I'll see you tomorrow, 'bout eleven."

"Good night, Priscilla. And thank you."

"What time do you want to leave for Waverly?" Scott asked Denise.

"If I had my way, we wouldn't go, but I promised. So let's take an early flight. Mom said that Daddy wants to announce our engagement this weekend."

"Great. I've been so tied down with policy issues, my first in this administration, that I've neglected to get with Judson and tell him how things are going. But I had better, or he'll be sore."

"I'm sure he knows about us, because I showed Pamela and Heather my ring."

"He needs to hear it from me. He's closer to me than my own brothers."

Clyde Miller met Denise and Scott at the airport. "I'm glad you took an earlier flight. I want to show Scott around San Antonio." He hugged Denise. "Scott said last time that it was his first visit to Texas, and I didn't show him very much of it."

"Whatever you say," Denise replied with a notable lack of enthusiasm.

Clyde seemed put out. "We should at least show him The Alamo, La Villita and the San Antonio River that runs through the city," he said. "People come here from all over the world to see that river, take a ride in the Yanaguana and to see the way the city looks from the River Walk."

"Okay," she said. "Let's go to La Villita first, so Scott can get a taste of the effects of some of our immigration laws."

Scott didn't like her tone. "I left my job back in Washington, and I'd appreciate it if it stayed there."

"Sorry," she said.

The Alamo surprised him. He had thought it was much larger, and asked himself why anybody would fight over it. He could easily have mistaken La Villita, a city within San Antonio, for a place in Mexico. He wasn't much of a tourist, but he wished the ride down the San Antonio River on that flat-bottom river taxi, known as the Yanaguana, had lasted for hours. He imagined an awesome sight at Christmastime, when the number of shops and cypress trees along the riverbanks were all lit up with colorful lights and decorations.

"It must be beautiful here during the Christmas holidays," he said.

"Oh, yes," Clyde replied. "It's wonderland, indeed."

"Mom must be holding supper for us. Shouldn't we head home, Daddy?"

"Yeah, I suppose so," Clyde said, in a lackluster voice.

Katherine met them at the door wearing a red jersey caftan. Clyde rewarded her with a warm greeting.

"I was beginning to wonder if the plane ever landed," she said airily. "Wash up, and let's eat."

After supper, Clyde produced several scrapbooks. "These will tell you something about our family, son." He pointed to a blue leather one. "Katherine put this together, when she was recuperating from a riding accident. This is Denise's life from birth 'til she left home."

"Thank you, sir. I'll go through these tonight."

"But Daddy, some of these pictures are too, uh, personal."

"Nonsense. There is nothing personal about a baby's bottom, and I know that's what you're talking about."

Scott laughed. In more appropriate circumstances, he'd have reminded her that he had already seen her without her clothes.

"What's funny?" she asked.

He laughed harder. "There are few things as cute as

a baby's bottom, and they all look the same." When her eyes narrowed, he got up from the chair and, carrying the large album, walked over and kissed her in a lingering embrace. "I can't wait to see these." He looked at Clyde. "Who's cooking breakfast? You or me?"

"We can do it together. Six-thirty all right with you?"

"Sure thing." He kissed Katherine's cheek. 'Night all."

"Anything wrong with you two?" Clyde asked Denise after Scott left.

"Nothing yet, but if he spends the entire weekend with you and ignores me as he did when we were here before, there'll be plenty wrong."

Clyde's frown should have warned her, but it didn't. "Surely you are not jealous of the time your future husband spends with your father. I don't have a son or a brother. Every man needs one or the other, and I'm so happy that you are marrying a man who wants to be a son to me and to your mother. You're with him all the time. Try not to act like an only child."

"He didn't kiss me once when we were here before."

"Well, he certainly did a few minutes ago."

"Not nearly as well as I know he's capable of." She knew she sounded childish, but she didn't care.

Denise would learn that her father could be as cross as she could—if indeed, she needed a reminder. "This house has nine rooms, a recreation room, five bathrooms and closets on three floors," Clyde said. "You ought to be able to find a place to kiss Scott in private."

"Sorry, Dad. I'd like the chance to introduce him to my friends," she said, feeling that she'd gotten the upper hand in the conversation.

"Then throw a party. I'm going to bed. Six-thirty will be here shortly. Coming, Katherine?"

Denise knew she had no right to be mad. But she wanted to show him off. She went to bed promising herself that she'd be in the kitchen at six-thirty to spoil their male-bonding fun.

Denise awakened at ten-thirty, and by then Scott and her father had caught, between them, nine fish—four rainbow trout and five bass. Having finished fishing, they sat under a wild pecan tree near the banks of the Guadalupe River picking up nuts.

"This place is so peaceful," Scott said, sitting beside the river, shaded by cypress, pecan and cottonwood trees. "No wonder people down here move slowly."

"'Til they get behind the wheel of a car," Clyde added. "You think you can get Denise to come down here for Thanksgiving? I expect you'll want to be with your folks for Christmas, so it would be nice if you split your holidays between Denise's family and yours."

"I can try. If she balks, and she's in a mood to do that, perhaps you and her mother will come to Baltimore. It's time you met my family."

He could see that Clyde agreed only grudgingly. "All right, son, we'll play it by ear."

When they got back to the Miller home shortly after one o'clock, neither Denise nor Katherine greeted them warmly. "I don't know where the time went," Scott said to Denise. "It was heavenly. So quiet and peaceful, the only sound was the breeze through the cypress trees and the rushing of the water. It was almost like a symphony. I wish you had been there."

"Me, too. Oh, Scott. Let's go for a ride this afternoon."

"Sweetheart, Clyde wants to take us to San Antonio this afternoon to see the annual street festival."

"I'll bet. He wants to fill up on souvlaki, Italian sausage and beer. I forgot about that. It's the one time Mom lets him pollute his arteries."

The weekend had gone by quickly. "What about Thanksgiving?" Scott asked Denise Sunday night after they arrived home. He'd waited until then, hoping to avoid any arguments.

"No way! Mom and I would spend the weekend alone except at mealtime." She showed him her left hand. "And this ring says I'm entitled to monopolize all your free time. No thanks."

"I can't believe you're jealous of your own father. It makes no sense."

"I am not jealous of him. He's the one who doesn't make sense."

"I had better go. After such a wonderful evening, we shouldn't part like this. I'll call you."

"Bye," she said, her voice so weak that he barely heard her.

At home, after checking his answering machine, he telephoned Judson. "Hi. I was out of town. You called three times. What's up?"

"Plenty. To begin with, who's your best man? If it's me, then when were you planning to let me know?"

"Man, this is a bad time. I hadn't planned to tell anyone until I put the ring on Denise's finger. Right now, she's furious with me over nothing."

"Join the club, buddy. If she's merely furious with you, you haven't done much. If anything, you probably deserve it. If it was serious, man, she'd just stop talking to you. So chin up. It isn't so bad. I've been calling because Drake and Telford told me to ask you to come down next weekend. We are celebrating Russ's thirty-fifth birthday on Sunday. He wants some books on ancient architectural design and Middle Eastern architecture as gifts. He told Telford that he needs a new Western saddle."

"Thanks for the tip. I'll see you Friday afternoon. Give Heather my love."

"Can we meet for lunch? I have a business engagement this evening," Denise said.

"I can meet you at the Willard. What time?" Scott asked.

Once they were at lunch the debate resumed, although Scott wasn't quite sure what the underlying issue was.

"I want to introduce you to my friends in Waverly," she said at lunch, "but my father doesn't give me a chance."

"I can appreciate that, but couldn't you resolve this easily by giving a party?"

"Oh, for goodness' sake. You men are all just alike. That's what my dad said."

Why should she get ticked off about that? "Well, wasn't he right?"

She speared an asparagus with her fork. "Is he ever wrong?"

"Sweetheart, I see that we have to let this issue cool

off a bit more before we can move on. What do you see when you look at me?"

She leaned forward and looked him in the eye. "When I look at you, I see my man and *not* my father's son."

He laughed, since laughing gave him a good feeling. "Tell him that."

She let out a long, deep sigh. "It won't do a bit of good."

"Too bad. I have to go. I'll call you when I get home tonight, provided it's not too late."

Denise telephoned Scott twice that afternoon. "I don't have anything to say," she told him during the second call. "I...I need to feel closer to you. I know it's my problem, and I don't know how to fix it."

"If I knew how, I'd tell you," he said. "You're not going to like this, but I keep thinking of the word *trust* even though I believe you trust me. Do you think your dad cares more for me than for you? It isn't possible, you know."

"I don't think that's true, honey, but when you are with them, I feel left out."

"How are you going to feel when we have children, especially if we have girls who will undoubtedly try to monopolize their father's time?"

"I know, but—"

"That's something for you to think about."

"Are you still sore with me?" she asked him.

"Put it this way. I'm not happy because I know you won't give in and allow us to spend Thanksgiving in Waverly, as we should, and as I want to do."

"Let's not go over that again."

"Of course not."

It wasn't until she was in Saks Fifth Avenue shopping for her wedding gown that she reflected upon the bitterness of those words...*of course not.*

"You need to get your act together," Katherine told her when they spoke later that day. "Clyde is so proud of having an ambassador for a son-in-law, and we both like Scott so much. Scott wanted to invite our families to get together for Thanksgiving dinner and your father is so disappointed."

"I'm sorry, Mom. Honest, I am."

"That isn't good enough."

If her mom was annoyed with her, her dad was probably even more disappointed and unhappy. After talking to her mother, Denise realized that if the three people she loved most were vexed at her, she had to do some rethinking.

She telephoned Pamela. "Can you stand a houseguest this weekend?"

"Sure. Where've you been lately? We're past thinking of you as a houseguest, Denise. Drake even refers to that room as Denise's room. Oh, I've been meaning to ask you to come over because we are celebrating Russ's thirty-fifth birthday on Sunday. Roast pork is Russ's favorite, so Henry is roasting a huge pig. Come Friday, so we can catch up on things."

Late Friday afternoon, sipping wine with Pamela and Heather, Denise could barely contain her misery. Scott would be in Eagle Park for Russ's party, and he hadn't mentioned it to her.

"Did you tell him you'd be here?" Heather asked her.

"You can't expect more than you give," Pamela said. "What's wrong with you two, anyway?"

Denise sipped her wine as she rolled her eyes toward the ceiling. "Mr. Ambassador is enamored with my dad, and vice versa. When we are in Texas, I can't even get a friggin' kiss. They're always together. You'd think he'd never bonded with a man. He'd have a fit if I hung out with *his* dad." She giggled. "Raynor Galloway is one fine-looking brother. He puts most thirty-year-old men to shame."

"Hmm. Looks like the apple doesn't fall far from the tree," Pamela said.

At her house after dinner that evening, Heather made the mistake of relating part of Denise's conversation to Scott.

"Why the hell would she tell you anything about it?" Scott asked.

"Please, Scott. I wanted to try and ease the situation, not to make it worse."

"Well, you missed the mark."

"Are you going over to Drake's house?"

As mad as he was, he didn't dare go there. "*No. I am not!* I'm going to bed."

"But she knows you are here," Judson said.

"Right. And I know she's there. See you in the morning." But he didn't see them the next morning.

At a quarter to seven the next day, Scott rang the doorbell at Harrington House, and as expected, Henry opened the door. "I had to clean the flour off me hands. Lock the door behind you. I'm in the kitchen."

"How are you, Henry? Mind if I watch you make the biscuits? I'd like to learn how you do it."

"You can learn some other time. Get the bacon and sausages and fry a pound of each. Sit down over there. You don't look so happy. How's Denise?"

"Where do I start?"

Henry broke four eggs into two cups of buttermilk, tossed the egg shells into the compost bucket and squinted at Scott. "Bacon and sausage. You can talk while you do that. What's wrong with you and Denise?"

Scott told Henry as much as he thought he needed to know. "Last night, I was mad enough to have doubts. Why can't she—"

Henry interrupted him. "But you didn't, and you won't walk away, because you ain't that stupid. Sit her down and tell her what you just told me. She's everything to ya. But you ain't gonna put up with her nonsense. She's an only child, and she ain't used to sharing. When is the wedding?"

"She hasn't set a date."

"Tell her you want to set the date. Now that that's settled, turn over that bacon, 'fore it burns."

"That simple, huh?"

"She's backed herself into a corner," Henry said, "and she don't know how to get out of it. Quit reacting, and be direct. Women are never completely sure of a man, and they shouldn't be. You can handle it. Brush some of that melted butter over these biscuits, so they'll brown evenly."

"Henry, I hope I can come to you for advice for as long as I live."

"Humph!"

A few minutes later, Scott wrapped six hot biscuits in aluminum foil and headed toward the river, eating them as he walked. He had to tape an interview that evening, and he needed to pull his thoughts together. He needed to see Denise, too, but he was tired of skating around the issue between them, and he didn't feel like pretending. He sat on a boulder beside the Monocacy River with his back against the cypress tree, took a small pad from his pocket and began to make notes.

"Is Scott down there?" Heather asked Pamela when she called at about eight-thirty that morning.

"No. We haven't seen nor heard from Scott. Denise is ready to climb the wall."

"Let me speak with Heather," Denise said. "Is Scott's car in your garage?" she asked Heather.

"Yes. I figure Scott is down at Telford's house," Heather said. "Are you two going to make up?"

"How do I know? He's acting as if I'm on an island somewhere."

"Well, you'll see him at the party tomorrow, Denise," she said.

"According to Drake, this is all my fault."

"I agree, but—"

"I don't know how to beg, and I do not plan to start now," Denise said.

"Atta girl! Scott's got a TV interview taping at five this afternoon, but he'll be back here for dinner. You want to join us?" Heather said.

"Thanks, but that smacks too much of outside interference, and he'll balk at it. There are other ways.

Scott left the television station exhilarated. He knew he'd done well, and the host and staff had applauded him when he'd finished taping. He wanted to send a gift to the host. In the elevator, he patted the inside pocket of his suit jacket for his iPhone, but it wasn't there. He remembered that the last time he had worn the suit he had on was the day he'd left Lithuania. He put his hand inside the pocket and found Helga's letter, which he had put there as he was leaving the embassy in Vilnius. It had been months since he had thought of Helga. As he drove back to Eagle Park, he was tempted—even anxious—to see Denise, but instead he went directly to Judson and Heather's home.

"How'd it go, buddy?" Judson asked him.

"It couldn't have gone better. We can watch the piece at nine-thirty tonight." He knew Judson would phone the Harringtons and tell them. He had already told his dad and Clyde, and he wanted Denise to see it. But he didn't feel like calling her. Hopefully, Pamela would tell her.

After warring with himself for most of the evening, he went to bed around midnight without calling Denise. For hours, he lay there staring at the ceiling and at the moon, which he could see through the blinds. Between thinking of Denise and trying to get to sleep, he remembered Helga's letter and got up.

Sitting on the edge of the bed, he read:

Dear Scott,
It's been wonderful knowing you. Unless you

come back, we won't meet again, because my son has grounded me. He's afraid something will happen to me if I continue to trek around the world by myself. But it's been a great life. Yours will be great, too. So you remember what I told you, especially the part about horseback riding. It's a very rewarding activity. Write when you can.

Yours,

Helga

He couldn't fathom the significance of horseback riding, so he reread the letter several times before it dawned on him. Helga had once told him that she hoped he liked horses. Suddenly he realized she had to have been pointing him to Denise, who owned a dozen of them and who loved to ride. He put on his robe and walked barefoot down to the kitchen, got a bottle of beer, opened it and sat down at the kitchen table.

His father had often told him that, if he ruined his life, it would be because of his stubbornness. And he had the fortune—good or bad—to love a woman who was just as stubborn as he was. He spent Sunday morning along the riding trail, near the Monocacy River, thinking of his life, of Denise and what mattered most to him. He could barely remember why he'd gotten so angry with her.

At one o'clock, he headed down the road to Harrington House. A recording of "The Honey Wind

Blows" by the Brothers Four—a song he loved—and the sound of human voices greeted his ears. When he walked around the back of the garage, colorful balloons, pennants and streamers greeted his eyes. In a far corner of the garden, beside the barbecue pit, a thirty-five-pound pig was roasting on a spit, as the tantalizing smell of seasoned pork and barbecue sauce made his mouth water.

His heart lurched when he saw her standing with her back to him talking to a man he didn't know. Was this guy the reason she hadn't tried to reach him when he'd been only a short distance away from her for the past two nights? Never one to second-guess, he headed straight to her. He didn't care who the man was; Denise Miller was *his* woman.

From his peripheral vision, he saw Henry drop his barbecue fork and stare at him. And from a glance to the side, he saw that everyone, including Tara, watched him—everyone except Denise and her *friend,* who couldn't see him.

"Hello, Denise."

At the sound of his voice, she whirled around, and he noted that she was neither nervous nor flustered. "Hi," she said and fully faced him.

"Aren't you going to introduce me to your friend?"

"Yes, of course. You totally threw me off. Ambassador Galloway, this is Charles Hamilton, one of the Harrington brothers' associates. Mr. Hamilton, Ambassador Scott Galloway is my fiancé."

He shook the man's hand and waited for him to make himself scarce. He glanced at Henry, who wore the widest grin he had ever seen.

"Excuse me, please, Mr. Hamilton. Scott and I have some catching up to do," Denise said. "I enjoyed talking with you." Drake appeared and soon walked with his guest toward the bar.

"If Drake hadn't pulled Charles away, I would have," Velma whispered in Scott's ear.

Soon, Alexis joined them handed them each a glass of champagne. "I've been so scared you two were breaking up."

"Not a chance," Scott said, accepting the flute.

"Thank God for that," Alexis said, releasing a deep sigh.

"Could I have a word with you, Denise?" Pamela asked just when he thought he could sneak away to Judson's house and take Denise with him.

"Can't it wait?" Denise said.

"Yeah, it could, but in the meantime, you could do something foolish."

"Not on your life."

Wide-eyed, Pamela left them alone and joined Heather. Holding Denise's hand, he walked over to Henry. "Can I get something for Denise and me? We're going to Judson's place, and we may or may not be back."

"Give me ten minutes. Meantime, tell Russ happy birthday."

At Judson's house, Scott opened the door with his key, and went into the kitchen. "We can eat right here as soon as I get us a beer and some forks. Have a seat. Henry fixed a plate for each of us."

Denise had missed him. As she watched him set the

table, open a can of beer and say grace, she wondered what was wrong with her. She had to do something. "Scott, have you made other arrangements for Thanksgiving? We can go see my folks, if you still want to. I've been thinking that if Dad hadn't liked you, I wouldn't have been happy. I don't know what got into me. We can spend Christmas with your folks." She waited for his response while he formulated his thoughts.

"Denise, I am not going to sugarcoat this. I love you, and I need you. Those are words I haven't said to a woman, since I was still wet behind the ears, so to speak. But I am not a slave to my emotions."

He reached over and lifted her hand from the table and caressed it. "Yes. I accept my role in it. Promise me that in the future, whenever something isn't right you'll do what we are doing right now. Sit quietly and talk to me about it."

"I will, and you will do the same."

He nodded. "Count on it." And as if the subject was over and done with, he said, "I hope you don't need dessert."

She couldn't help laughing. "Boy, do I ever!"

Both of his eyebrows shot up, and his eyes widened. "You mean?"

She nodded. "Nobody's here but us."

He cleared the table and put the dishes in the dishwasher. She'd never seen him move so fast.

"Come with me?" he told her.

"Yes!"

They ran up the stairs to his room. At the door, he picked her up, carried her inside and placed her on her feet beside his bed. She kicked off her shoes, and it just got to him. She could see it in his entire demeanor. His eyes darkened, and his Adam's apple bobbed when he swallowed heavily.

"Do you love me, sweetheart?"

"Oh, yes, I love you. You are my whole world. I know that now."

He opened his arms, and she was in them. His hands roamed all over her. And his mouth, oh, Lord, his mouth! He ran his tongue along the seams of her lips, and she opened them, anxious for the taste of him. She pulled his tongue into her and suckled it, feasting on it as if starved. He grabbed her buttocks, tightened his grip on her and plunged his tongue in and out of her, demonstrating what he planned to do to her. Frissons of heat plowed through her, and her nerves were on end. Frantic for more, she undulated wildly against him. The pulsing began in her vagina, and she took his hand and rubbed her left nipple with it. He yanked her top over her head, threw it on the bed, pulled her breasts from her bra and drew her nipple into his mouth.

"Yes. Oh, yes. Yes!" she said, holding his head as he nourished himself. She tried to unbutton his shirt, but couldn't. Instead she took off his belt. She caressed his penis, and he bulged against her.

"Get in me. Honey, I don't need all this. I want to feel you in me. It's been so long." When she unzipped her slacks, he eased them to the floor, picked her up and placed her on his bed. She unhooked her bra, and her breasts fell free. He got out of his clothes, quickly, and she reached for his hand and offered her breast to him. She spread her legs, and with a hoarse groan, he

stumbled onto the bed. When she felt the warm mois-
ture of his mouth, her hips thrust upward toward him.

"Slow down, sweetheart. I am going to enjoy every
second of this, and I aim to see that you never forget
this day." He licked the valley between the globes of
flesh that he loved so much, kissed his way down to her
navel and anointed it with his tongue, while his hands
skimmed the inside of her thighs.

She didn't try to control her undulating hips when
he locked her knees over his shoulders and kissed her
thighs. She knew what to expect, and lifted her body
to his mouth, but he continued kissing and licking her
thighs.

"Stop teasing me. You know what I want."

"Tell me. I want you to tell me."

"Scott, please!"

"Please what?" She moved up to him, but he
thwarted her effort.

"Kiss me. I want to feel you stroking my clitoris."

"You like that, do you?"

"I love it. Scott, honey, I'm so hot. I think I'll die if
you don't do something to me."

He parted her folds, rubbed her clitoris until it was
swollen and ready. "Oh, I can't stand it. I want you in
me." His tongue went into her and she felt the liquid
flow from her, but he didn't stop. "Honey, I'm going to
come. I feel it. Get inside me. I want it good and hard,
Scott. Oh, Lord! You aren't letting me come."

"You will, baby," he said, trailing a stream of kisses
up her body. "Take me in."

She took him in her hands and gloried in the feel of
him, big, hard and heavy, as he thrust into her. Slowly

he began, in and out, side to side until he found the spot. "Yes!" she said. "That's it. Right there."

"All right, baby." Minutes after he began his rhythmic motion, heat spiraled up from the bottom of her feet, to her quivering legs, to her vagina. He accelerated his pace, unleashed his power, and the pumping, squeezing and contractions began.

"Relax, and I'll give it to you," he said.

"I know. Why won't it come?"

He put a hand between them, found her clitoris and unleashed a double-barrel assault on her senses. She couldn't stand it. He was in her, on her, over her, under her and all around her. She didn't know her flesh from his. He dropped her a thousand feet, and flung her up just as high. Screams of delight pealed out of her as she burst with the blessed relief.

"I love you. Oh, I love you," she moaned as she descended from her climax. "You are everything to me."

He gripped her to him, gave her the essence of himself and came apart in her arms. "You're my life, my everything."

Denise awakened about an hour later to find him still locked inside of her and smiling as he looked down into her face. "When are you going to marry me?"

"February the fourteenth. I've already chosen my wedding gown."

He kissed her eyes, her cheeks and her lips. "Where are we going to live?" he asked her.

What was happening to her? Could it be that after all of their problems, it would really come to pass? She couldn't believe it. "I always thought that we'd live in your fancy three-story condominium in Georgetown and my place in Frederick, unless you want to join the Harrington clan."

"I say Georgetown and Frederick for now. Frederick's only fourteen miles from here," he said. "Do I understand that it's all right with you if I called Clyde and told him we're having Thanksgiving dinner in Waverly?"

"Yes."

"I love you, Denise. You and our children will be my first priority always."

"I know. By the way, Second Chance has split. I'll be heading the group that supports the administration's policies, and my group will retain the name Second Chance."

"Thank God. That was my next question. Is there anything else that we have to settle? If so, now is the time, Denise."

"I'm happy and impatient to start a life with you, love."

"So am I, sweetheart. And we had better vacate this bed before Judson or Heather decide to find out if we're all right."

"Gotcha. Where do they keep the sheets?"

He looked at her and grinned. "You're wonderful."

"And I've got a man of my dreams."

* * * * *

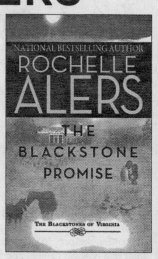